THE DISCOVERED

MAGGIE SUNSERI

Copyright © 2021 by Maggie Sunseri.

All rights reserved. No part of this publication may be reproduced, distributed or transmitted in any form or by any means, including photocopying, recording, or other electronic or mechanical methods, without the prior written permission of the publisher, except in the case of brief quotations embodied in critical reviews and certain other noncommercial uses permitted by copyright law. For permission requests, write to the publisher, addressed "Attention: Permissions Coordinator," at the address below.

Maggie Sunseri
PO Box 1264
Versailles, Kentucky 40383
https://maggiesunseri.com

Publisher's Note: This is a work of fiction. Names, characters, places, and incidents are a product of the author's imagination. Locales and public names are sometimes used for atmospheric purposes. Any resemblance to actual people, living or dead, or to businesses, companies, events, institutions, or locales is completely coincidental.

Cover design by K.D. Ritchie

THE DISCOVERED/ Maggie Sunseri. -- 1st ed.

ALSO BY MAGGIE SUNSERI

THE LOST WITCHES OF ARADIA

The Discovered

The Coveted

The Illuminated

The Hunted

THE AWAKEN SERIES (Young Adult Series)

Awaken

Arisen

For those who choose love over fear.

CHAPTER 1

The winds of autumn brought a chill into the heart of the city, whistling against windows that revealed a stunning cityscape view. I swiveled around on a stool and faced my roommates, glancing every so often at the glittering lights of towering buildings and backlit figures moving within. I absentmindedly ran my fingers through Steph's faux fur coat that was draped over the marble counter. She hummed softly beside me as she blended out Rena's smoky eyeshadow with her fingertips.

"Áine," Rena said, careful not to move her head as Steph worked. "Are you sure you don't just want a girls' night? It's *your* twenty-second, babe."

"Yeah honestly," Steph added. "Are you still feeling up for going out?" She peered over at me, setting down the eyeshadow palette and studying my face.

"Of course," I assured them, smiling. "I'm glad the guys are coming over. It's going to be a memorable night. I can feel it." What I didn't say was that the more people who came out with us tonight, the easier it would be for me to pull an Irish goodbye. However, the way Steph was looking at me, I wondered if I didn't need to say it.

The guys in question included the man Rena was seeing, two of Steph's friends from her fashion magazine internship, and the only other person in our friend group who'd stayed in New York City after college, Nick.

"Fantastic!" Rena typed furiously on her phone with one hand and sipped on Chardonnay with the other. "Because Cole's here."

Steph and I exchanged glances, raising our eyebrows at each other and then laughing as Rena went to buzz him in, completely oblivious to our reaction. We weren't Cole's biggest fans considering how often Rena had gone from smitten to disappointed and back again, all within a couple weeks' time. She wasn't the greatest judge of character, but then again, not everyone had my gift.

"Shot?" Steph asked me, already pouring tequila into the cheesy NYC shot glasses we got from street vendors during freshman orientation. The deep brown skin along her cheekbones glimmered, creating an iridescent dance of color as she turned her head beneath the kitchen pendant lights.

"Sure, why not?" I tapped my glass to hers and threw it back. The burn of the liquor traveled down my throat and pooled into an enveloping warmth in my stomach.

Rena opened the door to a tall, blond man with a strong nose and lightly freckled skin. He looked like he'd come straight from Wall Street, and he walked with a kind of lazy swagger that threw his center of gravity off as if he was leaning back on his heels.

"This is Cole," Rena said after he entered. She beamed ear to ear.

He waved at us with a short flick of his wrist. "Hello, roommates. Who's the birthday girl?"

"That would be Áine, the one in that gorgeous little red dress," Rena said animatedly, making an exaggerated gesture with her arms.

"Ahn-ya," he attempted to repeat back to us. It didn't sound right on his lips.

As Cole stepped closer to me, his energy coursed out from his body in wisps of red and murky gray hues. It reached for me, bubbling up and overflowing into the space between us. It was lustful, but not entirely directed at any single target. It was just a general state of being, longing, dissatisfaction. It felt like frustrating attempts at getting warm on a cold night—icy hands reaching toward flames that continuously moved out of reach at the last second. It was an uncomfortable, restless aura, and I had to try hard not to make a face.

I met Steph's eyes, coming back into the present moment and letting Cole's energy slither back to him and away from my perception. She lifted her eyebrows slowly as she discerned my judgement. Then she gave me a small nod, as if to say, *I knew it.*

Rena scrunched her face at us, sending me a sharp glare from behind Cole.

"Hey, nice to meet you," I said quickly, extending a hand to him. "You want a drink?" Who was I kidding? Of course he did.

He didn't seem to notice the wordless conversation that

had just taken place. "Yeah. For sure, but could I use your bathroom first?" he asked.

"Of course," Rena said, her excitement slightly deflated. "It's just down the hallway." She gestured to our right. As soon as he shut the door behind him, she turned to me and crossed her arms. "I told you I didn't want you to do that anymore."

"I'm sorry," I said. "Sometimes I can't help it." Okay, maybe I could've helped it.

Steph cast a glance down the hall before leaning in. "We're just trying to protect you. Why would you want to be with someone with bad vibes, dude? Not just regular bad vibes either, but like psychically, cosmically bad vibes..."

Rena sighed dramatically but looked back at me in spite of herself. "How bad?" she asked.

Before I could open my mouth, Steph gestured to the front door. "Be right back."

"Well, I don't think he's a serial killer or anything," I started. "But possibly some kind of addict? And certifiably... horny."

Rena rolled her eyes. "Right, well, that's more than half the people in this city." She stared me down.

"Fine! I'm sorry. I'll stop. Just be careful." It wasn't going to end well. But *free will*, and all that, right?

Multiple voices echoed from the hallway as Steph opened the door. At the same time, Cole came back into the kitchen, sniffling loudly. He helped himself to a tequila shot and tilted his head back to take it in one decisive gulp.

Nick's voice rang out. "Hey, witch bitch!" He sauntered over to me.

"Stop calling me that," I hissed at a clearly tipsy Nick

before pulling him in for a hug. Leave it to him to pregame the pregame. "How are you?"

"Fantastic, darling," he glanced behind him at Steph's work pals. "Oh my god. Who are they?" He fanned his face.

On cue, Steph introduced them as David and Reagan, who, to be fair, did look like fitness models. Cole was not amused by Nick's antics as he drooled at the two men, and his unwavering, judgmental gaze was really starting to get on my nerves. We all gathered in the kitchen talking and waiting to head out to the club a block over.

"Is no one going to say anything about how nice this place is? How in the world are you guys affording this?" Cole gawked, looping his arm around Rena's waist. "I know that a fashion magazine intern, a social media manager and whatever the hell it is that you do," he continued, lazily pointing to me, "do not make enough for *this*." He laughed, looking for support from Steph's friends who politely smiled and averted their gaze.

Steph and Rena fell silent and looked over at me. I cleared my throat and opened my mouth before being cut off by Cole.

"Oh," he said, "trust fund baby then?" He stared me down with a crooked grin.

Rena crossed her arms and shot him a look. My cheeks felt hot. A vision of my mothers' faces overwhelmed my vision, smiling down and warning me:

Never take off your special bracelet, Áine. It will protect you and keep you hidden...

I twirled the silver band around my wrist. "My parents passed away and left me some money," I said simply, meeting

Cole's gaze and holding it firmly until he looked away, the color draining from his face.

"Oh, I'm sorry, that's my bad," he said, scratching his head and looking down at the kitchen tile.

"Alrighty then," Nick said, laughing nervously and giving my hand a squeeze. Under the façade of chaos and messiness, his energy was warm and light, like the feeling of sunlight trickling through blinds on a morning with nowhere to be. "Shot and then go?"

Everyone quickly nodded their heads with more than enough enthusiasm.

"To the birthday girl!" The room cheered.

By the time we made it to the club, the line to get in was all the way around the corner from the entrance. Cole groaned and rolled his eyes, which the rest of us tried to ignore as we made the best of it. His energy was becoming more and more draining and hard to ignore. Blocking out his negative vibes was even more important to someone like me—a clairsentient—who could feel the emotions and psychic baggage of others. Clubbing could be an intense and overwhelming experience for anyone, but for me it could either turn into my own personal hell or an orgasmic high. It all depended on the kind of energy I intercepted from the hundreds of people around me.

"Hey." Nick nudged me. He brushed his light brown curly hair out of his face. "You feeling up for this?" He swayed a little, resting a hand on my shoulder.

"I would tell you if I wasn't," I said.

"You didn't last time..." he trailed off, referring to the night I'd just been dumped and had a full-blown mental breakdown as I felt the pain of three hundred people. He saw the look on my face and quickly spoke again.

"You look *so* hot though, seriously." He grabbed my hand, lifted it above my head, and twirled me around. "Like yes, honey!"

I laughed and rolled my eyes at him. Rena and Steph joined in to hype me up as I blushed and grinned. I felt the red flashes of anger coming off of Cole like sparks, for reasons I couldn't begin to imagine.

When we finally made it inside, Steph led us to the coatroom and then to the dance floor. Somewhere along the way we'd lost Rena and Cole, and I felt a bit guilty at my relief. The energy around me was overwhelming. It was bright, multicolored, and pulsating, overpowering my senses. I allowed myself to get drunk off of the collective effervescence as I danced in our little circle.

After a while, one of Steph's friends, Reagan, approached me and started dancing in front of me, eyeing me up and down. He had dark brown skin, well-defined muscles that peeked through his thin white shirt, and a mischievous smile. We started to dance, Steph squealing, "Get it, girl!" in my ear. I reached out for his energy, trying to separate it from the crowd. Deep in its core it was breezy but reserved, complex like a fine wine, but at the surface lay palpable lust. I had to taste it.

I moved my face closer to his, and he met my lips. But as soon as his tongue grazed mine someone pulled me away.

"Áine!" Steph yelled over the loud music. She pulled on

my arm, her eyes urgent. Dread swam to my gut. "We need to go find Rena!"

The four of us linked hands and started moving through the crowd back toward the entrance. In the wake of my fear, my high dissipated and dropped into the cavernous abyss. Suddenly the people around me reeked of pain, anger, and destruction. I could see the darkest parts of them billowing around like smoke and shadows.

When we hurried into the street, I gulped in fresh air, trying to breathe and center myself. Reagan shot me a look of concern, reaching out to steady me.

"What's going on? Is Rena okay?" Nick asked.

Steph was staring at her phone, leading us further down the street in the opposite direction of our apartment. "I don't know. I think she drank too much and now she's arguing with Cole. Her texts don't make much sense."

I took a glance at her phone's screen, where Steph was tracking Rena's location. We seemed to be approaching.

"You can sleep it off at my place." Cole's terse voice rang out as we rounded a corner. He had a firm grip on Rena's arm. When he saw us approach, his demeanor shifted into the defensive, and he let go of her. "She's fine. Sorry about the *drama*." He raised his eyebrows and glared at Rena like he was scolding an errant child. "She just got too drunk —*shocker*—so I was taking care of her." His eyes darted around, the streetlamps illuminating a throbbing vein in his forehead. He wiped at his nose and then at his bloodshot eyes.

The hair on the back of my neck stood up, my whole body suddenly vibrating like the booming bass of a rock concert. I was barely aware of Steph and Nick starting to argue with Cole as I watched a very drunk, wobbly Rena dart into the road just as a taxi turned the corner and sped down the street. As if in slow motion, Rena tripped. Her body sprawled right out in front of the vehicle. The sound of screeching tires rang through the night. Reagan clutched my arm painfully as David yelled.

Time slowed down as my mothers' silver bracelet burned my skin and then dissolved into ash. A monumental surge of energy I'd never felt before entered through the crown of my head and shot out through the palm of my instinctively outstretched hand. At my direction, the cab flew through the air and into the vacant building across the street, smashing through heavily vandalized glass.

A chorus of screams erupted and mixed with the boom of the collision. I was relieved to see Rena sit up, confused but unharmed. I stumbled as darkness washed over my consciousness, and before anyone could catch me, I fell hard to the pavement.

I'd always known I was different from the other children in my Northern Irish village. I started willing flowers to grow and bloom right before my mothers' eyes at age five, and by the time I was ten, I brought lightning and hail with each temper tantrum. I tried my hardest to contain it. I witnessed my mothers' terror with each display of raw power, but I couldn't stop.

One day, I overheard Momma Jane talking to Momma Celeste in hushed tones in their bedroom. "They're going to find her soon. We need to act."

They sensed me lurking at the door and ceased speaking, immediately coming to console me. Hot tears streamed down my cheeks as wind gushed through an open window and extinguished the candles on their dark mahogany dresser. I closed my eyes as they held me, trying not to give in to the enthralling energy reaching out to me from all directions.

Channeling that power was the greatest high I'd ever felt, but honoring my mothers meant never searching for it again.

Aware of my unconsciousness but unable to force myself awake, I thought of my mothers and our quaint, rural life among the rolling hills, where they braided flowers into my hair and told me stories of witches and magick. They sang to me in an ethereal, ancient-sounding language as we gardened. Sunlight warmed the back of my neck and I giggled as—

You need to run. You are in grave danger. Don't trust anyone. A man's deep voice rang in my mind, sharply cutting through the mirage of memories and replacing them with unstable darkness behind my eyelids.

Who are you? I asked into the void.

A friend. I will find you. Run.

My eyes flew open. My friends and a couple of strangers were gathered around me, a mix of fear and confusion in their eyes.

"Hey! Get back, guys. Give her some space," Steph said, her voice strained and shaking.

Cole's mouth was agape. "What is this? The motherfucking Avengers?"

"Ma'am, are you okay? Don't move. An ambulance is on its way," a man in a police uniform urged.

"What on earth just happened?" Reagan asked, looking at me in pure terror. His energy recoiled from me and went cold.

Something about me felt naked. Disoriented, I instinctively reached for my silver bracelet, only to wince in pain as my fingers brushed over festering red and white blisters where it used to rest. Tears brimmed in my eyes from the pain, soon replaced by hot panic as I realized my source of protection had disintegrated—as well as my only tangible connection to my mothers.

You need to run now, the male voice said again.

I lifted myself off the ground with my good hand, ignoring the police officer reaching out to me in protest. "Ma'am, I'm going to need you to stay seated."

"Don't touch me," I yelped, adrenaline—and something far more potent—coursing through my veins. Sparks flew from the streetlamp above, making everyone jump back. I met each of my friends' eyes before brushing dirt and debris from my suddenly far too revealing red dress.

"I love you guys." My voice caught in my throat. There was nothing else I could say to explain to them why I needed to go. I didn't have enough time, and I refused to say goodbye. I didn't want this to be *goodbye*.

I took off running as my friends called out after me, and for some reason the police officer decided to follow—his heavy stride pounding on the pavement in unison with my labored breaths.

"Fuck!" I muttered, my feet aching as I registered how impractical my high heels had become. He was going to catch up to me.

I shot a confused look back at the slightly overweight

officer on my tail, then threw up my unburned hand and shot a bolt of energy back at him on instinct. I needed him to stop.

He grinned at me, and with a flick of his wrist he seemed to deflect the shot into a nearby car, shattering its windshield. I gulped. This was no cop, and I had absolutely no idea how to use my newly regained power.

It only took that one second of inattention toward the ground in front of me for my heel to catch in a dip in the pavement, sending me tumbling. A shot of pain erupted from my ankle, and I heard some kind of popping sound. I cried out, catching myself on my forearms so I didn't break a wrist too. The pain from my blistered wrist hitting the hard cement was nearly unbearable, causing my tears to overflow.

The man came to a halt in front of me, his police uniform dissolving from him like a cloud of mist to reveal jeans and a plain black T-shirt. His face and body thinned out, and hair grew where he was once bald. I gasped at the emptiness of his icy, dark energy as it sent off a cacophony of warning bells through my system.

"You feel... evil." I let his aura snap back to him. I wanted nothing to do with it.

He knelt down beside me, feigning shock. "Well, that's not very nice, now is it?" He now spoke with an accent similar to a heavy Southern drawl.

I attempted to crawl away from him, but he grabbed my injured ankle. I screamed, helpless and unable to keep more tears from streaming down my face. His grip tightened, and he closed his eyes. From his palm came a horrible pulling sensation against my skin, and soon a look of pure bliss washed over his features.

He let out a gasp, his eyes fluttering open. "I've never felt anything like that. You're the one they've been looking for, aren't you?"

I could hardly focus on his confusing words as unconsciousness threatened again. As my vision drifted in and out of focus, another man appeared from behind my attacker. His face was strong and angular, with steady brown eyes, and his dark hair had a slight wave to it. He swiftly locked his arms around the assailant's neck and pulled him away from me.

As he did, my head fell back onto the sidewalk, the pain from my injuries and sudden exhaustion overwhelming me. Lying there, I listened to the sound of muffled pleading, grunting, and then quiet.

"Nice dress," a familiar voice purred as I felt my body being lifted into the air. It was the same voice that had told me to run. "Sleep now." Fingers brushed over my eyelids and the world went dark once again.

CHAPTER 2

When I was a young child, my mothers told me bedtime stories about the place they came from—a place filled with magick and wonder, where the colors were brighter, the trees were taller, and the people were kinder. They said there were beaches with sand made of shimmering crystals and water clearer than translucent glass. They told me I was a gift from the Goddess herself, and it was out of unconditional love and devotion that I grew in Momma Celeste's belly.

"You were so loved that people feared you," Momma Jane whispered, stroking my deep copper locks of hair. "We had to take you away to keep you safe."

"But one day," Momma Celeste whispered as a tear escaped her eye.

"A very long time from now," Momma Jane cut in. "When you are ready…"

"You will go back home and learn of who you are."

I dreamt of them nearly every night. Whether it was the

soft, delicate contours of their faces as they sang to me in the garden, or their frenzied panic as they chanted words in an ancient tongue, tracing shapes on my wrist where the silver band rested, when the front door to our cottage flew open and—

I awoke in a cold sweat, sitting up quickly. I shuddered as I looked around at unfamiliar surroundings. I was in a bed with unbelievably soft sheets. I quickly looked down and saw I was still in the red dress that now clung to my damp skin. The walls were grayish purple, with a white bedside table and a dimmed lamp. The bedroom was lavish yet also looked barely lived in, with very few markers of personalization. It was far bigger than my bedroom in New York.

I jumped when a tall figure appeared in the doorway, but as I shifted to get up, a searing pain in my ankle reminded me of my injury. I winced as I began to recollect all of the very strange events that took place on my twenty-second birthday.

The man who saved me—whose voice told me to run after I destroyed my source of protection—approached me cautiously, his face pensive but relaxed. He appeared to be in his late twenties, an athletic build with striking features that seemed carefully controlled.

I was able to hoist myself up to rest against the headboard, reaching an outstretched palm in the space between us. My power curled around me, like a snake poised to lash out and bite hard.

He raised a brow but stopped his approach. "I'm not going to hurt you. I think you'd know by now if that was my intention."

"Who are you and where are we?" I cleared the hoarse-ness out of my voice as I assessed his every movement, from the way his fingers unclenched at his sides to his long exhale.

"My name is Daelon. We're in Aradia—the witch realm—in a remote cabin where you will be safe. You were asleep for about a day after we made the jump, I suspect because you weren't used to channeling that kind of power."

"The witch realm," I repeated dumbly. So it was all true. All of those stories my mothers told of the land from which they'd escaped came flooding back to me. They were fragmented into bits and pieces, scattered by the trauma of their deaths and time long passed. I was only a child then, and after so many years living a relatively normal human existence, they felt more like a mélange of dreams and mythic bedtime tales than reality.

Not to mention, I wanted absolutely nothing to do with the realm my mothers' murderers came from. Or the power I'd held inside me that led them to us.

It had all been my fault.

The deep, dark wound opened up and festered, and like a great tide, my power began to flood. The lamp beside us shook, and heavy rain began to pour and batter against the windows.

Daelon watched me carefully. "Breathe," he said. "Give me a deep breath in and out."

His tone was commanding enough to earn my narrowed gaze. I still had no idea who he was or what he wanted, and as I reached out to his energy, I realized there was nothing to feel. His aura was like a solid brick wall of impenetrability. In my moment of distraction, the furniture settled and stilled.

"Why can't I—feel you?" I stuttered.

He raised his brows again, an amused grin taking shape. "Maybe buy me dinner first," he said.

I crossed my arms. "Your energy. Aura. Soul. Whatever you want to call it."

"You're an energy reader," he said, somewhere between a statement and a question. "Interesting."

"Well?"

"That's your gift, and mine is that I'm a shield. I can mask energy, power, and spells, and I'm more in tune with defensive magick. That's why you're safe here. Witches like the one who attacked you, energy vampires, will be drawn to the enormity of your power like moths to a flame. And your flame burns much, much brighter than most."

I mulled over his words, looking through the windows to the rainy forest landscape below. Not being able to read him was going to be a problem. It was like losing one of my senses, leaving me vulnerable and shrouded in darkness.

"Well, then how am I supposed to trust you?"

He snorted, and the dirty look I gave him only seemed to make him more amused. "Maybe by judging my words and actions like everyone else?"

Yeah, I wasn't so sure about that.

"Can I get more of an explanation on whatever the hell energy vampires are and why they're after me?"

He leaned against the wall by the windows as he faced me, mirroring my crossed arms. A flicker of disgust rolled through his features. "Well, they're not after you, specifically. They're just after power, and you have a lot of it. They take from others as a way of life, living on the outskirts of society and getting high off the act of stealing energy. Or some seek to use others as kinds of power batteries, because they weren't born with much ability for channeling themselves. So they steal. Some of them were banished to the human realm for their crimes, so they prey on human energy instead. They're the scum of Aradia and Earth." He spat out the last words like they were spoiled.

I thought of my friends, and anger swelled in my chest. "What happens to the humans?"

"Fatigue. Depression. Insanity. They grow weak. Or ill," he said softly. "To witches it's a grave violation. Syphoning away power and gifts without one's consent. I'd imagine many would seek to use you as an infinite power battery. Or the greatest high of all time."

My heart rate picked up, the tightness in my chest growing heavier. How did I know that wasn't what Daelon was doing?

"Well, thank you for saving me. But I can't be here. I don't want to be here. I want to go back," I said.

My mothers died protecting me from this realm. I wanted nothing to do with it. I was an orphan from Northern Ireland who lived in New York City with my friends, my anthropology degree, freelance writing, and doing normal, human things. This power suddenly felt like a sickness, pressing up against me from all angles and squeezing the air from my lungs.

Daelon walked closer, his hands raised in the air in a silent *don't shoot*. Wind bore down on the cabin's foundations, the furniture beginning its haunting rattle once more. My palms grew hot, begging for release as I struggled to gulp down air.

"Hey," he said softly. "I need you to listen to me." He sat down on the edge of the bed, his features hardening into the air of someone with authority. Someone who knew all the answers. "I know you're scared. But I will prove to you every day that you can trust me. You can't go back. Going back now would only put you and everyone around you in grave danger. You belong here. I know you can feel it."

He was right. The energy of this realm was different—less stifling, less rigid—like it was where I was always meant to be. Like it was *home*. But I wasn't ready to admit any of it.

I also knew I didn't want to put my friends in danger, which meant I was stuck here with a stranger in a realm I knew nothing about.

Daelon's unwavering gaze and steady, assured voice pulled back my focus, enough to halt the panic for the moment. "Right now, you're free-channeling. Your power is bound up to your emotions, which makes you kind of a wild card. It will burn you up from the inside out. But if you learn to detach your power from your impulses, urges, and feelings, you can use and direct it exactly how you want. I can help you."

"Why? Why do you want to?" This power felt like a storm, and I was caught in the eye of its hellish cyclone. The idea of control didn't sound too bad at the moment, but I couldn't let go of the feeling that it was more curse than gift. It had only brought me pain.

It stole away my parents and now it had taken away my chosen family of friends, too. A tsunami of grief began to build in the periphery, reminding me that I was alone, again —just like the day I arrived in America—and maybe this power would mean I would always be alone in the end.

He sighed, his jaw tensing. "Because I think we have

common enemies. And... it's just something I was called to do. I heard your cry for help, and I came. I can't explain it."

Can't or won't? Common enemies... the image of the cottage door blasting open—a recurring nightmare reconstructed from memory—was still fresh in my mind's eye, along with the cacophony of screams that followed.

I shifted positions, wincing and gritting my teeth as pain shot through my ankle.

"I set a couple pills for the pain on your nightstand," he said. A flash of anger flitted across his features as he inspected the blue and black bruises on my swollen skin. "They're more magick than medicine. And you'll heal much quicker than a human now that you're connected back to so much power."

I glanced down at my once-scabbed wrist, marveling at the healing that had already taken place. Only a faint red line encircled my skin now. I grabbed the two blue pills on the wooden table, noting the mark of their energetic makeup, as if they had a slight aura of their own. The aura of painlessness. I took them with a gulp of the accompanying glass of water, and the relief was instant.

Daelon and I stared at each other for a few long seconds.

"Okay. I will stay here. For now. But I'm going to need a lot more answers, and if I find out you're lying to me in any way, I will unleash this untrained witch curse on you so fast," I warned.

He blinked. "You think being one of the most powerful witches in the realm is a curse?" he asked incredulously, ignoring my threat. "We'll have to work on that."

I pursed my lips. I wasn't ready to talk about my mothers with this stranger. "I just want to take a shower." As my power simmered down like the hiss of steam from an extinguished fire, all I could feel now was exhaustion. My mind raced, but my body was as heavy as lead.

"There's a bathroom attached to your room there." He gestured to the double doors across from the bed. "But you need to stay off your ankle if you want it to heal right. Which means you need help. And I would be more than happy to oblige."

My stomach fluttered as his eyes moved from my ankle, up my body and back to my eyes. I might as well have been naked already given the state of my dress. I narrowed my eyes.

"Áine," he said. "Let me help you. I promise not to peek." The faintest tinge of mischief clouded his eyes as he cocked his head.

I let out a breath, the smirk he was biting back doing little to assuage my unease. It was hard not to get lost in his steady, controlled voice, which seemed to consistently teeter on the edge of commanding.

I uncrossed my arms and shook my head. "Fine." I paused. "How did you know my name?"

"Sometimes, we witches just know things," he said, shrugging a shoulder. "Come on, then, little witch."

I bristled at the patronizing pet name, but the tips of his mouth only shifted up. He rose, offering me his arm—taut muscles peeking out from beneath the black fabric of his T-shirt. I looked away quickly, grabbing ahold of him as he helped me to my feet.

He led me into the spacious bathroom, which was white with gold accents and all kinds of elegant. A luxurious, free-standing bathtub sat against the far wall. The mirrors in the front were tall and meticulously clean, the counters a shimmering gold and white marble. A spacious shower with glass doors was in the right corner, with a detachable shower head and a shelf built into the wall at sitting height.

"It's nice, isn't it?" he said softly.

I nodded, assessing my best course of action as I leaned on him and hobbled to the shower.

"I think I can take it from here," I said curtly.

He watched me for a few long seconds as I grabbed onto the towel rack for stability. He was so close I could smell the faintest woodsy, clean scent from his clothes, like fresh pine and soap.

"Are you sure?" The half-smirk was back.

I rolled my eyes. "I'm sure."

He nodded, turning and moving to stand with his back to me at the front of the bathroom, leaning against the open doorway.

"Maybe witch customs are different, but I prefer to shower in private," I said, my eyes boring into the back of his head.

"First of all, you *are* a witch. No amount of time with the humans could change that. Second, I don't particularly trust you not to fall, and I'm not going to let you crack your skull open on my beautiful white marble floor. It would be terribly inconvenient to me."

I clenched and unclenched my fists, motionless until I finally decided this particular hill wouldn't be the one I died on.

"Fine. But any funny business and I will annihilate you."

Daelon laughed, and I was startled by the pleasant sound

of it—nearly pulling an instinctive smile of my own to my lips. "I have no doubt."

I unzipped the side of my dress and pulled it up over my head, trying not to lose my shaky balance. I shimmied out of my panties and peeled off my adhesive bra. I cast glances to the double doors every once in a while, but Daelon stood motionless, eyes forward. I wished now more than ever I could break through his shield.

I was surprised at how well the magick pills worked, coursing through my veins like a warm veil over my ankle's throbbing. Medication on Earth never seemed to work right for me, which was just another reminder of just how much I didn't belong.

I stepped carefully into the shower and closed the glass door behind me. I balanced myself on the cool, white stone and grabbed the golden showerhead above me, facing it away from my body as I let the water warm. I cleared back the toiletries from the shelf and sat against it, sighing in relief as I was finally able to get clean.

I stole a glance toward Daelon through the steamy glass. He still faced the bedroom, his arm outstretched to lean on the door frame. Despite my inability to use my clairsentience on his psyche, I couldn't deny the calm and security his presence evoked. It was actually very soothing not to have an aura constantly reaching out to my line of perception. It was like he was surrounded by solid walls—a walking armory of security. I had no idea if I could trust this stranger, whose alleged abilities were conveniently exactly what I needed right now. Maybe he really was someone I could trust... or maybe it was all a mirage, a trick, or a trap.

Steph, Rena, and Nick's shocked and fearful faces overwhelmed my mind's eye. I let a tear slide down my cheek, where it was swept away by a stream of water from the showerhead. Daelon was right. I couldn't go back. I didn't know when—or even if—I would see my friends again. Through the waves of grief, of which I was well familiar... there was something else, lurking, like a sliver of light through a long tunnel or a line of dominoes lying in wait. It was a feeling I couldn't put into words.

As reluctant as I was to have anything to do with the realm of the people who murdered my mothers, I knew in my heart that my return was as inevitable as the sunrise. Not only did energy of this world seem more natural to me than the denser, colder flow on earth, but I also remembered my mothers' words: *One day you will return home and learn of who you are.*

Who was I? Daelon seemed to think I was one of the most powerful witches in the realm, and the ebb and flow of energy all around me seemed to suggest that he was right. It was as if I were tuned into a million different frequencies, and they all yearned to be broadcast at my will and direction.

I turned over a palm, glancing at my slender fingers as they pulsated with electricity. Never in my life had I felt so alive—like I'd been living in a world without color since my mothers' deaths. It felt wrong to think, but this newfound vitality shone much brighter than the deep wells of grief.

No matter his true intentions, I could at least use Daelon as a way to learn about my power and the landscape of the witch realm. Because if I had to be in Aradia, with this uncontrollable, accursed power, the least I could do was use it to avenge my mothers. I took a breath, a certain determination bleeding from the cracks of my disorientation and sadness. Someone—or something—had now stolen two lives from me. Two sets of families. And that couldn't go unpunished. This was what my mothers wanted. It had to be.

After I was finished, I carefully stood up and turned off the water. The floor was slick. I wasn't in the mood to fall again after the other night, so I let out a breath and sucked up my pride. "Daelon," I called.

"Yes, little witch?"

I scrunched up my nose at this new nickname. He was awfully brazen for someone who knew what I was capable of.

"I need your help. Eyes closed. And don't call me that," I snapped.

He laughed lightly. My heart fluttered when he turned and strode toward me with his eyes shut tight. He handed me a towel, which I quickly wrapped and secured around myself before clinging to his arm. I rose to my feet, cursing as I slipped on the slick floor and tumbled into him.

He caught and steadied me. "Can I open my eyes now?"

"I suppose," I sighed, eyeing him defensively.

"Hold onto your towel," he ordered, and I gasped as he lifted me into his arms bridal style.

"Hey!" My cheeks heated up, and I focused all my strength not to lose control of my power. I couldn't very well unleash it on the man who was holding me above the hard floor. I glared up at him instead. "Put me down," I growled, squirming in his arms.

He just shook his head, the corners of his lips turning down. "You're very demanding." He set me down on the edge of the bed. "I'm only trying to help."

"Demanding?" I repeated incredulously. "You're the one who just manhandled me."

"That's one interpretation," he muttered, and the look on his face appeared a little too scolding for my taste. He opened up an intricately carved wooden wardrobe, his back to me. "What dress would you like to wear?"

"Oh, I get a choice?" I said sarcastically.

He smiled to himself, like he told a joke that I wasn't privy to. He flipped through the articles of clothing lining the hangers.

"A dress would be easier to put on and take off yourself, wouldn't you say?"

I was silent, still reeling from his off-putting, domineering attitude. This ankle needed to heal as soon as possible, and then I would reconsider shacking up with a mysterious stranger. At least there was a perk to being some kind of ultra-powerful witch.

"Wait, how'd you get all of my stuff?" I asked, peering over at the familiar dress he was currently inspecting. I'd worn that one to my college graduation.

"Magick."

I sighed. "The gray T-shirt dress will be fine," I conceded.

Daelon regarded it disapprovingly before handing it to me. "Not the one I would've picked."

I quirked a brow. *Weirdo.* He moved to the dresser, grabbing a black lace thong and simple nude bra from the top drawer. I glared at him in a stunned silence, anger bubbling up at the intrusion. That seemed very, very unnecessary. He tossed them onto the bed with a purely stoic expression and then exited the room, softly closing the door behind him.

Daelon helped me sit down at a sleek, gray wooden table in the kitchen. As I took in my surroundings, I had to admit; wherever the hell I was, it was impeccably decorated and designed. The modern, black and gray kitchen bled into the chic and comfortable, yet slightly rustic living room, separated by the dining table at which I sat. The rug beneath me was white and soft under my bare toes, contrasting with the dark, hardwood floors. Opposite the kitchen to my right, two tall windows stretched floor-to-ceiling. The scenery outside—tall evergreen trees, mountains off into the distance, and the sun disappearing below the horizon—didn't seem at all otherworldly.

"This is your house?" I asked, unable to keep the awe out of my voice. If I was being held captive, at least it was in style, right? I watched Daelon move around the kitchen gracefully, pulling out various utensils and produce. He had all but dragged me out of my room to eat and to *stop pouting*. Which hardly seemed fair considering I was just forcefully dragged into a dimension I hadn't been to since I was in the womb. A little pouting was surely in order.

He glanced around nonchalantly and shrugged. "Suppose it is quite nice, isn't it?" he murmured.

That didn't answer my question.

"Are you okay with pasta?"

"Sure," I said. I fidgeted with my fingers, inspecting the painting across from me of an ocean with multi-colored sand and clear water. "It's a real place?" I wondered aloud, remembering the beaches my mothers told me about as a child.

More memory fragments swam to the surface like hauntings, coalescing into the scene of that primordial trauma. My mothers chanted power into my silver bracelet, and the door swung open—

"Áine!"

I snapped out of my daze to see flames leaping up from the stove in front of a very shocked Daelon. He set down the tray of chopped vegetables he was holding on the white marble island and strode to me.

"Look at me," he commanded, bending down to stare into my eyes. "Close your eyes and take a deep breath. Think of any time, place, or person that has made you feel calm. You need to get yourself on that frequency. You've felt that kind of peace with your clairsentience. Tap into it."

I swallowed, shutting my eyes and listening to him without protest. I combed through my memories, reaching out for the ones that felt serene. Visions flitted across my mind's eye, some personal to me and some that felt more universal. Steph knitting on the sofa, a warm cup of tea, my mothers singing, light touches from a lover on my bare skin—

"Good," Daelon said. "Keep your eyes closed." He tentatively touched my hand, pulling back when I flinched. "Sorry."

I had only flinched out of surprise, but I didn't say anything.

"Describe what you're feeling now. The frequency. How does it taste, smell, or look to you?"

I furrowed my brow, letting imagery pass through like a montage. Its energy traveled down the length of my body in waves.

"Like warmth," I said. "Shivers down the spine. Soft sweaters and blankets. The light of golden hour. Chamomile, pastels, ocean waves. The security of a mother's love. Like belonging." My voice faltered. I opened my eyes and looked away, flushed with embarrassment. Tapping into this energy with Daelon—this stranger—felt intimate. It was also a rush, but a softer, more controllable form of power than the other bursts I'd felt while angry, scared, or overwhelmed. It was like I was in tune with a current that ran through the entire universe.

A look resembling awe, or maybe just shock, brushed over Daelon's features. He cocked his head, studying me for a few long seconds before clearing his throat.

"Now let's see if you can use that energy for something more constructive, rather than a knee jerk reaction from free-channeling at the whims of your emotions." He offered me his arm and led me to the kitchen, the stove now bereft of angry, spitting flames.

I took a deep breath, holding on to the pleasure of this so-called frequency. As wary as I was to dig into the power that my mothers feared—the power that for some reason made me and my loved ones so vulnerable to attack—I felt nearly giddy to wield the magick I felt now. Here in this place, it felt right. Like it was always meant to be.

And like Daelon said, it was different than what coursed through me when I was backed into a corner. It filled a hollowness inside me I'd spent many years in the human realm ignoring and suppressing. I knew at its core that this energy was good in the truest sense of the word. It was transcendent and... connective. I sensed my mothers in this power.

I smiled, maybe for the first time since I woke up in this foreign realm.

Daelon's eyes lit up, the corners of his mouth tipping upward. "I think we're making progress already, little witch."

I feigned annoyance and scrunched my nose. "Whatever," I said.

He gestured to a pale purple candle on the kitchen island.

"Let's see if you can channel just a touch of this energy to light this candle. Emphasis on *just a touch*. I quite like this house, as do you, it would seem." He narrowed his eyes at me, and I tried not to let his scolding tone mess with my buzz. "For all intentional magick, from the casual and small-scale to the more laborious spells and rituals, it's best to visualize your intent as if it's already occurred. You need to believe the candle is already lit, not that it will become lit. That's where the true power lies."

I concentrated on the tingling in my skin, gathering it in the tips of my fingers to focus my intention. It was like I already knew on some level how to do this—and to do so much more. I followed this mental roadmap of instinct as I gathered up the energy I had channeled, calling on visions of fire in particular. I tried to be careful not to let too much rush out at once, but the power was harder to control than I thought as I let some pass through my fingers.

I grinned. Sure enough, a flame encircled the candle's wick and flickered wildly.

Daelon sighed as light flowed in from the living room suddenly, a dull rumble of flames erupting. I peered over at the grand fireplace now alight, along with the line of tall white candles on the mantle above. The flames reached up emphatically.

"Well, close enough," he muttered, extinguishing the flames with a gesture.

I couldn't help the satisfied giggle that escaped my mouth. Daelon regarded me with bewilderment, as if surprised by the sound. He cocked his head ever so slightly, and the sudden intensity in his chiseled features made my stomach churn. I had to stop myself from getting lost in it.

His eyes softened as I hobbled over to the bar stools behind the island, huffing when I realized they were too tall for me to climb without help. I was growing tired of this helplessness.

Daelon let out a small breath and hoisted me up, his face frustratingly unreadable again. I tried to ignore the electricity of his hands on my waist.

"Now that our impromptu training session is over, I'm going to need you to behave while I cook. Think happy thoughts," he said. "You'll need your strength to heal quicker."

I narrowed my eyes at him, which he only met with an amused half-smile as he got back to cooking pasta. Funny that he thought he could talk to me this way when, from what I've gathered, I could destroy him with the flick of a wrist.

Or could I?

"Wait, you said you were a shield, and that's why I can't read your energy... so if I were to say, grow tired of you and want you to perish, would you be able to stop me?"

Daelon paused for a moment and then laughed, nearly snorting. It was a laugh that made me want to laugh too, but

I didn't. It was fairly deflating that he didn't even seem intimidated by my threats.

"No," Daelon finally said. "Rest assured that you have access to enough power to end me whenever you want. I'm just better trained than you, for now." He turned from the stove to study my face, his eyes coaxing. His admittance reassured me. "You won't ever need to test that out, though. Believe me when I say I have your best interests at heart. I'm here to help you."

"So you say," I muttered. "Also, where exactly is Aradia? Like in relation to Earth? And how can we go between them?"

"Full of questions, are we?"

I scoffed. "How can I not be?" I had plenty more where those came from.

Daelon dished up the now completed vegetable pasta wordlessly and slid the bowl in front of me. Staring down at the fusilli topped with tomatoes, onions, and fresh basil made my mouth water. I was suddenly aware of my ravenous hunger, lifting a forkful to my mouth self-consciously as Daelon stared.

"Is it good?"

"Yes," I admitted, looking at him expectantly as he let my unanswered questions hang in the air between us.

Daelon's shoulders relaxed, seemingly satisfied. "Aradia isn't exactly in a different place than Earth. It's more like layers. They exist in the same space, at the same time, but the witch realm is on a higher frequency that humans simply can't access. The human realm is made up of denser metaphysical matter than us. That's why you probably feel like the energy of this world is lighter and more fluid. It's where we belong and where we are most powerful. Witches have learned ways to go between, but it's unnatural, and it requires a great deal of power."

I swallowed my mouthful of food and took a sip of water, still bursting with questions.

Daelon ate standing up at the counter. He seemed to always be alert, scanning the room occasionally, as if looking for someone to appear out of thin air. The silence between us should have been awkward, but it wasn't.

I let my mind wander, stealing a glance at the painting to the right again, where the sand seemed to shimmer and glow in multifaceted iridescence. My mothers' fairytales were coming to life before my eyes.

"I can take you there sometime," Daelon said quietly. "If you want."

I blinked out of my daze and turned my head to find Daelon staring intently at me. A flicker of vulnerability flashed in his eyes, but it was soon gone. I swallowed, surprised at the rush of emotions bubbling up. I felt closer to my mothers here in this place—more than I had in years.

"Who am I? Why am I so powerful?" I asked quietly. I felt the pull of a rising tide, and shivers ran down the length of my spine. In my mind, faint voices joined in a song that rang painfully familiar. I braced myself, straining against the current of power threatening to overtake me.

Daelon sighed and scratched the back of his neck. "You're special, to put it mildly. I don't know *exactly* why, but I know that you're here to help the witches of this realm. I can just feel it—just as I know that I'm here to help *you*."

I heard my mothers' voices echo in my mind as he spoke those words, telling me I was special and loved—so loved that people feared me—so loved that bad people were chasing us, unrelenting, until they burst into our home and—

"Hey, deep breaths," Daelon said. He reached out for the hand I was balling into a fist so tightly that my knuckles were white, but he stopped, seeming to remember my reaction to him touching me before. The wind howled outside, and the candle's flame in front of me grew taller and violent.

I relaxed my fist and took a deep breath, hesitating before slowly inching my hand closer to his in a silent granting of permission. He looked at me then closed the gap, placing his hand over mine and giving me a slight squeeze. The shielded nature of his energy was soothing, and it distracted me from my traumatic flashbacks and ruminations. Its stability was a comfort to the turbulent nature of my own.

"I will never lie to you, Áine. There is a lot you need to understand about this realm and the darkness that has overtaken it, but right now you're completely untrained, uncontrolled, and unpredictable. I need to focus on teaching you how to control and harness this power before all else. Otherwise, your emotions will let the power consume you," Daelon explained, his hand still on mine.

I knew he was right, but I didn't want to admit it. I knew that there was a terrifying amount of power available to me, and I sensed that it was completely dependent on my emotionality. I couldn't avenge my mothers without some semblance of control.

However, Daelon's arrogance in acting like I couldn't handle something when he didn't even know me was frustrating.

He'd now spoken both of common enemies and a darkness that had overtaken the realm, which meant he might know exactly who had been responsible for my mothers' constant fear and eventual murder.

"Fine," I said finally, pulling my hand away from his. "We'll do this your way." I paused, narrowing my eyes to indicate I wasn't just merely falling in line. "For now."

Daelon chuckled, yet again infuriatingly unaffected by my intimidation attempts. He looked bemused, but his lips tilted upward. "Are you threatening me?"

"Yes!" I exclaimed, exasperated. He said I had enough power to end him, easily. What wasn't clicking? I couldn't tell if he was being arrogant, just putting on a good poker face, or maybe something far more sinister.

"You're very endearing," he said. "Did you have a human boyfriend or two back on earth?" He searched my eyes, waiting for me to answer.

I scoffed, my eyes widening. Then I blinked at him, incredulous. "Are you flirting with me?"

"No, just curious." He shook his head slightly, almost as if he was scolding himself, and just like that, his features returned to stoic. The muscles around his sharp jawline tightened, and he picked up my plate to take to the sink.

I sat helplessly in my seat, wishing my ankle was healed enough to retreat to my room without any help. If only I could read his energy and figure out what the hell he was playing at. Rena always said that my gift was cheating, but with so many people in the world with concealed bad intentions, I saw it more as a necessary line of defense. I usually knew who was up to no good. But all I felt from Daelon was only what he wanted me to perceive, or what he let slip in his body language. It was maddening.

I regained my composure as Daelon turned back around to me after cleaning up. The witchy painkillers were working a little too well, and I was suddenly exhausted again. My eyelids began to droop. At least it was dark outside now.

"I'm tired. I'd like to go to bed."

"Okay." Daelon was impassive. "I'm surprised you lasted this long, honestly. You obliterated one of the most powerful protection spells ever cast in order to channel an extreme amount of energy impulsively... without any sort of invocation or preparation." He sighed. "Just unbelievable. That had to leave you pretty drained."

"My mothers' bracelet," I murmured to myself. And what did he mean by invocation? I opened my mouth to speak but Daelon cut me off.

"Okay, time for bed," he said curtly. Then in one swift motion he scooped me up.

"Daelon, enough! Stop doing that," I squealed, brushing my long copper hair out of my face. "You don't need to—"

"It's just easier." He strode into the bedroom I awoke in earlier and set me down gently on the bed's plush comforter.

"Are you going to tuck me in too?" I mocked.

Daelon smirked. "Would you like me to?"

"No. I want you to go away." That sounded way more childish than I intended, and I cringed as Daelon stared at me, quirking an eyebrow. I pulled down my dress that had bunched up slightly, revealing more of my legs than I wanted Daelon to see.

"Goodnight, Áine," was all he said before he left me bothered and confused in this dark, unfamiliar bedroom.

CHAPTER 3

I glided through the air like a ghost, below the clouds but above everything else. I peered down at the barren trees below, whose branches stretched out toward me as if to pluck me from the sky. The air was cold and dry, prickling my skin like tiny needles. I soared quicker now, and the scenery began to shift as a massive, dark castle loomed in the distance.

I didn't want to fly anymore. I wanted to go back to the earth where I was safe, but a force stronger than gravity pulled me past the forest, above the castle, and then sharply toward one of the many towers. A light flickered in a window near the top, and in an instant, I took a swan dive like a fallen angel through an open window.

I rolled gracefully onto a velvety, golden carpet. The inside of this place held an energy I had never felt before. It reeked of pleasure and pain and sheer power that felt unnatural, cold, and blinding. Candles lined the wall of this lavish interior, their flames suddenly growing and moving erratically. Down the hallway to my right, I heard a rising din of laughter and voices, and to my left was silence. I chose the silence, levitating so that my feet hovered above the ground. The hall was bathed in mostly darkness other than the occasional candle lamp jutting out from the walls and the flickering chandeliers above. The walls were intricately carved stone with golden accents. It was like something out of a fairytale, if not for the rotten, decaying energy that seemed to ooze from the stone like blood.

I halted before a large set of dark, wooden double doors with lavish detail. They flew open suddenly, startling me to the ground.

I hesitated as I faced the darkness, but a force—a sinister, bone-chilling power—pulled me toward the abyss. I wanted to scream but couldn't as I reached out for something to grab onto. I dragged my fingernails across the carpeted floor.

Hello there, a deep voice boomed in my mind with acoustical prowess, and in a single moment of pure panic and desperation, I was sucked through space and into the void. My ability to scream had been restored, and soon I was caught in an endless, deep well of pain.

You're so weak, the voice mocked as I struggled against the darkness. *You are nothing. No one. And there is nothing for you in this realm but more suffering and grief.*

I couldn't see anything but obsidian black, and thick smoke burned through my lungs like fire.

You are all alone. And you always will be.

The voice wrapped around me like a boa constrictor and squeezed and squeezed until I was hollow. Until I was nothing. Just like it said I was.

"Wake up, Áine," a voice urged.

I jolted awake. My breath caught, and beads of sweat formed along my hairline. I felt like I was in the abyss still—where both my psychic and physical senses had been completely overloaded, and all of my deepest desires and hidden thoughts rose to the surface—where I was mocked and called weak and pitiful. *What was that place?*

Where was I now? I sat up quickly, my confusion and panic waning as I brought myself back to reality.

Daelon stood over me, his face etched with concern. "It was just a dream," he murmured.

A dream? I didn't think so. I hadn't had a dream so vivid in my life. I guessed this was just another witch thing I was going to need to get used to.

I began to shake, overwhelmed and feeling lost. The dream—or nightmare—had been so realistic, and it had struck a chord deep within my psyche. Something powerful was out there in this realm that I didn't understand, and it yearned for me. It had always yearned for me, and now I was here on its home turf. I was wholly unprepared to confront whatever—or whoever—it was. This was all too much.

"Hey," Daelon consoled, clearly sensing I wasn't fully focused on him yet. "You're safe." With his steady eyes locked on mine, he willed me back into the present. The way he spoke with such authority made it hard not to believe him.

"How—" I couldn't finish the question. I hugged my knees to my chest. I hated how pathetic I probably looked right now. I needed to keep up my front to protect myself from Daelon and his carefully concealed intentions, but I was scared and exhausted. I couldn't shake the sinister voice from the dream that told me I was weak. That I was *nothing*. And that there was nothing for me in Aradia but loss and pain.

I stared at a spot on the comforter in front of me. "Why are you here?"

"I heard you scream. I wanted to make sure…"

I lifted my head up to look at him when he trailed off, seeming to self-censor. His normally impassive, in-control vibe had been shaken, worry etched into features that seemed out of proportion to a nightmare. What wasn't he saying?

He broke our gaze, composing himself. "I could lay next to you, if you want. Above the covers, of course."

I hesitated, unable to admit how soothing his shielded, protective presence had been when I'd returned from that hellish void.

"I promise not to bite." And just like that, he was back to his usual antics, his eyes gleaming with mischief.

Absolutely not, I thought, but I said, "Okay," instead. Frustrated with myself, I laid back down and let out a sigh.

Daelon seemed surprised, but quietly walked to the other side of the king-sized bed. I felt his weight settle into the mattress next to me.

"You can get under the covers," I said, feeling guilty about making him uncomfortable in his admittedly sweet gesture. "But don't try anything."

"How generous," Daelon taunted. "And I wouldn't dare."

He didn't have to make it sound like *that* preposterous of an idea. I shook my head at myself. I needed to go back to sleep.

As we lay quietly together in the darkness, I resolved to ask him more about where he came from and why it was his purpose to help me. I knew that it might've been insane to allow this stranger to get so close, especially when I didn't know my friends from my foes. I knew I had enemies here; my nightmare was a good reminder of that. The sooner I got to the bottom of who they were—and who *I* was—the better.

And where did Daelon fit in? As much as I wanted to remind myself that without my clairsentience he was as good as an enemy to me, I couldn't deny the sense of safety that washed over me as he lay beside me.

And with him there, I drifted off easily into a dreamless sleep.

This time when I awoke, I was calmer. Working through grogginess, it took me a moment to realize there was a weight on my chest. I opened my eyes to see Daelon's arm wrapped around me like a vine. He was fast asleep, his head buried into the comfortable silk pillow. So much for not trying anything... maybe he wasn't as immune to me as he let on.

I slipped out from under his grasp, and he stirred but didn't wake. I was surprised to find that my ankle wasn't aching. I pulled it out from under the covers and sat up to rest on the edge of the bed. I gasped in astonishment to see that the bruising and swelling had disappeared. Tentatively, I stood, putting some weight on the once-injured joint. It felt tight, but not painful. Delighted not to be so helpless anymore, I made my way to the lavish en suite bathroom to brush my teeth.

The witch realm seemed to agree with me, I thought, as I studied myself in the tall, gold-framed mirror. The reddish hues of my long copper hair shimmered, and my green eyes looked bright and alert. My fair skin with golden undertones was clear and practically glowing. What was in the water here?

Somehow Daelon had obtained most of my belongings from my apartment, and I wondered if his mysterious, magickal ways included a run-in with my roommates. What must they think of me? And everything that had happened? Their terrified faces flashed in my mind, and my heart ached. I missed them more than anything, but with my power returning, no one around me was safe anymore. The best thing I could've done for them was leave. Who knew how many witches like the fake cop were already on their way to me as soon as that taxi crashed through the glass? I shuddered, remembering how it felt to have him syphon my energy. It was cold, intrusive, and cruel—like a leech digging its teeth into my soul, draining me. Daelon was right. Anyone who had the gift of magick and chose to use it for *that* was the scum of the earth.

I went back into the bedroom to pick out clothes for the day. I wasn't really sure what *witch training* would entail, but I thought it best to ensure full range of motion. I settled on black athletic leggings and an olive-green tank top. Although Daelon seemed to be fast asleep still, I slipped back into the bathroom to change. To get my hair out of my face, I swept my long locks into two French braids that rested at my shoulders, with a few strands left out to frame my face. I stole one last glance into the mirror, my eyes jumping to the lace trim of my bralette peeking out from beneath the tank. I pursed my lips and pulled the fabric up.

Daelon was still sprawled out in my bed when I returned, his arm resting where my body used to be. I walked slowly to him, studying his relaxed features in the morning light. I was perplexed by how much softer and more innocent he looked this way, as unconsciousness kept him from putting on any carefully constructed—and often downright domineering—fronts. His facial muscles were relaxed, the hollows of his cheeks shifting slightly with each slow intake of breath. His dark hair was a bit messy from sleep.

I wanted to read him so badly. It was a compulsion. Maybe he was more vulnerable in his sleep. I moved to stand over him, closing my eyes in concentration as I reached out with my mind, feeling around his energetic field for anything perceptible. I was met with only resistance, like an impenetrable steel wall. The hairs on the back of my neck prickled in warning before a psychic shockwave knocked me out of my concentration.

My eyes fluttered open, and I gasped in surprise to find Daelon staring straight back at me.

"What are you doing?" he snapped. He glared at me, and what was once soft in his features hardened. As if remembering where he was, he quickly pulled his outstretched arm back from my side of the bed and sat up. He stretched and flexed his taut muscles as he frowned at me.

I tried to replace my shocked embarrassment with a smirk.

"Did I—" He looked appalled.

I crossed my arms. "Try to spoon me? Yes," I teased, feigning the scolding tone he'd been all too comfortable using with me.

"Sorry about that." He shook his head, but then narrowed his eyes again. "You were trying to get inside my mind," he accused.

My cheeks heated up, but I tried my best to remain impassive. "Can you blame me?"

He considered my words for a moment. "Don't try it again," he ordered. "Not that you'd ever be able to."

How frustrating. I shrugged as if unbothered. "We'll see."

Anger flashed in his eyes. He got up from the bed quickly and strode to the door. "It's in poor manners to force your way into another's mind, on par with energy syphoning without consent."

I frowned, considering an apology as the weight of his words sunk in. But he had to understand how impossible of an ask it was for me to trust him on his words alone, given everything that had happened.

"Eat some breakfast, and then be ready to train," he said without turning. "Glad to see your ankle is healed already."

I crossed my arms, flustered by him ordering me around like that yet again. The phrase *hot and cold* seemed to have been created just for him. But he was my only hope of surviving this new world at the moment. As soon as I had a better grasp of my abilities and the nature of this realm I wouldn't need him anymore—or anyone, for that matter.

And I couldn't help but grow excited to feel the rush of my power again.

After I made coffee, I waited for him in the living room while considering the fireplace I had lit yesterday with my magick. I leaned back on the plush, black suede couch. Daelon had disappeared into what I presumed to be his bedroom, and I made a mental note to explore the rest of the cabin later. Growing impatient, I set my coffee down on the table in front of me and walked over to the tall windows to gaze at the beautiful scenery. It reminded me somewhat of the Pacific Northwest, or maybe Colorado, with its tall evergreens and mountainous terrain.

Suddenly a chill slithered down the length of my spine, carrying with it a familiar feeling of a dark, alluring power. Power that didn't belong to me—yet was just as intense and all-consuming. I scanned the trees, taking an instinctive step back as a figure emerged in the distance. Its outline was hazy as if made from blackened smoke.

My breath caught in my throat. "Daelon?" I called, trying to quell the rising panic in my voice. In an instant the imperceptible figure vanished, leaving me to wonder if I had really seen it at all. But I couldn't deny the energy that had called out to me from deep within the woods—strikingly similar to the abyss in my dream. It was such a fleeting energetic read that I couldn't be sure, though.

At the sound of footsteps, I whipped around to face Daelon, who studied my face with just a hint of worry. He straightened, his features tensing at my no doubt bewildered expression.

"Yes?" His right eyebrow shot up.

"I thought I saw someone out there, but I'm not sure," I

said, peering out the window again. The trees swayed slightly in the wind, and a hawk flew in the distance to land on a jutting branch.

Something flashed in Daelon's eyes. Concern, maybe. "That's impossible."

"But—"

"You're probably paranoid right now. Which is perfectly understandable after your nightmare. The witch realm can be highly... impressionable, especially by someone as powerful as you. Your thoughts, and especially your emotions, can have a tangible effect on Aradia's physical reality. Don't let it go to your head. The cabin and its surrounding land are heavily protected by multiple spells. I've completely masked your power. No one can find you here."

I was skeptical still, but his words seemed to resonate. If the power mirrored my own, maybe it really was just an extension of myself—the darker part of myself—the part I feared loved this power despite the pain it had caused in my life. Or maybe it was just the nightmare resurfacing to haunt me.

"Okay," I finally said, but I was still going to keep an eye out.

Daelon visibly relaxed. "Have you eaten?"

"I don't eat breakfast. I drink it." I gestured to the coffee.

He scowled. "You need your strength, Áine."

"You can't control everything," I snapped. "I'm sure caffeine will be more than enough fuel for ninja warrior witch training."

Daelon looked like he was debating on whether or not to

force food down my throat, but he settled on a slight roll of the eyes and a disapproving look.

"Come on, then." He spun on his heel and walked away. "*Ninja warrior witch training*," he muttered under his breath, chuckling quietly.

I smiled, feeling a bit triumphant in amusing him. He led me past the kitchen, past my room on the right where the door was ajar, and then past a closed door further down the hall to the left that I figured was his. The home opened back up again in design, with the far wall in front of us made completely of glass, overlooking a vast deck with a firepit and seating. There was a bar with tall barstools, another seating area, and possibly more space that wrapped around where I couldn't see. It seemed like a home I figured celebrities owned—sleek and modern, yet comfortable and built for entertaining. Yet, it was just Daelon and me here.

He stopped in the hallway just before the vast, open living room. To our right, a door. I peered past his frame when he opened it and saw stairs leading down into darkness.

"Yeah, I don't know about following a stranger down into a dark basement," I said. "Talk about Serial-Killer-Victim 101."

Daelon snorted. "Do I really strike you as a serial killer?"

"Ted Bundy was attractive and charming. Appearances are of no consequence." I sighed, then followed him down the steps. He probably had no idea who I was talking about.

"You think I'm attractive and charming?" Daelon threw me a wicked grin as we descended, though his eyes told a different story, as if he was surprised... and maybe a bit hesitant. *Nervous?* He didn't seem like the type to get nervous.

I rolled my eyes. "Well, that isn't exactly what I said," I stammered. "I think you're difficult and confusing." *And attractive, yes.*

"Right back at you, little witch."

Before I could remind him that I could kick his ass, we'd reached the bottom of the stairs to a breathtaking basement. I gasped audibly to see that the glass wall from above extended below, revealing that the house was built on the side of a hill. The glass was clear, letting in an abundance of soft, natural light. The basement itself was mostly bare, with some plush gray, low-seated chairs in the corner, wooden flooring, and pillows, mats, and black storage containers off to the side. There was a closed door underneath the stairs, which I assumed led to more rooms, given the size of the upstairs.

"Not really what I was expecting," I said.

Daelon grabbed two of the pillows and set them in the middle of the floor, gesturing for me to sit across from him.

"Most of your training will take place in your mind," he said with a shrug.

I scrunched up my face as I plopped down on one of the pillows. "Well, that sounds boring."

"We'll get to the fun stuff soon enough." The corners of his mouth tipped upward, scanning my body for a moment. His eyes lingering a second longer than I expected. "That shirt makes your eyes look... very green."

"Are you complimenting me?"

His eyes hardened. "Possibly." He allowed a ghost of a smile on his lips. "Are you going to be cooperative now?"

"When have I not been cooperative?" I batted my eyelashes. "Maybe you're just too demanding."

"Or, you're too defiant," he said, a hint of exasperation in his voice. He didn't seem used to being challenged. "Now, then, let's begin. For most witches, the key is learning how to raise enough energy to bend to one's will. You don't have any trouble summoning the power," he explained. "You have access to plenty of it. You just lack control. You allow your emotions and impulses to free-channel, which can be highly draining, not to mention outright dangerous to you and others."

"Maybe I want to be dangerous," I said quietly, flashing him a warning look.

Daelon was unbothered. "Be that as it may, you're not going to be very effective when your emotions can be used against you so easily. Your enemies will seek to use any weakness to their advantage to make up for being outmatched."

"Who are these enemies, exactly?" I tried.

"Áine," Daelon said in warning. "You agreed to focus on training before we discussed the rest. Once you have better control, I promise I will tell you everything I know. I don't need you on a revenge path before you're ready. You would get yourself killed. And me, for that matter."

I studied him, looking for any sign of deceit. His gaze was steady and earnest. He might've had a point, because the sharp pushes and pulls of my power already reached for me as I thought about my budding plan for revenge. The room's energy grew as intense and volatile as a tropical storm.

"You're angry. Why?" Daelon implored. "If this is going to work, you're going to need to be honest about what you're feeling."

"Because these enemies you won't tell me about killed

my mothers," I blurted. I looked away. My fingernails dug into my knees through the thin fabric of my leggings.

Daelon was silent for a moment. "I'm sorry. I, too, know that kind of loss and grief." His eyes were soft and sincere, a layer of vulnerability peeking out through the cracks of his shield. "Sometimes we lean heavier on anger when we're in pain, but I promise revenge will be much more satisfying if it comes from a place of strength and transformation rather than destruction." He suddenly looked surprised by his own words, like he was trying to convince the both of us.

I wanted to ask him who he'd lost, but he leaned closer.

"I will help you on this path, should you choose it. You have my word." His voice was barely above a whisper, yet I heard each syllable with glaring intensity. Something dark and heavy brewed in his eyes, mirroring the storm I felt beyond the horizon, awaiting my command to come rolling in.

I swallowed, unsure of what to say. "Okay. Let's get started."

He nodded, the muscles in his face relaxing.

"Where does this power come from?" I asked.

And just like that, the power stirred at the mention, tugging at me from all directions and whispering to me in a tongue more universal than any human language. The source felt timeless—utterly transcendent—as sure as the moon rising each night and the grass collecting dew in the spring.

"From everywhere. It's the current that runs through all things. From the moon, the stars, the seasons, every living thing, every action and reaction, from earth, water, wind, and fire, from death, birth, hatred, and love. Witches do not create power. We harness from and transform forces that already exist."

"Okay, Yoda," I laughed.

I wasn't used to being around someone who understood who I was and what I was capable of—someone who not only accepted my magick—but was in awe of it.

Daelon frowned. "I'm afraid I don't follow."

I scoffed. "Witches aren't Star Wars fans, huh?"

"Is this television?" Daelon cocked his head, his cluelessness sort of endearing to behold.

"Yes," I giggled. "It's *television*." Not making cultural references after living with Steph and Rena for years was going to be difficult. They were like walking pop-culture encyclopedias. At least I was no longer the one who couldn't keep up. I felt a pang of sadness as I thought of them, but loss and change were not unfamiliar to me. So, I stifled it.

"Sorry, my human knowledge is sorely lacking. You'll find that witches have much different forms of entertainment here." Daelon smiled to himself as if remembering another inside joke. "Are you ready to focus now?"

I nodded reluctantly, my gaze still narrow with skepticism.

"We're going to go through some exercises that will help you connect with and manage your power. You were born with more access to these natural forces than the average witch. It's like you're an energy beacon—constantly channeling an extraordinary amount of power freely with your mind alone, rather than ever having to use ritual, invocation, or the help of other witches for aid."

I tried to follow Daelon's words, but it all seemed so foreign and complicated to me. All I knew was the raw intensity at my fingertips, and the wealth of emotions, impulses, and intents emanating from everyone who had ever—or would ever—live, feel, and breathe. I was itching to feel their rush again.

Daelon sighed and shot me a pointed look, probably noticing that I had mentally jumped ship. "Patience, little witch."

I wasn't entirely convinced he couldn't read my thoughts.

"Close your eyes," he ordered.

I hesitated but then obeyed. *Fine.*

"Good girl."

Are you kidding me? Why was he so patronizing? I was going to punch him if he—

At the sound of a gust of wind my eyes flew open just in time to see Daelon fly backward onto the hardwood floor, catching himself on his forearm. The look in his eyes went from bemused to enraged quicker than it took me to realize *I* had just done that, somehow.

"I—"

Before I could apologize, he'd dragged himself back to his seat in front of me.

"Whatever was that for?" he asked, his anger dissipating as he shook his head. "Don't make me restrain you."

I glowered at him. "You're going to make me send you through that glass wall, next, Daelon," I hissed.

His face was now unreadable, as if made of stone. He just stared at me with his head cocked to the side, deep in thought. I squirmed under his gaze, holding my breath.

For a moment I wasn't sure what was going to happen next. Was he actually angry? Did he understand why *I* was so angry? Had people allowed him to act like this his entire life?

"What am I going to do with you?" he finally asked, clicking his tongue. "Close your eyes again, and this time be *a bit* more aware of how your thoughts and emotions are guiding your power."

I complied wordlessly, utterly confused by the whole interaction.

"Good. Now slow your breathing."

This was about me and my training, not Daelon and his mood swings, shielded aura, suspicious lack of backstory, and oscillation between being repulsed at the thought of flirting with me and being blatantly sexual. Did he even realize he was doing it? Maybe this was just a classic case of witch-human cultural difference.

Focus, Áine, I reminded myself.

"I know when your energy shifts," Daelon said. "I feel the ebb and flow of power in this room, as if you're warring with yourself for control. That's good—that means you're at least, on some level, already self-aware. I want you to work through it. Continue to slow and deepen your breathing, from your stomach. Think of something on a smaller scale than your mothers that brings out your anger, or another negative emotion that's hard to control. Something manageable. Then move through the energy that calls to you. What does it feel like? Where does it want to go? Don't let it take you. Just observe."

"Like getting stuck behind someone walking very slowly?" I joked, but I was ignored.

I wanted to say that this felt like a corny New Age guided meditation, but I held my tongue. I retreated within myself, following the trail of my annoyance toward Daelon's attitude. But it was too overwhelming a force, difficult to conceptualize and focus on. It was just an elusive reddish hue in an entire field of color, intensity, and shape.

"It'll help to create a metaphor within your mind—something tangible that will help you psychically organize and understand what you feel and how you channel. Think of it like visualizing an elaborate, functional daydream. A library of energy maybe, or a garden, or an—"

"Ocean," I said softly, unsure of where this word arose from, but it felt like more than a mere metaphor. That was what my power was. It was a vast blue ocean that spread out infinitely.

I let Daelon's words guide me as I wrestled with all this power, allowing it in so it could take shape. The landscape of my mind was chaotic and unorganized, whirring with visions and impressions waiting to be perceived.

"Let it carry you away," Daelon said, but his voice was growing more and more distant now. "I'm going to focus my magick on helping you into more of a trance-like state. But it'll only help if you allow it in," Daelon stressed.

His own magick swam toward me, and I could read its intent to aid me. I let it in, and my skepticism, self-consciousness, and doubt melted away into a quiet stillness. Soon the sound of crashing waves rose from the depths, and my body felt as though it was swaying back and forth.

I let go. Fully and completely.

I waded in a pool of infinite energy. The water was clear and iridescent, and as I reached its center, I felt currents reaching for me from all directions. I again considered my frustration with Daelon, though I was more detached from the anger than I had been moments ago. As I homed in, one of the currents before me grew stronger. It was anger. These streams were feelings or frequencies, not just mine, but *all*. Normally I surrendered to these pulls without even realizing it, following impulse, but now I was fully conscious. I was merely an observer.

Within my anger was the anger of millions—witches and humans alike. This ocean was endless, and it contained multitudes. It was every desire ever bloomed, every thought ever conceived, every spell ever cast, and every action ever undertaken. It was all things, and I had access to it all—like a vibrant cosmic tapestry depicting the fabric of all of existence.

My anger toward Daelon was his anger toward me. It was my anger toward myself, toward this world, toward my mothers, and toward the people who killed my mothers. I saw it all within the energy, like watching a universal drama play out before my eyes. Waves began to lap, growing violent and tall, and I was pulled into the chaos of the tide's violent ebb and flow. In a panic, I realized that my metaphor had taken on tangible shape as I gulped down very real water, salty and strong against my tongue. The anger wasn't detached anymore. It was within me and I within it. I—we —needed revenge. A wave of energy grabbed hold of me and dragged me beneath the surface.

I held my breath to avoid swallowing more ocean, opening my eyes to see visions playing out before me like a hologram amidst the shimmering water. I saw the cottage door fly open, seeing in third person the look of terror on my face as a ten-year-old child. My mothers chanted and my silver bracelet glowed with murky, defensive energy. Two men entered. They shoved past my mothers and reached out for me, but they grasped nothing as I vanished before their eyes.

"Where have you sent her?" one man snarled, striking Momma Celeste square on the jaw. He held magick in his palms that was black and evil, holding within its depths the screams of tortured witches.

I screamed underneath the water, shockwaves from my outburst dispersing the mirage to reveal tempestuous, dark water. I ran out of air, and water entered my lungs as I gasped and spluttered. I lost control of the rage swelling up within me, making it even more difficult to swim back to the surface as currents pushed and pulled me in all directions. Within the storm and struggle I felt a presence.

You're weak. I can feel you struggling and grasping for control that you will never obtain... you might as well give up now.

My vision went blurry as I suffocated, and I could make out a figure like the one from the woods—the outline of a man—but it was gone as quickly as it had appeared.

Then I heard Daelon, and I had never been so grateful to hear his voice.

"Come back to me," he said. "Come back to the room. See it in your mind."

I envisioned the glass paneling and the hardwood floors. I was draining rapidly. I saw Daelon's sharp jaw and dark eyes. I grabbed onto the sound of his deep, commanding voice, using it as an anchor to pull myself up from the abyss.

My eyes fluttered open to find Daelon over top of me as I lay on the hard floor. He pressed rhythmically on my chest as I choked on water, turning my head to the side as I coughed it up. After I had hurled half an ocean, I finally started to breath in unadulterated oxygen.

"Goddess above, Áine," Daelon muttered, breathing hard. "Are you all right?"

"Um, I guess so," I managed to sputter, still gasping. "How…" I trailed off, trying to piece together where I just was and how something within my mind ended up happening to my actual body.

"Like I said, Aradia is highly malleable and sensitive to energy. There often isn't a clear separation between our consciousness and material reality, especially when this dimension begins to blend with the astrals. It's hard to explain, but that's not important right now," Daelon said softly, his brows creased as he gazed down at me. He looked terrified, scrambling to build up his usual composure again. "Where were you? I thought I told you to focus on something manageable."

Was he seriously scolding me right now? And what the hell were the astrals?

"I did," I snapped. "But then I lost control of it. It was an ocean, but the water was also energy, and I just got swept up in the whole world's anger. I was doing so well at first." I shook my head, struggling to even comprehend what had just happened. "Are you sure you didn't slip me LSD? DMT? Shrooms?"

Daelon drew back, as if I'd mortally offended him. "I would never drug you," he hissed.

"It was a joke, jeez." I sat up, still trying to catch my breath as I hugged my knees to my chest.

His eyes softened, blinking at me. "Right. Well, witches don't really need drugs to trip." He shrugged. "You can't be taking on the whole world's anger, Áine, at least not yet. Baby steps."

"It wasn't exactly intentional." I paused, remembering my encounter within the dark side of the energy. "There was someone there, I think. In the anger. He told me I was weak."

Daelon looked away for a moment. "Strange," he said. "It could be anything, really. A part of yourself, another metaphor, or someone you've met or will meet. If you saw this person, or thing, only in your anger then I would steer clear. It's nothing good. I'll help you with defensive tactics soon."

I opened my mouth to say that I'd felt this being before—within my dream and out in the woods—but Daelon cut in again.

"You thought of your mothers, didn't you?"

I swallowed. "Yes. I saw the day they died. When they somehow spelled my bracelet to send me away before I could save them." My voice cracked a little, and I looked away.

Daelon nodded, reaching for my hand and giving it a squeeze. He looked unsure of himself. I accepted the gesture with a small smile. I noticed something familiar in his eyes, if only for a moment, but I couldn't quite place it.

This experience had lessened my anger toward him, as I realized it may have more to do with my deeper trauma than Daelon. I may not have known much about who he was, but I knew he didn't belong in that darkness. All the witchy intuition I had wanted me to believe he was an ally, despite my doubts.

"Will you tell me more about yourself?" I asked. "Like

where did you come from? How did you know I was in trouble?"

He was quiet for many long seconds, and I almost wondered if he would say anything at all. "I'm an orphan. I was taken in by some questionable people, and I'm a witch trainer of sorts. I felt your beacon of power when you saved your friend, and like I said before, I just *knew* I had to help you. It was instinct, like it was a part of some kind of higher purpose. I don't know how to explain it. As a shield, I knew I could keep you concealed from the people who wished to do you harm, as well as teach you how to wield your power constructively." He lowered his voice once again, which was strange considering it was just us. "And I know that your enemies are my enemies."

"I'm sorry about your parents," I said, reaching for his hand slowly like he had done for me. He looked at my hand over his pensively for a moment. "I want to trust everything that you say. But I don't know how to yet. At least not completely."

"I know. It's just hard to tell you certain things about myself because I fear it would trigger that anger within you, and it should be obvious now you're not equipped to deal with it all yet. You'll find that our stories run very parallel."

He peered out the glass paneling, which made me realize it was pouring down huge droplets of rain, flooding the earth. I wondered idly if that was my doing.

Probably.

"And it's hard to explain how I got here. Like I said, it was instinct—like a force beyond my rational understanding, built into the fabric of my DNA. I still don't quite understand it. You needed me and I came. I knew that you were special, that you were brought into existence to bring hope back to this realm, to right the wrongs committed against both of us. You feel that don't you?"

I was taken aback at how vulnerable he looked in this moment, staring out at the storm. His voice was low and conspiratorial, as if we were planning a coup, and his words mirrored my mothers' in ways that didn't seem all too coincidental.

"Yes," I sighed. "I feel it."

CHAPTER 4

"I'm sorry, Momma," I cried. "I'm sorry." I begged them to meet my eyes, clenching my small fists so I wouldn't unleash any more magick. I'd seen the lamb limp onto our property, covered in blood, and I just couldn't let her die. I had to heal her.

"You can't save every animal, Áine," Momma Jane whispered. Her long dark brown hair reached her chest, wavy and scented lavender like her shampoo. She wore a smoky quartz amulet that hung low against her deep purple blouse. "You have to let nature take its course."

"But aren't I nature, too?" I asked. That was what they always told me. *I was nature and nature was me.*

Momma Jane pursed her lips, shooting a look at Momma Celeste, who was staring out the window, tears streaming down her sun-kissed skin, chanting in a language I couldn't understand but still felt in my soul. She wore a delicate white summer dress, nearly the color of her cool blond hair. The two of them often reminded me of night and day personified, yin and yang, the dark and the light.

"You are also from the Divine. From the Goddess Herself," Momma Jane sighed. "And you need to accept that all living beings get sick, all living beings grow old, all living beings die."

"She wasn't sick, Momma," I said earnestly. "Something hurt her."

Momma Celeste stopped chanting and turned to face us, pressing her palms down on the kitchen counter. Her many silver rings clanked together as she tapped her long, pastel pink fingernails on the granite. I saw magick move beyond the window above the sink, like a forcefield expanding out into the horizon.

She stared at me with enough intensity to make me stop crying. "There is evil in the world. There are people who want to hurt others—to hurt us. Using your magick will attract that evil."

Momma Jane shot her a look. "Áine, baby," she cooed, pulling me in for a hug. "You will banish this evil when the time is right. Never lose your heart." She pressed her palm on the left side of my chest, and a comforting warmth spread throughout my whole body. "You will be able to use your magick again someday. All of it. And with it you will make the world whole and lovely again. Just not today."

The memory faded, and I became lucid of my dream state. My mothers and the inside of our cottage vanished, leaving me in an open field of tall grass. I was back in my adult body—no longer a frightened eight-year-old—and the scenery became just as clear and real as if I were awake.

A gust of wind danced across my skin, then continued to

ripple out among the foliage, the grass bending and swaying. I wasn't alone. There was something here with me, a familiar being with magick of a magnitude that matched my own.

Who are you?

A dark figure shrouded in a blackened cloud of smoke appeared in the distance. I couldn't make out any features.

Hello, Áine. It was a deep, distorted male voice that rang in my mind.

Smoke swirled around him like a cyclone before slithering out like snakes among the grass, inching closer and closer. It picked up its pace, but I stood my ground. This wasn't real. This was just a dream. I choked back my fear as I glared into the distance. I would not be intimidated.

The sky turned obsidian black, and the tall grass withered and died upon contact with the dark cloud, which smelled of fire, decay, and death. It turned my stomach sour with nausea. I couldn't see the being anymore as the smoke surrounded me and entered my lungs. It descended upon me, making my eyes burn as I coughed and grew dizzy.

No. This wasn't real.

Then I felt it in my mind, polluting and corrupting everything good about me and everything beautiful about my magick.

You killed your mothers, the figure taunted, his distorted voice as grating to my ears as the metal-on-metal impact of a car crash. *For power that is weak and dying. You are nothing. No one. Daelon will betray you. He sees how pathetic you really are.*

The darkness coiled around me like a great serpent, and I felt my body levitate off the ground as it tightened its grip. Flashes of suffering, torture, and death played in a loop in my mind. Witches in tattered clothing, crawling all over each other in a pit beneath the earth, reached for me, their mouths contorted into silent screams. I felt their suffering as if it were my own, and thus it became my own. I lost all sense of time, all sense of self. I was trapped in endless pain and destruction.

But within the darkened pit arose a sliver of light, gleaming from the end of a long tunnel. I fought my way toward it, scraping and digging and pulling myself through the cacophony of screams and packed dirt and sinister laughter.

This was an intruder. *I could fight this.*

In a burst of resistance, calling on every time I'd ever felt strong, every time anyone had ever felt strong, I bellowed,

Get out of my mind.

The crack of light opened up, and soon everything was illuminated. The smoke lifted, and I dropped from the sky into my ocean of energy, treading water and desperately breathing in salty, fresh air. I looked up at the deep blue sky, full of stars and constellations. I was safe. The dark force was gone.

He was gone.

I was pulled back into reality by Daelon's voice yet again, coaxing me out of my subconscious. My bed was soft and comforting in the wake of such a horrific nightmare.

"You're okay," he said, stroking my cheek.

He jerked his hand back when I opened my eyes. I took a

moment to adjust to this new change of scenery, as grateful for it as I was.

"I heard you scream again," he said. He cleared his throat. Whatever wall he'd so carefully constructed was starting to crack.

"I'm okay," I breathed. "Just another nightmare." Whoever that figure was—I seemed to have cast him out. I hoped he would stay gone, but if the enormity of his power was any indication, I knew it would be far from the last time we would encounter each other. Was this the enemy Daelon hoped to shield me from?

The light from the moon shining through my open window illuminated the contours of Daelon's face, his dark hair falling onto his forehead. He was shirtless tonight, which I had to admit was a sight to behold. His upper body was defined and rigid, and I wondered if his job as a witch trainer had anything to do with that, or if he just worked out. *Do witches work out?* His joggers hung low on his hips, revealing the V from his abs disappearing below the waistband.

"Like what you see?" Daelon smirked.

I blushed scarlet. *Busted.*

I hesitated. "Yes," I answered because it was the truth, and I knew it would catch him off guard. "It's not a bad view."

His eyes widened, regarding me with surprise before letting an amused grin spread across his face.

"Do you want me to stay with you again?" he asked, quieter this time. His grin faded, and his eyes narrowed, intense and imploring.

No, Áine, you absolutely do not, I scolded myself. *You still don't really know who this man even is.*

"Yes," I murmured, barely audible. My breath caught as he crawled over top of me rather than walk to the other side of the wide bed. For a moment he hovered over me before rolling over, leaving a gaping space between us.

"Well, as long as you don't end up trying for a cuddle like last time," I said, daring him.

"It's times like these I wish I could force you silent," he muttered.

I tensed. He really did have some audacity. "I'd like to see you try." Something dangerous stirred within me, and I couldn't tell whether we were threatening or flirting anymore.

I lay on my side to face him. He was on his back, his jaw tense as he stared up at the ceiling.

"Don't test me," he said, his voice low and rough, throwing me a side-eye. I couldn't tell if he was being serious or if we were still toying with each other.

"Test *you*? I'm the one with all the power."

His mouth twitched. "Power is a social contract between you and others. It can be exchanged, given, and taken at your will. What good is your magick if you don't desire to wield it on me?"

"Is this a philosophical riddle?" I asked, attempting to piece together what he was trying to tell me. I wasn't conscious enough for any of it.

"Go to sleep, little witch." The corners of his mouth curved upward, and his eyes closed. His hands clasped over his bare stomach.

"You're used to ordering people around, aren't you?"

"Yes, actually. And they generally obey, too."

I huffed and turned over to face the window. I gave my head a little shake. I didn't understand what game we were playing, and I sure as hell didn't know the rules.

I also didn't understand the feelings Daelon stirred within me—a longing, an understanding, and as much as I didn't want to admit it—desire. He knew who I was, and he didn't run. He didn't want me to become less of anything, not less powerful, less of a witch, or less *different*. I didn't feel different at all here in this place with him. Not like I did back on Earth with my friends, as amazing and loving as they were. They weren't capable of understanding me. Not fully.

It was perhaps too good to be true that he was exactly what I needed right now, but here he was. He was a protector, a mentor, and maybe even a friend. But this growing fire between us was dangerous. I knew he felt it too, despite his attempts to remain impassive and controlled. It was raw, like the energy I felt from Reagan as we danced in the club. But it was more serious, like one misstep and we could crumble.

I reached out to feel Daelon's energy instinctually as I crept closer to unconsciousness, meeting the same wall as before. It was because of this defense that I was safe, and for that I was grateful. Time passed and I found myself unable to drift off again. As I studied the moonlight on the gray rug next to the bedside, I felt Daelon stir next to me.

I tensed at first and then relaxed as fingers stroked through the long strands of my hair, slowly and delicately. The gesture was so unexpected that I wasn't sure if Daelon thought I was asleep or knew that I was awake. I let out a long breath as his fingers brushed back the hair behind my ear, sending shivers down my spine.

"Go to sleep, Áine," he whispered. His hand trailed down from my hair to the side of my neck, lingering for a moment before pulling away. "You're safe."

Training was more of the same over the next week. Daelon insisted I wasn't allowed to graduate to actually wielding magick until I learned how to detach my emotions from my power. I found myself nearly drowning in my metaphysical ocean over and over again all on my own. The mysterious intruder had been absent from the shadows of my mind since I banished him the week before. Despite those brief moments of intimacy and vulnerability, Daelon was just as domineering and hot-and-cold as ever. It felt like we were playing a game that neither of us could win.

Today, as I treaded amidst all the energy of this world and the next, I bathed in a sense of calm. I was a part of all things, and it was a privilege. I lost sense of where *I* began and others ended, with all the forces of the cosmos at my fingertips, gently pushing and pulling me with each cresting wave. The water was warm against my skin as if infused by the soft rays of a morning sun.

Daelon's voice from beyond the confines of my psyche boomed, *Now I want you to think of your mothers.*

I did, and the crystalline water revealed the fragments of my most cherished memories, my most feared memories, and my most hated memories. I let them come, and the familiar currents of anger, pain, and sadness called out to me, begging to be transformed into magick. They made promises of absolution.

If only I gave in, I could avenge myself and avenge us all.

Daelon's voice reached me again. *No, Áine. Not yet. It's time to come back.*

But this energy was intoxicating. I wanted the rush. I had never made it this far before, to this space between emotion and action, where limitless possibilities spread out among the waves and into the horizon. I was in the center of a whirlpool, growing taller around me like a fortress of water. I heard so many voices, each a thread that weaved through the universal tapestry. In the waves played a cosmic story—of war, greed, and fear, but also of love, sacrifice, and devotion. It was the story of my mothers; it was my story, it was Daelon's story; and it was *our* story.

All of us.

Come back Áine.

The water collapsed all around me, sending me spiraling into the ocean's depths. I was not afraid.

I opened my eyes.

I blinked in confusion. I was no longer sitting on the floor cushion, instead suspended midair three feet above it, my legs still crossed. "Oh, what the—" I let out a small squeal as I dropped back down to the floor ungracefully, bruising my backside.

Daelon snorted, but his eyes were filled with awe. "The energy in here has been... intense. How do you feel?"

"Weird. It was like I lost who I was for a moment." I furrowed my brows, shifting and shaking off the pain of my landing. "Like I was a part of a whole, rather than a single witch."

"An ego death," Daelon mused. "A lot of mystic witches

see that as the ultimate state of existence—where the purest forms of magick are practiced."

Sounded like what stoners bragged about when they ate too many edibles to me, but I saw how it could apply here too. I wanted to delve deeper, but a wave of exhaustion hit me with full force. "I feel lightheaded." I rubbed my temples.

"I told you to eat beforehand for a reason," he sighed. "You did really well today. I'm proud of you."

"Aw, thanks coach," I said. "Does that mean I get to play in the big leagues now?"

He rolled his eyes as he helped me to my feet. Do witches play sports? *Oh, no.* A sudden headrush almost made my knees buckle. Spots danced in my vision. I swayed, taking in a sharp breath.

"Okay, maybe I should've eaten," I admitted.

"Uh huh." In one swift movement he scooped me into his arms with surprising ease.

I squealed, glaring up at him. "Not this again," I said. "Put me down."

"You should've listened when I told you to eat," Daelon growled, but I could hear the smile in his voice. "I'm not going to watch you faint."

I knew I should've been angrier than I was, but I was weary from today's session. Also, a part of me just might've warmed up to Daelon's antics, now that I knew that they were primarily out of a concern for my safety. His story still had its gaps, but as a witch, it was hard to believe in mere coincidences. Things happened for a reason. My mothers told me that I was born for a specific purpose, and if all that Daelon said was true—then he seemed intertwined in this mysterious fate as well. Is that why he was beginning to remind me of a home I'd never seen?

He set me down in the kitchen. "Sit," he commanded. "What do you want to eat?"

"I can make my own food."

"Duly noted. Sit down," he repeated. "You can barely stand."

I rolled my eyes, but I ended up hoisting myself up on the barstool facing the island. "I guess those sandwiches we made yesterday were good," I sighed.

Daelon's face softened, and I thought I glimpsed a shy smile as he turned toward the refrigerator.

"What exactly is the plan?" I asked. "Like, after I'm more trained and learn what we are up against."

"One step at a time, Áine. You won't be here forever if that's what you're worried about. You're getting better at control every day."

I studied Daelon as he chopped an onion. This was one of those moments I wished I could read his emotional state. The confident ease of his body language didn't match the tinge of worry in his voice.

"I'm just trying to maximize the time we're allowed," Daelon said, something almost bitter in his tone.

"That we're *allowed*?" That was a strange wording. "Did all witches feel my beacon, as you call it? Are our enemies looking for me right now?"

"Drop it, Áine," Daelon snapped. "I wish I could tell you everything, but I can't. Yes, they're looking for you, but I have it handled."

The edge to his voice caught me off guard. I swallowed, sensing the rise of emotion that generally predicated a magickal outburst. I wasn't strong enough to fight it right now.

"I'm sorry," Daelon said, halting the buildup. "I didn't mean to snap at you. You're not who I'm angry with."

I sighed. "I know I agreed to focus on the training first. It's just frustrating to be so in the dark. Especially when I feel and see what I do in those waters. Something horrible has happened in this realm, and I'm supposed make it right."

"Yes. You are. This realm has been waiting for your return—I can feel it too. I know it's hard. I wish things were different," he said, holding my gaze. There seemed to be multilayered meanings embedded in those words. He looked suddenly uncomfortable and raw. "I cannot protect you forever. Not against some things. I wish terribly that I could."

I opened my mouth to speak, but he stopped me.

"I need you to know that when our little bubble here bursts, and the chips begin to fall, I will always be on your side. Always." His voice was softer and pleading. It was like he was telling me a deep, dark secret while searching my eyes for understanding. "Like I said, we share a common enemy. I want to help you fulfill your purpose, whatever it is, after I do what I can to teach you everything you've been shielded from down in the human realm. I need you to know that I'm only doing what's best for you."

What was he trying to tell me? All his secrecy, his moodiness, and his offhand comments were like a pile of scattered clues, and I didn't have enough pieces to put the puzzle together. I didn't know how much longer I could wait for the answers.

But that look in Daelon's eyes was so sincere, so desperate. It softened me to my core.

"I believe you." And I did, despite the part of my brain that wanted me to run far, far away and figure it all out for myself. I only grew fonder of Daelon as the days passed, even though I knew that trusting him was still a gamble. It was a risk I was willing to take. Like he said my first day here, all I had were his words and actions, and everything he showed me pointed to his reliability as my protector and guide.

He sighed a breath of relief. "Now, eat."

***

When I awoke in the middle of the night to get a glass of water, I heard Daelon's voice coming from down the hallway in his room. Why was he awake? Or did he talk in his sleep? I had never heard him when he stayed with me after my nightmares, but I wasn't a light sleeper.

I crept forward; the dark floorboards creaked beneath my weight. He spoke in a hushed tone, too quiet for me to comprehend. I took a step closer, almost to his door, when a sudden clatter followed by a thud erupted. It sent chills down my spine.

"Daelon?" As soon as his name left my lips, the door flew open to reveal a shirtless, sweaty Daelon on the other side.

My eyes widened as I took in the sight of his muscles shining with sweat, the veins in his arms bulging. He gave me a once over, lifting a brow. I realized in embarrassment that I wasn't wearing any pants, since I expected him to be asleep at this hour. I was clad in a pale pink satin cami that mostly concealed my panties. As his eyes traveled back up to mine, he smiled mischievously, leaning on the doorframe.

"I was getting water, and I heard a voice, and then a, uh, loud noise," I spluttered in clumsy explanation, tugging at the bottom of my top for more coverage.

"Just working out. Dropped something." Daelon said, his eyes stony.

"In the middle of the night?" *And while talking to yourself?*

"It's not the middle of the night. It's the early morning," Daelon muttered. "Go back to sleep, and I'll see you in a couple hours."

Before I could react or say anything more, he shut the door in my face. Incredulous, I backed away. *What just happened?* I wasn't awake enough to decipher any of it, so I grabbed a glass of water and went back to bed.

CHAPTER 5

Tossing and turning, my mind ran in circles. In my disorientation, between waking and dreaming states of consciousness, I saw Daelon at the foot of my bed. His head was tilted to the side, staring down at me as if he was fully entitled to the act. My heart thudded, and I couldn't decide if the look in his eyes was unnerving or devastatingly exciting. I wanted to speak, but my voice was caught in my throat. He walked to the side of my bed and reached down, stroking my cheek with the back of his hand.

I stared up into his dark eyes, mine narrowed at first then widening as he climbed over top of me. *What was he doing? And why didn't I stop him?*

He straddled me, hovering just above my body. His chest was bare, and I wanted desperately to run my hands along his skin. The urge felt just as strong and irresistible as the pull of my power, begging for me to let go, give in, and submit to my most innate instincts.

"Then do it," he said, his voice low and husky.

Still unable to speak, I wordlessly lifted a hand to his skin and trailed my fingers down from his chest to his torso. His eyes were fiery, like they got when I didn't do as I was told.

"I told you I could force you silent," he said, his lips close to my ear.

His breath on my skin sent a shiver down my spine. Resting on his right arm, his left hand stroked the side of my neck and gently turned my head to the side with his fingers. In a sudden movement his lips were at my throat, his teeth lightly tugging on my skin.

I drew in a sharp breath as he trailed kisses along my collarbone, his left hand moving down the side of my body grabbing at my waist.

It was at this point that I became lucid enough to understand this was a dream.

"But it feels real, doesn't it?" my very realistic Daelon asked. "Admit you want it." He leaned in close to my face, brushing my upper lip with his thumb. He looked from my eyes to my lips and back again, dangerously, utterly seductive.

"I can't," I said, barely audible. I shook my head slightly, and my breath hitched. *I don't know who you are.*

"But you do." There was less than an inch of space between our lips now.

With the smallest movement, I leaned in and met him.

When I awoke, soft rays of light streamed in from the windows. I breathed in shallow gulps of air, and I jumped and nearly screamed when I saw Daelon standing just past the doorway.

"Fuck, Daelon." A flash of hot embarrassment flooded my system as I covered my face with my arm. "Ever heard of privacy?"

There was the hint of a smirk on his lips. "You were sleeping the day away. I was only making sure you were alive."

I attempted to collect myself. There was no need for all of this paranoia; he couldn't see into my dreams.

"What on earth were you dreaming about?"

No, no, please, no.

"Nothing," I said too quickly. This just might've been worse than my nightmares. "I don't remember."

"You are a terrible liar." He raised his eyebrows, regarding me with calculation. "Hmm. What I would give to know..." Compared to his demeanor in the early hours of the morning, this was like night and day.

"Well we don't always get what we want," I shot back. Something dangerous flashed in his eyes. "Now go away so I can get dressed."

He leaned against the door frame, his arms crossed. "You didn't seem too concerned with that earlier."

For a moment I panicked, until I realized he was referring to my lack of pants on my way to get water.

"I didn't think you'd be awake," I said, but the words came out far too exasperated and flustered. "Now get out before I force you out."

His eyes narrowed at my threat, but he obliged with an obnoxious grin and shut the door behind him.

For a moment I just lay there, working to slow my breath

and racing heart. My power called out to me, frenzied and chaotic, but all I really wanted to do was pull the duvet over my head and hide.

No, screw this. If the boundaries of our working relationship had been breached, he was just as much at fault as I was—with all his little innuendos, flirtations, and weird pet names. I was supposed to be uncovering the source of the evil that haunted my dreams, hunted me, and *killed my mothers*. Flirting with the secretive, mercurial witch trainer didn't seem like it fit into this grand, cosmic purpose they'd laid out for me. I also wouldn't soon forget his sketchy late night work out session.

When I emerged from my room, Daelon was waiting in the kitchen to practically force-feed me toast. He also had a cup of coffee for me, which was admittedly sweet of him. I still regarded him with caution, grateful he seemed to be back in business-mode after our exchange.

"You're going to need to grab a jacket. We're going outside," he said.

I couldn't contain my smile. The autumnal weather was in full swing; the tall evergreens, trees with red and orange leaves, and breathtaking mountain landscape were more than inviting. It was my favorite time of year, as it reminded me of some of my most cherished memories with my mothers—holidays, baking, snow, and the changing of the seasons in our cozy village nestled among sloping hills. They taught me little rituals and traditions that reminded them of home, whispered to me as they guided with gentle hands, as if they were passing on the language of a dying world. I hated that I could barely remember any of it.

"Okay, be right back." I took one last chug of the tepid coffee.

Daelon looked taken aback by my childlike enthusiasm, smiling back in spite of himself. He wore a chic charcoal sweater with faded jeans and hiking boots.

I shot into my room and then re-emerged in a soft, white faux-fur coat to go with my flannel shirt and dark jeans.

"Those shoes aren't very practical, Áine," he chastised, eyeing my black wedge ankle boots.

"I don't care. They're cute."

He sighed and shook his head, giving up. He gestured for me to follow him, and we passed through the hall to the other side of the house. We pushed through the door that blended into the glass wall and onto the deck. There was a firepit and outdoor living area to the left and an outdoor bar and more seating to the right, with a tall staircase descending between the two.

I stopped in my tracks. "Sheesh. This looks built for entertaining. Is that... something you do?" I eyed him, watching as his guarded features revealed absolutely nothing.

He shrugged. "I more so use it as an escape from my life. I come here when I need to be alone."

That seemed like a waste of architecture. "So your life is... stressful?" I probed.

He glanced at me, pausing for a moment before nodding. "Life in Aradia is stressful for most witches these days. I'm just... happy to be here with you, away from it all." The rare flash of vulnerability floated up in his eyes.

I offered a small smile, though we both knew he'd said far too little. There were just too many unanswered questions, and I had only my imagination to fill in the gaps. Was he embarrassed about his past? Ashamed? He'd said his life was parallel to my own, orphaned just like me. I had to assume it was by the same force that my mothers ran from—that they said was destroying the realm—and that Daelon wanted to tell me about *after* I'd gained control of my power. Maybe where he came from was simply depressing, and that was why he was so eager to leave it all behind to help me.

If only I could read his energy.

I pushed away my wandering thoughts, choosing to instead focus on the present moment. It was all we had, and my focus was necessary if I ever wanted to progress to actually being able to use my magick.

I followed Daelon down the steps, careful not to falter in order to prove him wrong about my shoes. Maybe they weren't the best choice, but they did complete the outfit.

The air was crisp and smelled of wood, dampened leaves, and pine. The energy was palpable, much stronger out here than in the house. The witch realm felt more comfortable than Earth's, and particularly New York City's, stifling and more viscous ebbs and flows. I was more in tune with myself and the world here.

We made it to the bottom, and he led me down a beaten path, our feet crunching on pine cones and fallen leaves. I could sense magick all around us, carried through the wind as it whipped through my long hair and whistled through tree branches. When we got to a fallen log, Daelon boosted himself over it effortlessly. I held out my hand and looked at him expectantly.

"You puzzle me," he muttered, holding out his arm for leverage to help me over.

"How so?" I batted my eyelashes at him. "And where exactly are we going?"

Daelon just shook his head, and I shivered as he put his hand on the small of my back to guide me off the path into a small clearing. The trees around us created a perfect circle. He spread out the plaid blanket he had tucked under his arm in the center of the area as I spun around to take in its beauty. There was a lot of magick in this area; I could feel it woven into the soil and coursing through the air.

He gestured for me to sit with him on the blanket. "This is where I cast major spells, like to use my shielding gift to neutralize your energy imprint, as well as to establish a perimeter to keep wayward witches from stumbling onto the property. We're in our own little microclimate of magick here, so that your outbursts aren't felt by the whole realm."

I nodded. "How does the shielding thing really work? Or my clairsentience? Like where do they come from?"

"That's a question for the mystics. Where do human talents come from? There's not a clear-cut answer really. Although it's generally believed that witch talents come from a place of need—the Universe's need for balance and symmetry," Daelon explained. "As a shield, I can tap into protective magick in a way that comes naturally. I'm just attuned to that frequency. It's useful when it comes to practicing covert magick that I don't want others to become aware of, since I can mask its energetic makeup. Then, of course, it can be useful in countering aggression and making tangible, energetic shields in the face of attack."

"Do you believe then that it's your gift that led you to take on this mission to help me? Like maybe gifts influence our purpose?" I asked, thinking about my own gift as an energy reader.

It was strange to think the Universe, cosmos, or whatever else was conspiring for Daelon and me to meet. I yearned to see the bigger picture. I was just starting to feel bits and pieces wafting through my vast ocean of magick, whispered in so many voices and so many languages that it humbled me. Somehow, I was at the center of it all, and it was far more daunting than my first thoughts of revenge. There was something bigger—much bigger—at play, and sometimes I felt its weight bearing down as if I were Atlas holding up the whole world.

Maybe I wasn't ready to face it all.

"Among other things, yes," he finally answered.

"Other things like revenge," I ventured. "Because you've lost people like I have."

Daelon shot me a warning look. "Yes." He looked away, almost as if he was searching for something among the trees.

"What are we doing today?" I asked, quickly changing the subject.

Daelon looked back at me, relief etched in his features. Whatever horrors we faced, he was clearly terrified of them.

"You're going to help me cast a spell."

I grinned, but Daelon's features were grave.

"A spell for more time."

"And that means what, exactly?"

His gaze unfocused as if he was looking right through me, deep in thought. "That the power I'm protecting you from is growing craftier. I need to cast a spell to distract him—it."

So, that thing was a *he*. Interesting. It would seem all of my nightmares and premonitions weren't all in my imagination, after all.

"This is going to require a lot of trust, Áine. I will take care of establishing intent, and with your consent, I will channel energy through you. You can harness more power than I ever could, so I know it will give us our best chance."

"And if I don't consent?" I asked, frowning. I wasn't sure I liked the sound of this. Was this not what Daelon warned me about, with people looking to use me as a witch battery?

Daelon reached for my hands. "Then I will accept it. I want you to feel something first though."

I quirked a brow, staring down at my hands now clasped in his. Suddenly a trace of energy travelled through his palms and into my field of perception, and I closed my eyes. It was a part of his aura slipping through the cracks of his shield. The energy was shrouded in a murky cloud of fear, yet at its core was light and soothing and safe—like the warmth of a fire after a long day toiling out in the cold. I felt his desire for security, control, and protection, not only for himself, but for another. For *me*. A flash of myself in third person passed through my mind, and I was smiling. I felt his awe, saw the way he was utterly mesmerized by me. I reminded him of something he lost, something that was pure and core to his entire sense of self—like *home*. My own energy reached for his, and it was as if it, too, believed in this inherent connection that transcended all logic and language.

There was something else swimming in his aura too, something murky and dark that was quick to shift and elude me like dissipating smoke. My hands tightened around his as

I searched for the source. I was met with a wall, blocking me from continuing further.

"No, Áine," Daelon said sharply. "Permission goes both ways."

My eyes flew open. "Sorry. I didn't realize," I said. "Well, that's not true. I'm just not used to it being that way. I'm sorry," I repeated, watching his eyes until he nodded and relaxed.

I was used to reading every part of someone at will, even the parts they desperately wanted to stay hidden. I knew there was more, but the part that he had shown me was genuine. Energy couldn't lie.

"So that's how you feel?" I asked, biting back a smile. I tried to come off as teasing, but it fell into a tone of shock instead. It was a surprising read of energy from someone usually so impassive and controlled.

Daelon tensed his jaw, looking away. Was he going to blush? I couldn't help but smile at the mere idea of it.

"Yes," he said finally. "Can you not tell how in awe of you I am?"

I scoffed. "No, I can't Daelon. Are you really not aware of how moody and cold you can be?"

"You have no idea what I'm risking with all of this. I took a jump into the void, like I was pulled to you by forces bigger than either of us." His voice was sharp, but as he looked at me his eyes softened, and he took a deep breath. "I'm sorry you feel that way. But what I'm doing here with you could get us both killed, and I can't bear to see you suffer that fate. I was *called* to do this, and I wasn't sure if I was even going to accept the calling... but then I saw you, and I just couldn't—" He trailed off, seemingly giving his next words careful consideration. "In order to continue protecting you and preparing you to protect yourself, I'm going to need to channel more power for a spell. You won't be able to see the specific intent behind the magick, but you will feel the energy I need as it moves through you. Does that make sense?"

"Protect me from people who don't want us working together?" I asked. The people who would kill us? The people who killed my mothers—and who maybe killed his parents too?

Daelon sighed. "Something like that, little witch. I wish I could explain more. I promise it's not out of malice that I can't. It's all for you," he said softy.

I looked down at my hands. All of the secrecy aside, what this really came down to was whether or not I trusted Daelon enough to use me as some kind of magickal battery. And, in the face of all logic, *I did*. Because energy couldn't lie, and what his aura showed me was nothing but care and devotion.

"Okay," I said. "I give you permission." I still eyed him with suspicion. I couldn't let go completely. Not yet. "If you really think it will protect us."

He gave my hand a squeeze. "Thank you."

He closed his eyes and chanted something unintelligible under his breath. I gasped as fire began to spread in the outskirts of the clearing, creating a trail of flames that encircled us.

"Casting a circle before practicing protects us while we're at our most vulnerable, and it helps to amplify the magick we release. Think of it like an energetic wall to keep power in, and negative forces out," Daelon explained to me. "Fire is a powerful element. Invoking it gives us a boost."

I nodded, peering around at the circle of blue-white flames. I felt the truth of his words reflected in their magick. The sky was overcast, and the trees rustled and swayed in the wind. The ground itself came alive with energy, as if remnants of old spells awakened to us. The land itself had power.

"This is going to be intense," Daelon said softly, concern in his eyes. "Maybe lying down would be more comfortable for you."

"Okay." I swallowed. I couldn't hide the anxiety crawling beneath my skin. Daelon watched me intently as I lay down, taking my hand in both of his.

"Slow your breathing," he instructed. "Don't be afraid. I would never hurt you."

I took in long, deep breaths. A sense of calm reached out to me through Daelon's hands, and I accepted it with gratitude. It bathed me in a light, airy warmth.

"You need to stay still and not interrupt the spell until I'm done. Doing so would be very, very dangerous."

I nodded, and soon a pulling sensation tugged at me from the hands that enveloped mine. It was similar to what I felt when the energy vampire grabbed my broken ankle, but it wasn't painful or draining, I assumed because this time I had allowed it. Power rose up within me, and Daelon began to chant in a low whisper until he went silent.

The flow of power grew stronger and stronger. It entered through the crown of my head and moved through my body until it spread into Daelon's palms, and as it did, I caught glimpses and impressions of its energetic makeup.

Most of it was protective in nature, like what I felt from his intentions earlier. Another part of it felt dangerous, biting cold as it passed through, coiling around me like a snake. My eyes rolled back into my head, the pulling sensation growing more and more uncomfortable. Not having control of the forces Daelon was channeling through me felt invasive and unnatural, especially the ones that whispered tales of chaos and confusion.

I gritted my teeth. I trusted Daelon. *I had to.*

I began to shiver as the warm, softer waves of defensive energy halted, and more dark, chilling currents took their place. Daelon wasn't just defending me. He was attacking someone, or something, and the energy he used was unlike anything I had ever channeled before. I'd felt it though, in the abyss—that place in the looming castle of my nightmares. I didn't know how much more I could take.

The shivers evolved into full-on convulsions. This energy burned, and I didn't want it anywhere near me. I pleaded internally for Daelon to hurry and finish whatever this spell was so I could be free from its icy, sub-zero grip.

The last bit of warmth in my body left as Daelon let go of my hand, and I feared that I would never be able to feel any heat ever again. I instantly sucked in air and opened my eyes, still shivering all over. Daelon's eyes were panicked and confused, and the circle of fire around us had vanished into smoke.

"I don't understand," he said, reaching to pull the blanket beneath us up and around my body. He hugged me to his chest, grasping my ice-cold hands to heat them up.

"You said you wouldn't hurt me," I accused. My teeth chattered violently. "What have you done?"

"I was just buying us some time," Daelon said. Worry seeped into his voice. "I don't know why you had that kind of reaction."

"Because that energy was *evil*," I hissed through my clenched jaw. I wanted to escape Daelon's hold, but I was too cold, and he was so warm.

Daelon stared down at me, grimacing and then looking away. "I—I don't know why—I promise Áine, I would've done it differently if I had known you were so sensitive to that kind of energy. I guess it makes sense, but I don't know…" He frowned, as if remembering something, his eyes darting back to mine.

"It wasn't an evil spell? Like to kill someone?" I asked. Even if it was to protect me, I didn't think I could tolerate being used in that way without more context.

"No," he said quickly. "I would never channel you for something like that without your express permission. I think this has to do with who you are. Some sources of power may run contrary to your very existence," he said, looking off, deep in thought.

Who am I? What kind of sources? My mothers always told me I was made up of everything good in the world. They told me I gave people hope, that I was conceived out of love, and a gift from the Goddess. But a gift to whom and for what purpose?

Daelon clutched me tighter, and despite what he had just put me through, I felt safe in his arms. I was just so cold.

"I'm so sorry," he whispered into my hair, and I found myself nuzzling into his chest for warmth. He smelled woodsy and clean.

"Was it at least worth it?" I asked, muffled by his sweater.

"Yes."

"Good." I wasn't ready to face whatever awaited us, not if it had anything to do with the pitch-black void of lifelessness and pain I felt today and in my nightmares. I didn't mind spending more time with Daelon here in our bubble.

"Let's get you inside," he said. "I'll start a fire."

I feared he already had.

CHAPTER 6

I sat on the floor facing the flames in the oversized fireplace, my body temperature beginning to regulate again. Daelon draped a blanket over my shoulders and sat down next to me.

"Want a drink?" He held up an unlabeled bottle of caramel-colored liquid with reddish hues. I assumed it was whiskey.

"Absolutely."

Daelon grinned and took a swig.

"Straight from the bottle, huh?" I asked.

"Would you like a glass?"

I grabbed the bottle from him, my fingers brushing against his. I took a pull and held his gaze. It tasted of vanilla, honey, spice, and fire, warming my insides as it left a pleasurable burn in the pit of my stomach.

"It tastes Irish," I said, handing it back to him.

"It's from a similar region, actually. Here, not on Earth." He paused, his face falling. "This is actually one of the last bottles ever made there." He looked mournful, taking another swig and staring at the bottle in deep contemplation. "A beautiful place."

"Thank you for sharing it with me."

He looked so angelic when he was vulnerable. It was such a stark difference between this and the mask he usually wore. Everything about him seemed tied to his role as a shield—constantly on the defense—as if showing weakness would destroy him. I knew how exhausting that could be. It was a tactic of the deeply heartbroken. Or people who lived in a world they didn't belong.

"What were your parents like?" I asked.

He shook his head and gave me a warning look as he passed the bottle back to me. There was so much of him that was off-limits. As I took another swig, I began to feel the familiar numbing flood my system. It was a nice break from the constant badgering from all the forces of the Universe.

"Do you miss Earth?"

"I try not to think about it," I said, realizing that wasn't really an answer. I sighed. "I think I've become very good at handling loss and sudden change. Having your mothers die before your eyes as a kid and finding yourself magickally teleported into the streets of New York City will do that to you."

"Is that why you saw your power as a curse? Because you blamed yourself for your mothers' deaths?" Daelon asked, but it sounded more like a statement of fact.

I swallowed. Now it was my turn to shut him down. "I don't want to talk about that."

"None of it was your fault. They saved you, Áine. They—"

He stopped when he saw the look on my face. He was right. I knew that deep down, but I couldn't think about it. I needed a break from feeling it all.

"Okay, sorry. What happened after they sent you to New York?"

I had to take another sip of whiskey, but this story I didn't mind telling, so I told it all as Daelon listened intently. It was liberating to finally be able to tell someone the whole truth. I told him I didn't miss Earth, but I did miss my friends. They taught me how to love and be loved again.

The State of New York didn't quite know what to do with the mysterious orphan with an Irish accent and a large inheritance in an American bank account. There were forces on my side though, from whatever spell my mothers had cast to protect me, and that magick somehow influenced people to help me when they probably wouldn't have otherwise. From the ages of ten to eighteen I was passed around from foster home to foster home, and most of the adults hated me and wanted access to my inheritance. They told me I was selfish, and I almost started to believe them.

It was a miracle I made it out with only damaged self-esteem. I saw what the system did to other kids my age, and I always knew it was my mothers' special bracelet that kept me safe. I sometimes wished I still had some of my power, if only to protect everyone else. But I didn't, so I kept my head down and white-knuckled my way through those eight years of displacement.

Most of the time I didn't miss my magick because I knew it had brought about my mothers' deaths. Even without it, though, I felt out of place and yearning for a place I saw in my dreams. I quickly learned not to talk about my clairsentience because it made people fear me, and they called me a freak. Actually, they called me a freak anyway for the way I talked and the way I saw the world, so I stopped talking, and I dropped my accent. I stopped thinking about the magick I felt as a child and my mothers' bedtime stories. I nearly convinced myself that none of it had been real in the first place. Despite my subconscious yearning for home and the power I had lost, I was determined to live life as a human to honor my mothers. I ignored their voices in my dreams that reminded me I would someday return home. I ignored the tingling in my bracelet that reminded me my power was never truly gone.

I met Steph one day in Central Park. I sensed her energy when I passed by her as she casually rolled a joint on a picnic blanket, unbothered and unashamed. Her hair was in many long black braids, cast into a bun on the top of her head. She wore a maxi dress and a leather jacket, and her dark brown skin sparkled along her cheekbones, nose, and eyelids. It was an intense energy, yet soft and warm and maternal. It had something I craved. She seemed to sense me too, and she asked if I wanted to join her. We talked for a very long time, and a year later I told her about my clairsentience as we applied for schools together. We met Rena and Nick, and I got a degree in Anthropology, which was a bit ironic now that I thought about it. It was basically my attempt at taking a crash course on how to be a normal human.

I didn't feel so out of place anymore. My friends may not have been witches, but they cared for and accepted me. They healed the damage of my years in the system. But there was always a part of me that knew that life could never last. As much as I tried to suppress it, I always knew there was this huge, gaping void inside me where my power was supposed to be. Nothing in the human realm was ever enough to quell the emptiness or the sense of unbelonging. I was caught between yearning for something more and convincing myself I was undeserving. *Because what I thirsted for had killed my mothers.*

When I finished telling the story, Daelon was silent for a moment, his eyes soft and open.

"Do you still think you're undeserving?" he finally asked.

"Sometimes. But not when I'm in that ocean. Not when I feel it all. There's something I need to do, but I don't know what," I said. My eyes watered, but I didn't let any tears fall. "There are people who need my help."

Daelon remained impassive but looked away and into the fire. "Thank you for telling me all of that." He set his gaze back on me. "You are where you belong now."

I nodded, letting out a deep breath.

"Look at me," he said softly. His eyes were warm and inviting. "You deserve it all. Everything in this world and the next. You are more deserving than anyone I've ever met."

Something about the fire, the blanket draped around my shoulders, the whiskey, Daelon's kind words, and everything I'd just revealed, led a tear to escape my eye.

My cheeks warmed as Daelon moved closer to brush the droplet away with his thumb. He sat back, but there was still less than a foot between us.

"It's me who is undeserving," Daelon whispered, so soft I could barely hear it over the crackling of the flames. "Undeserving of you."

I was speechless. Was this why he was constantly shutting himself down with me? Daelon didn't ever act undeserving. If anything, he acted like he deserved it all. It was hard to reconcile all these parts of him—the domineering, the protective, the vulnerable, the controlling, the caring, the broken, the unworthy. Who was he really? And why did it not matter how confused he made me, or how much he didn't tell me, or how irrational my feelings for him were... None of it mattered as he sat facing me, his face so close to mine, my skin tingling at the ghost of his touch on my cheek.

My breath caught in my throat, and I remembered my dream in the early hours of the morning. When Dream Daelon had looked at me like he owned me. When he climbed on top of me, I felt his bare chest, and he had dared me to admit I wanted to kiss him. When I did admit it by leaning into his lips—

"Is it frustrating not being able to read my energy?" Daelon asked, pulling me out of my dangerous reverie. His gaze reeled me in, and his tone dared me.

"Very."

"Triple that frustration and yearning," he leaned in closer, his breath tickling my skin, "and then maybe you could begin to fathom how badly I want to read your thoughts right now."

Although the whiskey helped to numb the pull of my power, it only made my irrational longing for Daelon grow stronger. I looked to his lips and then back to his eyes. His jaw tensed and a flash of the untamed gleamed in his eyes, eerily similar to the look I saw in my dream. It was commanding of all my attention. The energy between us was palpable now, distracting and all-consuming. I could nearly taste it.

He closed his eyes, fighting a battle with himself I'd watched him fight many times now.

"Maybe we need to stop thinking," I thought aloud, emboldened by the warmth in the pit of my stomach.

His eyes flew open. I considered making the move myself to close the gap between us, but no sooner had the thought crossed my mind had Daelon grabbed my face in his hands, forcefully meeting my lips. The kiss was urgent and desperate, like we had waited a thousand years to touch each other and would wait a thousand more to do it again.

Daelon pushed me to the floor in one swift movement, careful to keep a hand on the back of my head as I fell back onto the rug. He was on top of me exactly as in my dream. His lips moved against mine as his other hand gently grasped my neck. He lightly tugged at my bottom lip with his teeth. I tangled my fingers through his dark waves of hair and stroked the side of his face. It was smooth aside from the light stubble along his sharp jaw.

He groaned, moving his hand off my throat and pushing up to hover over me. Both of us gasped for air. "We can't do this, Áine." His eyes told a different story, staring at my body greedily. "*I* can't," he repeated, more to himself than me.

"Why not?" I furrowed my brows, confused and frustrated in more ways than one.

Daelon shook his head and looked away. He started to rise, and I grabbed his wrist, staring him down until he met my eyes. He looked at my hold on his arm and then to my eyes, anger flashing in his. *Surely that wasn't directed at me?*

"Stop," he growled, his features returning to their natural state of perfect control and display of strength.

I let go, feeling my own anger rise within me—with a

splash of shock and embarrassment thrown in for good measure. Had I misread this entire situation? Did he only kiss me because he knew I wanted it?

I rolled out from under him.

"Áine."

Pushing myself up, I glared at a weary looking Daelon. His features softened as I did, his eyes pleading. I clenched my fists, my heartbeat loud and fast as blood rushed to my head.

"Wait, let me—"

"No," I said, mirroring his tone from before. I wanted to yell at him. I wanted to unleash the power that now roared in my ears like the crashing waves of a stormy ocean. I wanted to make him feel the way he had just made me feel. I wanted him to kiss me again.

In a burst of whooshing air, the fire snuffed out completely, leaving only smoke in its wake. The already overcast sky grew darker, and wind whistled and bore down against the windows. The familiar rise of power swelled within me, looking frantically for release. I had to close my eyes briefly to gain back control.

When I opened them, Daelon was in front of me, placing his hands on my shoulders. I backed away and shrugged him off.

"Calm down and just listen to me for a moment," he begged, but his eyes showed irritation.

"Daelon, with all due respect, you can fuck right off," I snapped. The last remnants of my Irish accent unleashed out of anger, reminding me of my mothers and our village among the hills.

Now he looked furious, which in turn only made me

more enraged, and after a second of silence I turned on my heel and escaped to my room. I didn't have to physically close the door behind me as it slammed shut at the mere thought. My anger was like its own poltergeist.

I kicked off my shoes and fell back on my bed. My breathing was erratic and my mind a muddled mess. Maybe Daelon was right. That would've been a huge mistake. I couldn't tell if I wanted to laugh or cry, but I knew I needed some space to think.

CHAPTER 7

I woke the next morning famished. I held my breath as I entered the kitchen, sighing in relief when Daelon was nowhere to be seen. He hadn't tried to talk to me since I cursed at him yesterday evening, an outburst that sober and less angry me almost regretted. Another part of me didn't regret it though, and I held onto that part for dear life to avoid the feelings of shame and embarrassment his actions had caused. It was far better to be angry than ashamed. Or at least it *felt* better.

After whipping up some coffee, I quickly retreated to my room to grab my faux leather jacket to pair with a red dress with loose long sleeves and a plunging neckline. Black suede ankle boots completed the outfit.

I tiptoed around the house, unwilling to face Daelon. I wasn't sure when I *would* be ready, but it seemed he wasn't leaping at the opportunity to see me either. The house was quiet, even as I passed by his room.

I slipped out the door into the crisp autumn air, and then I descended the winding steps. I wasn't sure where I was going. I just knew I needed to be among the trees and search for some guidance in the calm. I felt more grounded and more connected to my power in the wilderness, and I wondered idly if that was part of the reason my mothers sent me to New York City, where even the greenspaces were unsatisfyingly disconnected and energetically barren. If the goal was to disconnect me completely from my witch nature, the location made perfect sense.

I ditched the beaten path, wandering for a while among the tall grass, browning wildflowers, and looming pines. I basked in the rush of wind as it whipped around me in welcome, blowing my hair and dress in every direction. Pleasurable chills swept over my skin, and a familiar energy tugged at my consciousness. I fell to my knees, fresh tears overflowing and streaming down my face. I felt my mothers. I felt their mothers. I felt all mothers. This current of power wrapped around me like a quilt, perfectly stitched from love and devotion.

On my bare knees, now scraped and dirty, I shifted into a crossed-leg position and brought myself into a trance-like state as Daelon had helped me into many times before. I stifled the pang of disappointment at the thought of my moody protector and trainer.

I plunged deeper into my psyche, accepting help from the motherly forces surrounding me, and soon I was in my clear, electric blue ocean with multicolored, iridescent grains of sand. I basked in the multitudinous waters, containing the depths of all natural flows. I called out for guidance, whispering this intent to the waves.

I dove under the surface, reminding myself that I could breathe underwater here. This was merely a psychic metaphor to help make sense of the infinite; I wouldn't drown unless I believed I could. I heard Momma Celeste's voice.

Hello, sweet girl.

You're not real, I thought, but here, thoughts were as good as spoken word. As I treaded, their faces appeared in front of me like a hazy mirage.

We never meant to make you ashamed of who you are, Áine. We just needed time until we could figure out a way to protect you from those who wished you harm. But you grew stronger and more unpredictable sooner than we expected.

The water grew warmer with my anger. *You didn't need to let yourselves die. There had to have been another way. Why didn't you let me save you?*

There was no other way. You aren't responsible for the choices of others, my child. No one let us die. We were murdered. And we used the force of that violence to protect you all these years, until we knew you'd be ready to return.

I will avenge you. I reached out for them, but the image dissolved as soon as my fingers made contact.

You will avenge us all, but not as an act of vengeance. As an act of salvation. You are made up of everything good in the world. Don't lose yourself in what you are not. Heed our warnings.

A flash of myself shivering on the ground of the clearing flashed before me. Daelon hovered over me, his eyes completely white.

The cold? What was that energy? Where did it come from?

It became harder and harder to tread as currents tried to pull my body in all different directions.

Who am I, Momma? Please tell me. Who am I saving? And from what?

My mothers' voices rang in unison. *You are hope embodied—the hope of thousands—the hope of this world and all the rest. You will deliver us. You will restore this realm to its former state of balance and goodness. Trust your intuition. It will guide you always, sweet girl.*

I realized these words were just a copy-and-paste from fragments of different memories, a compilation of things they'd told me as a child. I was alone.

A wave of grief crashed into me. It was the grief of thousands, and it was too much. It sank into my heart and dug and dug until I was hollow and cold. I gasped for air and was met with water, pouring into my lungs like liquid fire. In a panic I remembered that Daelon wasn't here to pull me out if I was overcome.

I thrashed and struggled, but soon flashes from the great beyond took shape all around me. I saw witches laughing, crying, begging, and singing. The din of their voices grew louder and louder, swelling into a melody that drove me to a peaceful stillness. The images and sounds faded out of focus, but I'd glimpsed enough to understand the truth my power wanted me to understand.

I wasn't alone, and I never would be. I had access to the loves, fears, desires, and intentions of all beings that had ever lived, begging to be transformed into magick. I borrowed some of their energy to propel myself back up, breaching the surface and coughing out every drop of water I could. My limbs were heavy. There was so much pain in these waters.

There was also enough hope to fuel a revolution. I clung to that current instead, shaking off the grief I'd worn as a second skin for too many years. My mothers' words illuminated the darkness of my guilt and shame, bringing it into the light where it withered and fell away. This power was a gift, not a curse, and the witches I sensed in these waters needed me to be strong.

Hello there, a new voice erupted, and I knew immediately it meant me no harm. His energy was soft and pure, his voice so close that I half-expected him to appear wading in the water nearby. No sooner than I could turn my head in the direction of his call was I transported somewhere else entirely.

A loud popping sound assailed my eardrums, but I was unable to scream as I was dropped into a familiar place. I knew it from my nightmare. I was inside the dark, sprawling castle once more.

This time I was in a dimly lit, medieval-looking room, with long, religious-looking tapestries and an altar set up at the front. As it came into focus, I jumped at the figure sitting on a green cushion to my right. It was an old man with a white beard, dressed in maroon robes. He sat up against a wall, his legs crossed.

"You're the one he's been looking for. Are you astral projecting, young one?" His eyes remained closed as he spoke.

That sounded like something Steph tried to tell me about after trying psychedelics. Was I still inside my head? Was this all some kind of weird metaphor?

"You don't know where you are, do you?" he asked. "That's okay. No need to be afraid."

Someone knocked violently at the door, and a booming voice erupted. "Amos. Are you aware of the chaos beyond your room? Or are you too busy communing with *the Goddess* or whatever the fuck it is you do all day?" the man sneered, anger dripping into each word. Even from here I could feel his heavy, cold energy. It was suffocating and... familiar. "I need your assistance. Now, old man."

"Maybe you do have reason to be afraid," Amos chuckled softly. "Off you go now. Until we meet again." He opened his eyes and smiled, and I knew he couldn't actually see me as he looked vaguely around the room. "Just think of your physical body, wherever it lies. That should be enough to guide you back."

"Who are you talking to?" the voice bellowed. Was this the voice from the abyss? From the field and among the trees? It wasn't distorted any longer.

I didn't want to find out.

The old man winked, almost in the right direction toward where I hovered, but not quite. He started walking to the door, and I quickly tried to remember where my body was. With Daelon? No. In the woods. I was sitting in the woods in a billowy dress. My knees stung.

I snapped back into my physical reality so quickly it left me with severe vertigo. As the forest came into focus, I became aware of someone standing over me. I lifted my gaze to see a very angry Daelon with his arms crossed.

"Where the hell have you been?" he hissed. "Do you have any idea the thoughts that went through my head when I couldn't find you? And then when I couldn't bring you back from wherever you just were?"

He was nearly yelling at me. I narrowed my eyes in petulance. "No, I don't have an idea of those thoughts because you won't tell me anything," I retorted.

Daelon offered a hand to help me up. I thought I'd seen him at his most angry last night when I told him to bugger off, but now I knew *this* was his most volatile, fuming state—or at least I hoped. I accepted his help mostly out of fear that the vein in his temple would burst. He looked down at my legs, and as I followed his gaze, I realized that one of my knees was bleeding. I must've landed on a thorn or something.

When I looked back up to him, he was glaring at me in a way that drove me to silence. Instead of letting go of my arm he moved his fingers down to encircle my wrist and pulled me behind him as he started walking back toward the house. His grip was loose, so I pulled my arm free from him and followed in silence.

I was still reeling from everything I'd just seen in my meditative state. What was my subconscious trying to tell me? Was this castle a real place? It seemed medieval and archaic, so that was doubtful, unless it was a glimpse into the past...

When we stepped inside, Daelon gestured to a couch. "Sit."

"When you talk to me like that, it makes me not want to listen."

"And how should I talk to you, Áine? How you talk to me?" His voice was level now, but still seething.

So, he was still angry about my words last night. I'm

the one who should've been angry—with his mixed messages and the confusion and humiliation his words caused. I sat down and fiddled with my fingers as they lay in my lap. I hated how he made me feel like an errant child.

"I have never in my life been spoken to so..." He paused as he searched for the right word. "Disrespectfully."

I scoffed. "Well maybe you should have been."

Daelon closed his eyes for a moment, and when he opened them again, he shrugged out of his jacket and tossed it on the leather chair behind him. He stalked off, leaving me to sit in silence.

When he returned, he clutched what appeared to be a first aid kit. He knelt beside me.

"Won't I heal soon?"

He ignored me, and I flinched when he took a damp cotton pad to wipe the dirt and blood off my skin. Despite his anger, his touch was soft and careful. I winced again when he applied some kind of antiseptic.

"You have no idea," he started. "What do I have to do to make you understand that I'm merely trying to protect you? Disappearing after last night—god, Áine. I thought you'd left or something. Made yourself vulnerable to kidnapping or worse. And going so deep into your mind that you couldn't even be reached as I yelled for you... which you did all alone I may add, something you aren't ready for." He glared at me again, wrapping a bandage around a cut that was deeper than I'd realized.

How had I not felt that? I sighed. I thought he was most upset about the cursing and the disobedience, but it seemed that most of his anger was just a mask for his worry. I let my guard down, if only a little. "I just needed some space," I said.

He stood. "You're not a prisoner here. But you can't just disappear like that after we had an argument." He ran a hand through his hair. When he looked at me again, his eyes softened, and some of the frantic tension in his features finally loosened.

"I didn't think about it like that," I said. "But I'm fine. It was just a scrape. And I just got too caught up in a visualization." That was putting it mildly, but I wasn't in the mood to elaborate.

Daelon studied me for a moment, his brows furrowed. "About last night—"

"No," I quickly stopped him.

"No? What do you mean *no*?"

"It means I don't want to talk about it, Daelon. I'm sorry I got the wrong idea," I muttered, flushing.

"It wasn't like that." He shook his head, cocking it to the side in mild confusion. "I—I just can't. It wouldn't be right. Not when there's so much you don't know about me." He seemed to consider his words carefully.

I heard him loud and clear. "You don't need to come up with an excuse. Like I said, it was a mistake. You don't have to do things you don't want to."

"Wait, but I didn't say—"

"It was probably just Stockholm syndrome," I joked with a shrug.

Daelon looked like he'd just been slapped, suddenly straightening his back, a flash of ice in his stare. I'd clearly struck a nerve. He stayed silent, his features now completely unreadable.

"Right, then," I said. "I'm going to go shower. We can go back to normal. Forget any of it ever happened." My face contorted with confusion as I cast him one last glance before walking away.

CHAPTER 8

The next few days were uneventful. Daelon was distant and untalkative, and I was still reeling from how quickly things had changed between us. Despite my attempts to return to our normal dynamic, the air was stiff and awkward. He began teaching me defensive magick—his specialty—and it was tiring to have to put up with his constant nitpicking and control issues. To make matters worse, he was wholly incapable of understanding my human culture references.

"The defense against the dark arts position is cursed, you know," I said at one point.

"I have no idea what you're talking about. Please focus."

And that was how our conversations went. He led me through ways to detect if someone was using magick against me, how to cast defensive spells, and how to make sure I was protected when I practiced my own magick. I was beginning to understand that my power somehow already knew what to do—how to tap into each individual current of witchcraft and launch itself to the desired outcome—and sometimes it was as though the magick itself was more in control than I was. The hardest part was centering and grounding myself so that the power could take the reins constructively rather than impulsively.

"Focus on the candle, Áine," Daelon instructed today. "Control. Don't get lost in your channeling. You only need just a hint of power for this. It's your intent that's most important." We sat on the floor in the living room next to the glass paneling, neither of us desiring to sit together in the room with the fireplace after the other night.

I had finally convinced Daelon that we should do a detection spell to reveal if the man who haunted my nightmares was still working against me, hiding in the shadows and in the darkness of my metaphysical ocean. I still caught glimpses of his sour, icy energy, as if he was watching us, lying in wait. I just couldn't shake it. And my mothers told me that my intuition was the most important guide I had.

I gazed upon the white candle, focusing on only letting a tiny bit of magick through. Even with all of the forces in the world at my fingertips, casting simple spells was harder than I'd anticipated. I wasn't used to directing my power into such specific magick.

"You can come up with your own short chant, which will help you cast this spell faster next time. It encodes an energetic imprint to the words."

Reveal this curse. I shrugged to myself. It wasn't exactly creative, but whatever. I repeated the mantra in my mind until it fused with my intent.

The candle flame soared, and the white wax began to

darken and turn black like a scorched piece of paper. I looked to Daelon, my eyes wide. That couldn't be good.

I frowned. "See? I told you. What does this mean, exactly? Is it the same witch you cast a spell against in the clearing? And if so, does that mean it didn't work?"

Daelon sighed, his features fixed and rigid. "No. My spell worked. Like I tried to explain before, a curse isn't always a cause for concern. No one can seriously harm you through all of my defenses." His tone was fiery, like he was deeply offended by the mere insinuation.

I tried to reason that if Mr. Overprotective wasn't concerned, then I probably shouldn't have been either. But I couldn't shake the nagging feeling that something wasn't right.

"So, you think we should just do nothing?" I scoffed. "A *curse* sounds pretty dangerous to me."

"For now, yes, we do nothing. Cursing someone can encompass just mild magickal workings and intentions for harm against someone, too. Not just overtly aggressive magick. Given all of our protections, I truly think it's just someone who doesn't want you here aiming blindly, attempting to intimidate you. They're just angry they can't get to you, and they're powerful. Their anger is bound to be felt in the fluidity of this realm."

I watched him carefully. He didn't answer whether this witch was the same he'd cursed last week, but it was safe to say my intuition was on the mark. It was hard to believe that someone was aiming magick at me just to be a nuisance, considering how dangerous Daelon made our enemies out to be. Then again, so far, the only evidence of a curse encompassed murky nightmares and evil-sounding voices saying mean things.

I watched him as he steepled his fingers to rest on his lips, a storm brewing in his eyes. I didn't understand why he was so dead set against learning more about a curse aimed at me, no matter how small. Was it really that he was just offended by my doubting his protective abilities?

"What next?" I asked finally.

"We're done for the day," he said without breaking his stare off into space.

He barely acknowledged me as I got up from the floor and headed through the hall to my room. I shut the door behind me, leaning up against it for a moment. I couldn't shake the sinking feeling in my gut toward how Daelon regarded me now. No more flirting or innuendos. No more looking at me with awe. All because of one whiskey-fueled lapse of judgement.

However, I was proud of myself for one thing that had also dropped off the last couple days—my uncontrolled magickal outbursts. Daelon had been leading me in more daily meditations to work on separating my magick from my emotions, which had worked surprisingly well. I was much better at recognizing when I was channeling power unknowingly or impulsively, and it was easier to tune in and out of these frequencies at will.

I shrugged out of my white sweater, dark jeans, and underwear, tossing them on the bed. I ran the shower and waited for the water to heat up to my liking. As I stepped in, I was immediately soothed by the heat on my skin, especially as the weather was growing colder.

Just like Daelon.

I sighed, leaning my head against the tile as the steam rose all around me. Daelon was just a distraction from what my mothers and—possibly even the Universe—wanted me to accomplish here in this mysterious realm. I grew more controlled and in tune with my power every day. Soon there would be no reason for him to keep the truth of my enemies from me. If I had that information, my path would become clearer. And then I wouldn't need Daelon at all.

I didn't like how willing he was to shrug off a possible attack from our enemies. If he wasn't going to do anything about whoever used intimidation magick against me, that was his prerogative. I, however, thought it may be prudent to send them some of their own medicine.

I finished up my shower and pulled a black, off-the-shoulder sweater dress over my head. Sitting on the floor, I cast a protective circle around myself with my fingers, watching as a hazy, barely perceptible translucent field encircled me.

"Reveal who cursed me," I whispered, closing my eyes. I sent my power out into the world through a point at the top of my protective field, searching for who matched the imprint of my nightmares and negative visions.

I opened my eyes and set my gaze upon the window in front of me, watching as the woodland scenery shifted into the field from my second nightmare. A figure appeared again in the distance, and I was certain it was a man, just as it had been in my past encounters. He was shrouded in black smoke as before, unmoving.

"Who are you?" I whispered.

A voice sounded in my mind, thick and distorted—like the way reporters altered the voices of anonymous sources.

Perhaps I'm the Devil. Or maybe a god. Either way, this realm is mine.

I switched over to telepathic communication, which seemed most natural when practicing magick. The words appeared in my mind like a kind of auditory hallucination.

Yeah, I don't think so. Why do you hide?

I'm not the only one hiding my identity from you, little witch.

My heart rate picked up at the sound of Daelon's condescending, but also growing-on-me pet name. How could he possibly know that kind of information? Just as he'd done before, this entity sought to challenge my trust in Daelon. But why? I figured it must've had to do with Daelon's shielding powers. If I didn't trust him and ran off, then I'd open myself up to attack.

You hide because you're the one who's weak, I retorted, ignoring his attempts to distract me and seed doubt. *You want to frighten me with all of these games. Because I've returned to Aradia and...* you're *scared of* me. *You know that I could destroy you.*

A sickening, bone-chilling laugh erupted in my ears.

How wrong you are...

The figure suddenly rushed toward me. As he came closer to the window, the smoke cleared to reveal skin made up of darkened, rotting flesh—a true embodiment of what I pictured the Devil to look like—his black robes whipping all around him. He bared his pointy, uneven teeth, and I couldn't help but let out a blood curdling scream, despite knowing this was all a show. I wasn't much of a horror movie fan, even if I knew the monsters weren't real.

Leave me now, I yelled, channeling all of my fear into an

intent to banish. My magick travelled up and out of my circle to carry away my intent. It swarmed the windows, and it melted away the field scene and my enemy to reveal tall pines and evergreens once more.

A loud thump at my door made my heart nearly leap out of my chest for the second time. I quickly dispersed the circle, releasing its energy back into the world, and went to investigate. My breathing was shallow as I crept toward the door, my hand shaking as I turned the knob. As I did, Daelon fell from where he'd been slumped against the other side.

"No," I croaked in a panic, reaching for him. His body was far too heavy for me to carry, so I carefully brought him down to the floor and dragged him onto the rug. "Daelon. You answer me right now," I begged, shaking his shoulders as I knelt over him. His dark eyes were wide open but empty, staring into the abyss. His body was rigid and lifeless.

I reached two fingers to his neck, searching for a pulse. As I found the right spot, my breath caught in my throat. His heart was beating, so soft and so faint. Tears pricked my eyes, threatening to overflow. If anything happened to him it would be my fault. Why couldn't I just do as he asked? I knew not to do magick under his nose. He told me to leave it alone, and instead I provoked something dangerous.

I made a silent prayer to the Universe, to the Goddess my mothers prayed to, to every deity ever worshipped by human or witch. I promised I would start listening to his guidance. *Just let him live.*

I wiped the tears from my cheeks and began to call upon the forces surrounding me, but before I could transform energy into magick, his pulse strengthened under my fingers.

The pounding moved quicker, his heartbeat jumping to meet my skin with vigor. I sighed a breath of relief, letting my head fall to his chest. "Oh, thank you. Thank you," I gasped to no one in particular.

I lifted my head up, watching Daelon's chest rise and fall. His eyes were still open and unfocused. I stared into them, tentatively raising my hand to touch the side of his face. I trailed my fingers from his temple down the side of his jaw. When I moved my fingers back up to continue the movement, Daelon suddenly caught my wrist in his hand. His grip was so tight it hurt.

"Ow," I yelped. "Ease up a bit, please." I started to smile, but it quickly turned into a grimace when his grip only grew firmer. A look I'd never seen before flashed in his eyes. They were fiery and hostile, and hauntingly devoid of any semblance of *Daelon*.

He let go of my arm, and in one swift motion sprung up and rolled over on top of me. I yelled out as my head slammed into the floor, blinking back tears from the impact. I fought back against him as he overpowered me, putting his full weight on my torso and pinning my flailing wrists to the ground.

"Daelon, stop," I cried.

But it wasn't Daelon at all. For the first time, I could read the energetic field around his body, and it held the screams of thousands, thick like blood and as sour as rotting flesh and charred land. My body rejected this energy like the plague. Hot nausea rose up in my stomach. I had to block it out completely.

He glared down at me, operating robotically like a wind-up soldier. "*Do you still think I'm weak?*"

It was the distorted voice of the witch who cursed me moving through Daelon's lips. He let go of my wrists and wrapped his hands around my throat, grinning sadistically. I tried to throw him off with my power but was met with an energetic wall that encircled his body. I could've found a way to break through it, but my ability to concentrate on my magick faltered as I ran out of oxygen.

I clawed at his hands, attempting to pry them from my neck, digging my fingernails into his skin. I searched his eyes, begging Daelon to come back to me as my vision blurred. I channeled whatever I could through my hands into his, but all I could seem to think about was my feelings for him—my foolish sentiments that weren't going to do me any good in this moment. My longing, my frustrating infatuation, my gratitude for his protection and expertise, and, as hard as it was for me to admit when I wasn't close to death... my incurable and irrational adoration of him. Despite all of the chaos and confusion, I couldn't deny this connection that felt just as natural to me as my magick did.

This connection that felt like the home I'd never seen.

My hands tightened around his one last time as I held my gaze steadfast, some of my energy flowing into him as the darkness descended.

I was on the beach my mothers told me about, overlooking the ocean that I used as my psychic metaphor. The rushing of waves and calls of birds flooded my ears. I wasn't quite sure how I got here or how this day began, but it felt too real to be a dream. The sand sparkled in multicolor, and I looked down to see I wore a long, white dress. I walked to the water and willed it to act as a mirror. I stared at my ethereal reflection with glowing skin and copper hair that shimmered with the tones of a sunrise. A crown made of white roses encircled my head like a halo. White roses were Momma Jane's favorite.

Chills danced down my spine as the din of a familiar song rose up around me, carried by too many voices to count. Though it was wordless, I knew it was a song of hope. It was a song about unity. A love song for a people who must overcome. This song had carried over mountains, through valleys, across deserts and snow-covered hills, and it crested over the tall waves that brought it to our shore.

I turned from the ocean to see witches dressed in white forming a semi-circle, like a crescent moon. I scanned their faces and saw my mothers, who looked youthful and radiant, smiling at me. Momma Celeste's blond hair was silvery and short, and Momma Jane's was dark, long and wavy, with the faintest tinge of red in its undertones. I ran toward them, but soon found myself falling to my knees in the warm sand. I wanted so desperately to get up and embrace them, but I couldn't move.

"No Áine, not yet," Momma Jane said, stepping forward from the group.

I knew she was right. This was not my time. I did not belong in this place. If I touched them, I might never leave.

"I miss you so much it hurts," I choked, clutching my chest. "I love you."

"We love you too, sweet child," Momma Celeste cooed, clasping her hand in Momma Jane's.

"And Áine—stop blaming yourself," Momma Jane said,

her face grave. "It is but a distraction from your grief, and a way to deny your destiny of a greater purpose... do you understand that?"

I looked at all the faces before me, young and old, and knew that they were family too. They smiled at me, beginning to chant softly, and I knew it was spells of protection, of strength, and of renewal.

A tear escaped my eye. "I know it wasn't my fault, deep down. But I wanted to save you, and you made me leave."

"You *will* save us. Just not in the way you thought. You cannot possibly fathom the entirety of your life's arc and influence from your own limited perspective. We knew we were going to die. We had accepted it long before those men came. The power of the cruelty of killing a child's parents right before her eyes forged a spell so powerful that it kept you hidden from them. It allowed you to mature and grow. It allowed others' roles in this story to manifest and develop. If anything had happened differently or on an alternate timeline then the whole plan would've fallen apart."

Plan? I shook my head, my brows furrowed. I struggled against the urge to run to them, to touch their faces, and to give in to the temptation that promised an end to my pain and all the pain that was to come.

This time Momma Celeste spoke, her voice soft and lyrical. "You don't see it all now, but you must have faith. This story has many chapters, and each piece will need to fall into place at the exact moment that it should and not a moment before. Like a road with many hills, you will not be able to see where it all leads. But know that it *will* lead."

"She needs to go back now," a woman said, with kind eyes, olive-toned skin, and dark brown hair. She offered me a knowing smile, almost as if she wanted to say more but couldn't. There was something familiar in her face, but Momma Celeste's voice cut through before I could place it.

"No matter how dark and cold, how difficult or impossible your journey becomes, know that we will always be with you. The whole world is on your side. You will always have friends where you least expect them."

The ground beneath me began to shake, like the very fabric of this world was crumbling. Suddenly my mothers and our people were much farther away, and they became more and more distant until they were merely specks of white light among the tall sand dunes. The ocean lapped at my heels as I knelt, and soon it was at my waist. I waited there in the sand until a large wave overtook me, and I was returned to myself.

CHAPTER 9

My eyes fluttered open to Daelon kneeling over me, begging as I had when I thought I'd killed him with my disobedience. His eyes were closed, his hands clasped around one of mine. I was still on the floor, and I realized that no more than a few minutes had passed. Or else I would be dead.

"Please," he prayed softly.

A soothing energy flowed from his hands to mine, but the pain and stiffness around my no-doubt bruised neck was raw and intense.

"Daelon," I croaked, my voice scratchy. I winced at the pain of speaking.

"Thank the Goddess." He didn't let go of my hand as he gazed down at me, his worry transforming to disgust as he studied my neck. "I'm so sorry."

"It's okay," I said instinctively, but winced. My mouth tasted metallic.

"Shhh," he soothed and lifted me up into his arms and

carried me across the room. He laid me down on my bed, so gentle and careful. "It's not okay." He slumped to his knees beside the bed buried his head in his hands, shame wracking his features.

"I know it wasn't you. It's my fault for provoking whoever that was," I said.

He looked up, and something flashed in his eyes, but he pressed a finger to his lips in a gesture for me to stop hurting myself by talking. I hoped this witchy super-healing would kick in soon.

My thoughts traveled to the dream that didn't feel like a dream, and I let that feeling of pure love sent by my mothers and the other people in white wash over me. It was real, wasn't it? It was becoming harder and harder to tell in the witch realm. Everything felt real on some level.

"This is all my fault, trust me," Daelon said, his last words laced with hidden meaning. He shook his head. "Let me get you something for the pain."

It was Daelon I wanted to be free from pain. I had never seen so much in him—in his eyes, in the lines in his forehead, and in his grimace. He had to know that it wasn't he who hurt me. How could he blame himself?

He quickly returned, holding out his hand where two blue pills lay. He handed me a glass of water with the other. I took them, reminded of a few weeks ago when I'd done the same. It was insane how quickly things had changed and progressed.

I just needed to be held. To be comforted. Having a near-death experience and seeing my mothers made me feel childlike and vulnerable. It was a feeling I rarely let myself indulge, but something about the words they spoke—that I still didn't entirely understand—filled a hole inside of me. A gaping wound of shame, denial, and faithlessness. This experience was what I needed in order to move forward, to see their deaths as a source of strength and sacrifice rather than a weakness I blamed myself for. I still didn't entirely know how to have faith in this path they'd laid out for me, which still felt as obscured and muddled as a hazy childhood memory.

I just knew I had to try.

"Could you lie with me?" I asked finally.

Daelon hesitated. He stood over me, his face frozen in worry.

"Oh," I said. "You don't have to." I wanted to cry.

"I don't want to hurt you further," he said quickly. "I've already failed you once." He studied my neck again, disgust rising back up to his features.

"Please."

He raised his gaze to mine and immediately acquiesced, crawling in beside me. I sucked in a breath as I moved onto my side, my back to him. I felt the bed shift as he took my cue and gently wrapped an arm around me, melding himself to me. I marveled at how perfectly our bodies fit together as his breath tickled the back of my neck.

"I thought I'd killed you," he whispered, his voice as hoarse as mine. His grip tightened around me, and he snaked his hand around mine.

"I thought I killed you, too." *Just like my mothers.* I thought I'd caused their murders because of my selfishness, disobedience, and thirst for power. But if they already knew they were going to die... if I was always meant to come into this power, and everything had happened exactly according to some grand plan, then I was absolved. They said I was meant to save them in a different way. Now it was up to me to figure out how.

We lay in silence for a beat, and I could feel an intensity bubbling up around us.

"You didn't fail me. Please don't blame yourself." It felt natural to be in his arms.

He chuckled in a way that was devoid of humor. "My cosmic purpose is literally to protect you, Áine."

The hairs at the back of my neck pricked up at his tone. I wanted to lift his hand to my mouth and kiss it.

"It must hurt to speak so please stop doing it. I can't bear to see you in more pain," he said, softer now.

"It doesn't hurt," I lied, "that much." I looked down at our intwined fingers. A vein bulged in his forearm, which was unsettling, considering the action that just strained his muscles. I frowned and shook the thought away. "I'm sorry for trying to seduce you," I blurted. After this experience, I needed everything to be out on the table. "When you didn't want to... you know."

Very eloquent, Áine, I chastised myself. God this was humiliating, yet again. I just wanted to put it all behind us.

Daelon nearly snorted. "Is that how you saw it?" he scoffed. "I thought you said your actions were due to *Stockholm syndrome*." The tone of his voice changed, revealing once more that that comment had cut deep.

"That was a joke!"

"Oh." He was silent for a moment. "It wasn't that I didn't want to. I mean, don't be ridiculous. I just didn't want to take advantage of the situation."

I drew my brows together. It seemed I had misread that

night in a completely different way than I'd originally thought. Heat rose to my cheeks, replaying his words in my mind. So, he *had* wanted me.

Now what?

"Oh," was all I could manage to say. I shivered as he unclasped his hand from mine and stroked through my hair just above the ear. "Do you believe in an afterlife?" I asked, veering quickly into a new conversational direction. I couldn't shake that image of my mothers, looking so proud of me in their white dresses that blew in the ocean breeze.

"Occasionally."

"I'm not sure that's something one believes in *occasionally*," I laughed.

Daelon's fingers paused in their brush through my hair. "I believe in what I experience. There are plenty of witches who believe in such things and claim to have seen them firsthand. But how can I trust in them? Two people can experience the same event and recount it completely differently."

I picked up on the embedded double meaning. "Fair point."

"Why do you ask?"

"I saw my mothers. When I was unconscious. Or at least I think I did."

Daelon sighed. "Maybe you did. It wouldn't be any less meaningful either way, would it? If it was *really* them, or some other form conjured through their energy and memory. I don't know."

I wasn't sure, either. I thought it would mean less in that I would like to see my mothers again, when it was my time to die. But if death was final and I snuffed out of existence, I guessed I wouldn't be conscious anymore to be disappointed.

"It's like that Mark Twain quote. Where he says he isn't afraid to die because he was dead for billions of years before he was born and had not suffered the slightest bit of inconvenience from it," I thought aloud.

"I quite like that," Daelon said, wrapping his arm back around me. I felt him move closer, his breath warm on my neck. "But can we stop talking about death, please?"

"Right. Yeah," I laughed nervously.

But the line of thought wouldn't loosen its grip. What I saw on that beach felt just as real as this moment. It lit something inside me that I knew would guide me for days to come, like I was being pulled through this life by an invisible thread—one that tied me to my mothers, our people, that place, and a power that was universal—magick that yearned for the completion of something I had yet to understand. My mothers wanted me to trust that one day I would. I would understand everything.

"Can we talk about whoever the hell it was that I provoked?" I asked, expecting yet another wall.

Daelon sighed, confirming what I already knew. "We can. Soon," he promised, and I wasn't sure whether to believe him. Even after we'd almost killed each other, there was still this barrier between us, one that he was entirely unwilling to break down. And I was tired of being put off.

We lay in silence, and my mind traveled to that beach until Daelon pulled me back to him again.

"What was that dream about, Áine? The one that made you blush and get all cagey?" And just like that, playful Daelon was back, his thumb stroking my palm.

"How did I know you would never let that go?" I muttered, glad to be facing away from him.

"Tell me."

I did sort of promise the Universe to obey Daelon more often if he lived. I groaned. "Fine. It was... risqué. And about you. But not a sex dream," I quickly added. My heart rate soared. "So don't get too full of yourself." As soon as it left my mouth, I instantly regretted it. What the hell was in these magickal pain killers?

I could nearly feel his grin. "Mmm," he purred into my neck. "I knew it."

I needed to use the bathroom. *And exit this conversation.*

I wriggled out of Daelon's grasp and started to get up.

"Hey, where do you think you're going?" he asked, more than amused. He grabbed my wrist and then quickly let go when I winced. It was the wrist he'd grabbed too tightly when possessed by whatever that malevolent force was.

I turned to look at him as I sat at the edge of the bed. His face had fallen, no trace of its former mischief. He grasped my arm lightly, inspecting the red, just formed bruising in the shape of a hand.

"I'm sorry," he said again.

"Stop apologizing." I wished I could banish the shame from his eyes. He looked like he'd failed the whole world. "I just need to use the bathroom."

He released my arm, watching me as I stopped in front of the mirror. I suppressed a gasp for his sake as I caught a glimpse of my neck, which was bright pink and beginning to swell. The bruises along the sides were red and splotchy.

I turned to Daelon, who looked positively mortified. "It's not that bad. They're sort of like, uh, hickeys." I shrugged and disappeared into the bathroom. Okay, maybe it looked way worse than that, but I needed to make light of it all so Daelon wouldn't shut down again.

Out of his sight now, I inspected myself further in the tall, golden-framed mirrors, smoothing down my messy hair and readjusting my thick knit sweater dress. My head throbbed slightly even through the witchy painkillers, and I remembered that I'd also hit it hard during the attack.

When I came back into the room, my stomach dropped at the sight of my empty bed. I was surprised at just how much it disappointed me. Even after all the cuddling and vulnerability, not to mention a shared near-death experience, I had absolutely no idea where we stood. I didn't know if I could suppress my feelings any longer.

I ventured outside the room, a bit loopy and lightheaded from the pills. They felt like a blanket of warmth around my every nerve ending, swarming my mind with soft, wispy clouds. I spotted Daelon in the kitchen chopping up what appeared to be herbs and fruit. He stopped when he noticed me.

"Go get in bed," he ordered.

"Without you?" I leaned my head to the side.

He narrowed his eyes, unable to hold back a smile. "Those painkillers are working, huh?" He shook his head. "I'll be there in a minute."

Were the magick pills really affecting my behavior that much? Oh, well. Who needed inhibitions anyway? It wasn't my fault he looked so hot right now, with his taut muscles and his chiseled face and his—

"Go get in bed," he repeated. I could tell he was trying not to laugh.

"Yes, sir," I said, biting my lip. "Is that how you want me to respond when you order me around?" I teased, feigning innocence.

Daelon set down the knife, utterly bemused before regaining composure. He lifted a brow. "Yes, that would be preferable to how you generally respond."

His eyes flashed something dangerous as he crossed his arms, as if he was daring me to continue. I decided to postpone the challenge for another time, spinning on my heel to get back in bed.

"How is it?"

"Kind of gross, sorry," I said, drinking the green smoothie Daelon had blended for me. It tasted exactly like its contents, which were a bunch of herbs and a banana.

"It will help speed up the healing. It's a recipe my mother taught me, one that was passed down for generations," he said thoughtfully, momentarily traveling somewhere else in his mind. He sat with me in the king-sized bed. "Plus, you haven't eaten in at least 6 hours."

"Holy shit."

"What?" He sounded alarmed.

"You're obsessed with me."

He rolled his eyes and sighed dramatically, but I could tell the corners of his lips wanted to tip upward.

"Listen. Only stalkers know how long it's been since someone's last meal."

"I'm both a kidnapper and a stalker now, is that right?" he asked as if he'd taken the insult seriously.

"Oh, stop pouting. It was a *joke*." I exaggerated the last word, shaking my head at him. "Stop being so serious."

"Keeping you alive and making sure you're prepared for what's to come is a serious job," he murmured.

"I'm not a child. I think I learned how to keep myself alive a long time ago."

"Well, you're not particularly good at it," he muttered.

I laughed.

"What is so funny?"

I shrugged. "You."

He flustered. "Glad I can amuse you." He looked like he wanted to say something more but didn't. Instead, he watched as I set my finished herb smoothie down on the bedside table.

I leaned back on the pillows. Across from me, he leaned back on his palms. We stared at each other for a moment in silence. When he moved closer, my breath caught in my throat as he gently lifted my left arm and kissed my wrist softly.

"Will that speed the healing, too?" I asked, my voice still scratchy.

"I figure it doesn't hurt to try," he said. His eyes were utterly seductive, but I could tell it still pained him to see my bruises.

"Well." I swallowed. "Then you should probably be thorough."

He smiled, crawling over me so that his face was mere inches from mine. He looked down at my lips, but then cocked and moved his head lower so he could reach my neck. I turned to give him better access as he left the lightest of kisses along my bruised skin. He moved from one side to the other, and I mirrored him. Each time his lips met my throat, a shiver went down my spine.

My breath picked up as he finished, and as his lips were so close to mine again, I was nearly ready to beg him to kiss me. He didn't. I must've given myself away because he looked rather contented with himself as he pulled back, leaving me yearning.

"I don't think I've ever been so gentle with someone," he murmured.

I quirked a brow. Why was that not surprising? Of course, Daelon wouldn't be into *gentle*. All of the innuendos he'd made came rushing back to me.

He smiled shyly, leaning on his side against the pillows. I turned so that we faced each other. "I just—this isn't something I'm used to."

I didn't have the gall to ask him to elaborate on whatever non-gentle relationships he *was* used to.

"I'm not used to feeling this way," he clarified.

"Oh," I said, barely audible. "Feeling what way?" My eyes probed his.

Daelon shook his head. "We really shouldn't, Áine."

"Shouldn't what?" Why must he always make things difficult? I didn't understand why he had all of these arbitrary rules for himself in place. I ignored the words of the wannabe devil that flashed in my mind, insinuating that Daelon was hiding his identity. I knew who Daelon was. Even without the help of my gift, I could sense it. "Nothing that you're hiding from me could change anything."

Daelon sighed. "It will." He looked so conflicted; his features racked with discomfort. "When I was close to killing you—" I opened my mouth to tell him to stop torturing himself, but he pressed a finger to my lips. "No, listen. As you faded out, you sent me what you were feeling. That's what brought me back, I think."

My eyes widened as I remembered those moments, and I knew I was probably flushed. My feelings for him had been the only thing I could think about. "And you don't feel the same way," I finished for him. Maybe this was all just lust for him.

"Áine, that's not what I'm saying." He took in a breath. "Like I said before, I just don't want to take advantage of this situation. I don't want to do anything that could jeopardize what we're working toward. It's all just—complicated."

"Stop treating me like I can't make my own decisions about how I act and feel. You are never going to take advantage of me, Daelon."

He sighed, and he moved a strand of hair behind my ear. "Maybe you're right. I didn't think I would feel this way. I've *never* felt this way," he said. He was angelically vulnerable again, like he looked only in his sleep. Fear gleamed deep in his eyes. "I don't know if I can stop myself anymore. Not now."

"I don't know if I can either," I whispered back, reaching for his hand. "So maybe we shouldn't."

He smiled hesitantly. "Your energy—it revealed that I reminded you of a home you'd never seen. I feel the same way. You—you remind me of home," he said, a long-buried sadness rising to the surface of his dark eyes. But hope swam there, too. "You need to rest. We can continue this tomorrow, okay?"

I nodded, reflecting his smile. Something had finally

shifted; a barrier crumbled at last. There were other walls to break and hurdles to clear, but for now, this was enough.

When I woke, Daelon was wrapped around me, his arm locking me in place. I couldn't help but smile. Even in his sleep, his instinct was to act as a shield. My dreams were normal and diluted for once, without any hint of hidden meanings, monsters, or magick. It was as if my mind finally blocked everything out to take some well-deserved time to recharge and rest.

I snuck out of Daelon's grasp, amused as he reached for me without waking. In the bathroom, I took a moment to inspect my neck in the mirror. Like my pain, the marks had faded miraculously overnight. The bruises had transformed to more blue and green hues behind my warm-toned skin.

Daelon stirred when I stepped back into the room.

"Áine," he said groggily, reaching out to where I once lay. He sat up quickly.

"I'm right here."

His momentary confusion and panic dissipated. He shook his head, and when I crawled back under the covers, he pulled me close to him. I rested my head against his bare chest, which was warm in contrast to the cold outside of our soft, blanket cocoon. He kissed the top of my head and held me tight.

I was still getting used to us being this close, but it didn't feel as strange as I thought it would. It felt natural. Destined. Like yet another piece coming together in this cosmic drama.

"How does your neck feel?"

"Better."

"Good."

I fell back to sleep pressed into the contours of his body, though flashes of those witches in white continued to dance in my mind in between states of consciousness. They whispered through the crashing of waves—things I would soon forget as sleep pulled me back under—but I held on to the feeling that I was exactly where I needed to be, with exactly who I needed to be with.

CHAPTER 10

Daelon and I sat in the dining room next to the kitchen, and I watched sleet pour down outside. I wished it was cold enough to snow, but the temperature hovered just above freezing. At least I wasn't the cause of the precipitation today.

"Now that we've regrouped," I started, sipping on coffee. "Can we discuss whoever the hell that was and how we are going to kick his ass?"

Daelon looked up at me warily and set down the book he was reading, which seemed to be on war strategy or something of equal dullness.

"We will be doing no such thing. At least not yet," he qualified. He gazed out the window, his features oddly impassive.

"Discussing him *or* kicking his ass?" I wasn't going to let this go. This man nearly killed him. And me. Why was Daelon hesitating? "Because last time I checked you said we were completely untouchable here. What happens when he comes for round two?"

He snapped his head back and crossed his arms, his face contorting like I'd offended him. Sometimes talking to him was like walking through a minefield.

"It *won't* happen again. It was a unique breach of my defenses due to extraordinary power and the element of surprise, but it will *never* happen again,"

Again, I couldn't tell if he was being arrogant and determined, or if he knew more than he was letting on. "You know who it was, don't you? And if he was that powerful, does that mean I'm not the only one of my... kind?" I frowned at the way that threatened my ego.

"There is no one like you, Áine. You can rest assured on that," he said with a smirk. "And yes, I do know who it was."

I was shocked at this candor. Was Daelon finally going to be honest with me about the evil that lurked in this realm? And even my role in defeating it?

"He's an enemy, of course. A powerful one. But I don't want you worrying about that for now, okay? I need you to trust me."

I huffed, narrowing my eyes. He was running out of *just trust me* cards to play.

"We will be studying offensive magick soon," he said, attempting to placate me and to change the subject.

It worked a little bit. I readjusted my turtleneck, which I wore to hide my fading bruises for his sake. We talked for a bit longer before training, but my mind was elsewhere, unable to let go of the man who wore the mask of the Devil. Was that how he wanted me to see him? Or was that how he saw himself?

He wanted me to know his strength after I challenged him, as if he was threatened by the mere suggestion that I was more powerful. If he was strong enough to overpower Daelon, who was supposedly built for shielding, then could he be more powerful than me? That would make Daelon a liar, or at least dishonest by omission. Maybe I wasn't the only omnipotent witch out there, in which case, I was not omnipotent at all. So, what was I? And who was he?

Despite what I'd told Daelon last night—that nothing he was hiding from me would alter how I felt—I couldn't shake these creeping doubts. I would be a fool to ignore them. But I also couldn't ignore the consistency in Daelon's words and actions, which all pointed to the idea that he was an ally who only wanted to protect me. Nor could I deny that the energy I'd gleaned from him had my best interest at heart even as he evaded my questions.

As I'd found myself doing more often than I felt comfortable with, I chose my heart over my head.

For now.

I sat facing Daelon in the basement, not bothering to hide my disappointment after he refused to train outside where he deemed it to be *too cold*. On the flip side, the first snow had begun to fall, which guaranteed my good mood. Winter and the holidays were tied very deeply to the most sacred parts of my childhood—times when my mothers and I were at our happiest. We celebrated Yule, or the winter solstice, rather than Christmas, but it was virtually the same besides a few witchy twists thrown in. We decorated a tree, gave gifts, baked sweets, and cooked elaborate meals. We celebrated with our neighbors in their homes and at the local pub, but I also remembered plenty of candle-lighting and spells, ancestral devotion, and a Yule log that burned with wishes for the new year. I just wished I remembered more of the specifics.

My mothers also made sure to tell me about their coven —our family, related through community if not by blood— and how much they all wished they could be with us during these holidays. My mothers cried when they told me, each year, that my people loved me so much that they gave up their chance of ever knowing me. I never quite understood what this meant, but I knew it had something to do with my mothers' escape from Aradia. If those witches in white were my mothers' people, all dead... did that mean I was the only one left? The only one who could preserve centuries of tradition?

I frowned. They did say that I would always have friends where I least expected them. Were some of my mothers' coven still here, somewhere? *And could I find them?*

"You're not paying attention."

"Sorry." I gave my head a shake. "I'm back."

"Learning how to defend yourself is the most important thing I can teach you," he chastised, finishing with a sigh. "I'm going to try to enter your mind again, and I want you to say when you detect me."

I cleared my ruminating thoughts and brought myself back to this moment. Today we were working on psychic defense, in particular my ability to detect external influence. I centered myself and waited, sending out probes to detect any sense of Daelon in the outskirts of my energy field. In a few moments, I felt the slightest shift, like a spider creeping through the tiniest of holes in the wall.

"I feel you," I said.

"Now block me."

He was searching for something. Instead of blocking him immediately, I followed him around the edge of my mind. His energy was unreadable by nature of his shielding gift, only detectable by its imprint that told me it wasn't my own. What was he looking for?

I grew distracted again, thinking of my dreams, in particular the dream where Daelon looked at me like I belonged to him, and his muscles flexed as he—

I suddenly realized it was Daelon who brought forward this vision. In a burst of strength, I banished him from my psyche.

"Hey!" Flustered, I swatted at his arm, but he caught my wrist midair.

He grinned devilishly, kissing my hand before releasing me.

"Talk about an invasion of privacy." I glowered.

"I would never seriously breach your mind in that way. You know that."

I did. Daelon was all about consent, if nothing else. He still looked all too pleased with his harmless intrusion, though.

As we worked through a couple more exercises, I realized that these lessons were very much tied to yesterday's attack. I'd always known we were preparing for some kind of battle, but it all felt real now. I needed to be ready for the pretend-devil and whoever else wanted us dead. So, we continued working, only partially distracted by the renewed and undeniable tension between us.

The snow continued to fall, and by the time neither of us could work any longer it had even started to cling to the ground. We faced the basement's wall of glass panels, and I sat in between Daelon's legs, looking out at the winter landscape. His arms snaked around my torso, a hand resting on my thigh.

"You fascinate me," Daelon said. He traced circles on my bare skin, drawing out a shiver of goosebumps.

"In what way?" I tried not to show just how much his touch affected me. How the skin-on-skin contact consumed my every thought.

"For reasons like getting so excited about the snow. It's... endearing."

I thought about it for a moment. "I cling to things that make me feel nostalgic and safe—that remind me of the part of my childhood I most cherish." I shrugged. "The part of my childhood before I learned that everything could change—that your loved ones could be there one minute and gone forever the next."

The difference between my early memories—memories where everything was magickal and untainted by the rise of my power and my mothers' growing fear—and my later memories of constant anxiety and confusion was astounding. It was like two completely different childhoods. I clung to the former whenever I could, to remind myself that things could be truly amazing in spite of their inherent transience.

Nothing was permanent. I wished I could live in these moments of warmth and security forever.

"Sometimes I get scared that the memories you and I

make now are like those—fleeting and liminal, as if we are caught in a happy limbo before the impending storm."

"I'm glad you at least think we're making some good memories," he murmured, sadness creeping into his tone.

"But they're bittersweet. Because I know that we can't stay here forever, and I feel the darkness and struggle that awaits us on the other side." And the selfish part of me didn't want to face that other side. I wanted to stay in Daelon's arms watching the fluffy white flakes fall to the earth.

He held me tighter, and when he kissed the top of my head I stilled, my stomach doing flip-flops.

"I know. I want to make this time count while we can, screw all the rest," he said, and I could tell he was convincing himself more than me. "Even when our path verges into the storm, I need you to know I'll still be there. I will always be on your side."

Before I could respond, a bird flew into a glass panel with a thump, startling me. I watched as it fell, still alive but injured. I pushed up from the ground, slipping from Daelon's grasp.

He peered up at me in confusion. When I darted toward the side door, he sprang to his feet and followed. "Where are we going?"

I ignored him as I walked outside. I headed around the side of the house, my attire not suitable for the biting wind. I wore a black wrap skirt with the red turtleneck to conceal my bruises. There was no doubt that Daelon would chastise me about my lack of clothing.

As if on cue, he admonished, "You are not wearing enough clothes."

I waved away his attempt to give me his jacket, but his glare held a certain finality as he wrapped me in the warm fleece. The air smelled crisp, and snowflakes floated down to melt on my cheeks and accessorize my hair.

I scanned the ground until I spotted the stunned bird, which was bright blue, small, and limping. I knelt, ignoring the bite of the snow on my bare legs. I conjured up a soothing, non-threatening energy so as not to frighten him away, reaching out slowly to scoop him into my palms. He climbed into my grasp willingly, staring up at me with his tiny black eyes.

"Hello there," I murmured, and for the first time since my mothers were alive, I used my powers to heal. Their voices echoed from the time I saved a lamb, telling me that one day I would be able to use my powers fully and unrestrained. That day was today.

I concentrated on the frequency of healing, invoking the power of a mother tending to a sick child, Daelon making gross herb smoothies, and any person who had ever mended another to health. This energy was pure and unencumbered by selfishness or greed, and it seemed to flow through nature like water in a stream. Healing was built into the fiber of every living thing's DNA.

Out of the corner of my eye, I saw Daelon drop down to my level, watching me with his fingers steepled at his lips.

It was growing easier and easier to tap into these natural currents without having to completely submerge myself into my metaphoric ocean. I couldn't deny that Daelon had been crucial in helping me to control and focus all of this power. It was also more effortless out here in the open, where the wind whispered its secrets and the elements had free reign. I gazed at the little blue bird, questioning wordlessly if he was ready to return home. In response he flew from my palms, chirping as he fluttered away.

"You find new ways to surprise me every day," Daelon said softly. He helped me up from the ground, frowning at my knees, reddened by the snow. "I—I haven't been around anyone with so much heart in a very, very long time."

"Then maybe you need new friends," I said. I remembered how he said he'd been taken in by the wrong crowd after he became an orphan. Were they the past he was so worried about telling me?

"I couldn't agree more," he muttered.

I crossed my arms for more warmth. "Let me guess, off limits?"

"Yes." He stepped closer to me. "Let's go inside. You're shivering."

The air shifted suddenly as I hesitated, ignoring his direction and watching as his features quickly turned stern in response. I smiled.

"So dominant," I whispered.

He blinked at me, breaking into a sly grin. "Yes. I think we've established that."

He grabbed my chin and kissed me hard, his other arm snaking around me and creeping down the small of my back. I was breathless by the time he pulled away, having completely forgotten about the cold. He clasped his hand in mine and led me inside and upstairs before pushing me up against a wall and kissing me again.

"No more stopping ourselves, right?" he asked, his lips at my ear.

"Correct."

And those words carried everything else away, leaving nothing but *us*. Here. Now.

He kissed me again, this time lifting my legs up to wrap around his torso. I held onto his neck as he carried me into his room, which was simple yet lavish like the rest of the house. The walls were a dark wooden paneling, and black and white abstract paintings hung above the black headboard. He dropped me onto the plush, gray comforter and stood in front of me, his eyes dark and... possessive.

Just like my dream.

"Take off your sweater," he commanded.

And for the first time since I'd been here, *I really, really liked him telling me what to do.* I yearned for it, even. It was seductive, but also safe and secure, like he had all the answers, and all I had to do was listen.

I took off my sweater and dropped it on the floor, revealing my lacy black bra. Daelon stood in front of me, still fully clothed in his dark tee and jeans. He leaned closer and stroked my cheek, then studied my body as if inspecting a painting at an art gallery.

He guided my head to the side with his hand at my chin, letting out a small sigh.

"I hate seeing these." His eyes met mine, staring at me deeply, probingly. "I would never hurt you, Áine. Well, maybe if you wanted me to."

I raised a brow. "Kinky."

He chuckled as he pulled off his shirt. "Is that what the humans call it?"

I nodded, in a daze. I just wanted him to touch me again. I had never wanted anything more.

In one quick movement he picked me up again and

moved me to the center of the bed. He straddled me. After first kissing my mouth, he trailed light kisses down my neck then moved lower to my collarbone, and then my breasts, tugging lightly at my skin with his teeth. I moaned softly, and as I reached to touch his hair, he grabbed my wrists and pinned them above my head. My breath caught in my throat as he kissed just next to my lips, teasing me.

"Don't move," he growled. He stared at me until I nodded, biting my lip. The corners of his turned up.

I felt myself falling under his spell, unconvinced there wasn't real magick at play here. Why else did I hang on his every command? As if he was the one tethering me to this realm—this universe.

He undid the clasp of my skirt, a guttural noise escaping his lips as I arched my back to help him as he tugged it down my legs and threw it to the floor. I didn't dare move my hands from their place above my head, as if he had physically restrained them there. This made me remember his strange comment about power:

Power is a social contract between you and others. It can be exchanged, given, and taken at your will. What good is your magick if you don't desire to wield it on me?

And I now understood what he meant. I wouldn't wield my magick against him for the same reason I wouldn't move my hands until he told me I could.

He unclasped my bra. "You can move, little witch."

This was also the first time I thought the pet name was sweet rather than condescending. I helped him get me out of the last of my clothes and watched as he shrugged out of his jeans. His body was captivating, with tight, defined muscles spanning every inch.

"You're so beautiful," he said. "Every inch of you."

"Funny, I was just thinking the same about you."

He moved back on top of me, trailing his fingers down the length of my body until they reached their ultimate target. He moved his fingers slowly, sending waves of pleasure that were never quite satisfying enough and left me yearning for more.

I was always yearning for more with Daelon.

"Please," I breathed against his lips.

"Please what?" His other hand stroked the side of my face, and I leaned into his touch.

"I want you."

"No, Áine," he said, the domineering tone of his voice was juxtaposed with the smile that played at his lips. "Not yet. We're making memories, remember?"

I frowned. The point of that conversation wasn't just about creating amazing moments with my mothers, it was also about the way those memories haunted me after the good times faded into grief and emptiness. We barely knew each other, and I already feared the void that Daelon could leave in my life when this all inevitably crumbled away.

"What is it?" Daelon stopped his teasing, searching my eyes. "Show me."

I hesitated, but then grasped his forearm and let the feeling pass from me to him. It was so intimate, even more so than being naked underneath him, to let this emotion pass from my mind to his.

His face fell for a moment as he received my psychic message, but he soon shifted back into seductive, in-control, and alluring. "Counterpoint," he said softly, pressing his hand into my cheek.

A different impression flooded my system, one that was teeming with reddish hues of desire, but also... devotion. This fortress of energy was built for the sole intent of keeping me safe. It was nearly overpowering—teeming with warmth and sincerity—but it was also strikingly thirsty for control. He just *couldn't* lose me, not when he'd already lost so much. He'd never wanted to hold on to anything more, like I was his anchor in a turbulent, murky sea.

Beneath his dominance lay a kind of desperation. He was desperate for me to know how much he wanted to shield me from the cold, the dark, the painful—his devotion to protecting me at all costs—and those costs felt great, almost insurmountable. What he felt for me mirrored what I saw in him, definitive and beyond reason, because we reminded each other of something we had lost and missed dearly, pulled together by a force that transcended conscious understanding.

This energetic kaleidoscope of color, thought, and emotion passed through my mind quickly, and began to ease my doubts.

"Yes," I said. "That is an excellent counterpoint." I couldn't stop my staring, and I could've sworn a flash of raw vulnerability passed through my fierce protector's eyes. I didn't think he was used to sharing his energy with anyone, not with his fortress of shields. But he knew how much I craved it. He knew how much I wanted to see him—all of him.

He kissed my forehead. "Now, where were we?"

I smiled. Whatever lay between us wasn't just lust. It ran much deeper, and despite it all, I needed it to. I needed an anchor of my own.

I sighed breathily as Daelon made a trail of kisses down my body once more, murmuring that I was beautiful in different ways every other kiss. I moaned as he reached the end of his path. This time, the waves of pleasure were nearly too much, and I dug my fingers into his hair.

"Hands above your head," he commanded again from between my legs, a dark smile on his lips. "No moving, and no noise. Or I won't let you finish," he challenged, a hard edge to his voice.

I took a deep breath. I had no idea how I was going to stop myself. It took everything in me not to reach for him, not to call out his name as he brought me to the brink over and over again. It was like he already knew my body and everything it craved. Even still, I stayed silent. Because his grip on my mind was somehow even sexier than his grip on my thighs, and I didn't know how much I'd needed the excuse to let go completely. But he knew. He knew exactly what I needed—and all I had to do was let his steady, commanding voice tether me to this earth, to this bed, to *him*.

After what seemed like an eternity of these pleasurable ebbs and flows, he stopped. I shivered as his lips brushed my inner thigh, his tongue flitting across my skin.

"Beg," he ordered, looking up at me through his dark lashes.

I hesitated, feeling suddenly exposed, vulnerable. "Please," I breathed. "Please, Daelon."

He started again, and this time there were no ebbs. The intensity only grew until I couldn't hold back any longer, clutching the sheets above my head as I let go completely. I trembled all over, and Daelon reversed his trail of kisses until he reached my mouth, smiling softly as he kissed me.

"Do you still want me?" he asked, stroking the side of my face.

"Yes." So much that it scared me.

He moved off of me to take off his boxers, and the look in his eyes was wild and primal. It sent a shiver down my spine. I marveled at his now fully naked body, my breath hitching.

Oh. My. God. Goddess? Whatever.

Daelon climbed over me, his gaze so sharp it stilled me. "Are you going to start listening to me?" he asked, catching me by surprise.

"Uh, within reason," I said. I did promise to do something like that when I thought he was dying...

He moved slowly at first, and then in a sudden movement he thrust inside of me, making me cry out.

"You're okay," he whispered.

He cradled my head with one hand and held one of my wrists to the bed with the other. I dug my fingernails in his back as he continued moving his hips against mine. It felt like I'd waited for this moment for years, all of the tension between us culminating in this long-awaited release of intensity. He lowered his head so that his mouth was next to my ear, his breath warm and tickling.

"Tell me you will," he growled. "Let me protect you." He moved up, pulling my legs to wrap around him.

"I will—" I could hardly speak as he thrust deeper and harder, maintaining eye contact as he did. His gaze was more intense than ever. I tried not to feel self-conscious as he moved me further and further toward a disorienting pleasure

—ecstasy that rendered me incapable of a single coherent thought.

I wasn't quite sure what I was agreeing to, but my promise earned me a small smile as he reached to brush his thumb against my bottom lip. He moved his hips slower now, giving me a chance to breathe. All of his off-hand remarks, glimpses into his heart and mind he'd allowed me to feel, and all of his actions and hushed promises—they all made at least one thing perfectly clear: he wanted me to change that social contract of power between us. He wanted me to surrender some of my control to him so that he could protect me from what lurked beyond this safe bubble. He wanted to help me become who I was meant to be, and this was the way he knew how.

He wanted some kind of submission, but I didn't know how much I could give. Half of me wanted to give Daelon everything, but the other wasn't going to be easily convinced to give up any sort of power in this foreign, tumultuous realm. There was still so much to learn. There was still a seed of doubt that I didn't want to think about, not when he was literally as close to me as he could possibly be.

"That's a good girl," he whispered. "I really do enjoy when you give in and do as you're told."

A comment like that would have ordinarily made me want to throat punch someone, but not when it came from Daelon's lips. All I could do was moan in response as he clutched me tight, nipping at the sensitive skin of my neck.

He flipped me over onto my knees, and he pulled me up to position my back to his chest. He picked up his pace again, and in this position the pleasure was intensely overpowering. He held my body close to his as he moved, his grasp tight and possessive. He tilted my head to the side and went in for my neck again. He kissed my skin softly this time, contrasting this gentle touch with the harsher tangle of his hand in my hair.

I moaned at the constant and varied assault of my senses and nerve endings, my entire body completely immersed in this gratification. I didn't think I'd ever had sex that was so overwhelming, so all-consuming, and endued with layers of meaning. It was like our desires were naturally in complement with each other's, and it created an undeniable impression of energy throughout the bedroom. It was intoxicating, stronger than any drug. Could Daelon feel it too?

My thoughts melted into pure feeling as Daelon held me to him, his mouth now at my ear. I was no longer falling under his spell. It had already taken me, and I feared no protective magick would be strong enough to free me of its hold.

Even after we finished and collapsed onto the duvet, Daelon refused to let go of me. He held me to his chest now, one arm around my head and another coiled around my back. I rested against him as we caught our breath.

CHAPTER 11

"One of the many ways I knew I could effectively silence you," he said into my hair.

I tried to struggle out of his grasp to smack him, but he easily overpowered me and wrestled me still. I giggled at my hilariously weak attempts to thwart him. I faced him now, and he watched me carefully.

"How was that?" he asked.

"Terrible. Worst sex I've ever had. Now that we tried and failed, we can go back to being reluctant friends." Despite the smile I had when I said it, his jaw tensed and his hold on me slackened.

He narrowed his eyes. "That's not funny."

I laughed, but I couldn't ignore that his tone gave me a bit of a chill. "Oh stop," I said. "I just didn't want how I truly felt about it to go to your head."

He brushed some of my hair behind my ear. "Too late." He smiled back, his features softening. "It certainly sounded like you enjoyed it. Or you're a fantastic actress."

I gawked, feigning great offense. He caught my wrist and lifted my hand to plant a kiss on my knuckles. We stared at each other for a moment, and I had the familiar desire to read him. Part of me was glad I couldn't, though, because I knew deep down that I'd often used my gift as a crutch to avoid true intimacy. As scary as it was, this was my first *real* relationship with someone without all of my usual tricks. I actually had to trust that the parts Daelon showed me were genuine and that whatever he hid wouldn't change how I felt. I had to take the plunge and hope he was going to save me from drowning.

"Can we just pretend we're normal tonight?"

He feigned shock. "Are you calling me abnormal?"

"Well, yes. But I mean… human normal."

"Well that just sounds boring."

I sighed. "Fair. But you know what I mean."

"Yes, I do."

A sadness crept into his eyes, and I somehow knew he was thinking about the dark and the cold—all of the things he so desperately wanted to shield me from. That was the sadness I wanted to avoid, at least for this one night.

"I'm in, although I don't pretend to understand what drives humans. Especially not their preoccupation with currency and fame."

"Kind of an oversimplification, but I guess that's one way of putting it," I laughed. "What are witches preoccupied with then?"

Daelon thought for a moment. "Currently, power. And pleasure."

"That doesn't sound much more evolved," I scoffed. "It doesn't sound like we're all that different."

He wrinkled his nose like the notion was preposterous. "We used to be much more evolved than *humans*, trust me. I guess not so much anymore." Something uncertain flashed in his eyes. "Some of us still are."

"As are some humans."

"Touché," he said. I could tell he was already moving back behind some of his walls, shielding me from the truths he'd decided I wasn't ready for. "Want to take a shower?"

I wanted to probe further, but his spell was still in full swing, and I said I wanted to feign normalcy tonight. So, I found myself holding back and following Daelon, questions and doubts be damned.

We stood in a massive walk-in shower against a rustic stone wall. Showering with Daelon was somehow more intimate than actual sex. He couldn't keep his hands off me, for starters. It was like he thought I might disappear, at any moment, if there was any space between us. I wasn't going to complain. Especially not after he insisted on washing my hair, lathering silky shampoo through its length and massaging my scalp more expertly than any hairstylist. He kissed my neck when he was finished and turned me back to face him.

Next, he ran soap across my skin, his fingers delicately trailing across my body's curves and contours in a dedicated silence. His touch was an act of devotion, like he was tending to a priceless piece of art. The intensity of his gaze when he refocused back to my eyes sent away my ability to speak.

"I want to do you now," I said when I finally found my

voice. I reached for the soap.

"And I want to give you everything you want."

Our eyes locked, and I couldn't help but smile. I didn't know what to say. So, I started to touch him instead. I moved my fingers along his body, appreciating the curve of his defined muscles, the firmness of his form. The parts of him that were smooth and the parts that were rough. There was a scar on his back, white and raised like the mark of a surgical incision.

"What happened here?" I asked, smoothing my fingers over the mark.

"Sparring accident."

"*Sparring?*" I giggled. "Like with swords?" So much for normalcy. Daelon stiffened. I didn't think he was very amused, so I dropped it and continued my admiration of his body.

After I finished, he pulled me in for a kiss under the warm water. His hands held my waist, and it almost felt like drowning as I ran out of oxygen with his lips thirstily moving against mine.

He pulled back. "Let's go make dinner. You need to eat."

I rolled my eyes. He was definitely *abnormal*. This earned me a light slap on my ass, which took me by surprise.

"So much for not hurting me," I accused.

He wrapped white towels around me and then himself, looking mischievous. He dried his long hair with a smaller towel, shooting me a devilish grin. "That didn't hurt."

True. It hadn't.

We got dressed and cooked together, still carefully avoiding any talk of evil witches, revenge plots, or reasons why we shouldn't be doing what we were doing. Now we stood in the kitchen, and I told him more about my friends and all that he was missing out on in the human realm, though he didn't seem all too convinced.

"Wine?" he asked, gesturing to a bottle of Bordeaux he pulled from a cabinet.

"See, now how can you talk so much shit about humans yet drink their wine?" I asked, giving him a pointed look. "And yes."

"I didn't say they do *everything* wrong." He poured some into two wine glasses. "I've been to many human cities actually, and I didn't even mind some of them."

I shook my head. "Wait, how do you hop realms, exactly?"

He hesitated, taking a sip from his glass and handing me mine. "With a spell. There are different methods, but it requires a great deal of power. It's not something the average person can achieve without help. It's usually only performed as a punishment to banish witches who have committed horrible crimes."

I took a sip, and before I could respond, Daelon spoke again.

"I'll show you sometime." Something in his eyes needed to reassure me, but of what, I couldn't tell. I thought it might've been about seeing my friends again. Or maybe he was still concerned I would think I was a prisoner here.

I offered a smile. "This is really good. So, you've been to France, then?" I gestured to the Bordeaux.

"Yes. I'm a fan."

"My friends and I studied abroad there." I smiled, remembering my time picnicking with them along the Seine and touring art museums.

I had many fond memories of traveling, but I'd refused to venture to any part of the United Kingdom or Ireland. Steph tried to convince me to visit my home village, but I just couldn't. I couldn't walk the earth my mothers used to walk. I couldn't hear the accents of my former neighbors, schoolteachers, and childhood friends. I couldn't see those sloping hills dotted with sheep—the place that held so much magick and so much fear and pain. I resolved to stick to France and surrounding countries, doing very human things and exploring with my very human friends, pushing aside thoughts of the power—no, *the witches*—that stole my mothers.

It was still my instinct to blame myself for their death, but ever since my experience on that beach, I stopped myself. Regardless of whether or not they were merely a construct of my subconscious, what my mothers had told me was true. I had been using my guilt and shame as a way to distract myself from feeling all of my grief. It was a way for me to avoid accepting inevitability—the understanding that sometimes bad things couldn't be stopped. I remembered their words on fate and a grand, cosmic story, urging me to have faith through the uncertainty. I wanted to believe I'd somehow made it to the great beyond in those moments, and thus had truly connected with my mothers again.

Next time I was on Earth, I would visit our little village in Northern Ireland. I would walk where my mothers walked and cry where I cried as a child. I would actually enact a proper ritual for their deaths, which was something else robbed from me by the nature of their passing and my thrust into the unknown streets of a foreign city.

"Áine," Daelon said, pulling me from my reminiscing. "What are you thinking about?"

"My mothers," I answered honestly. "I can't stop thinking about seeing them."

"When I…" he trailed off, and he pulled me to his chest, refusing to voice whatever thought came to his head. "What all did you see?"

I pulled back from him and sipped my wine. "I was on a beach. Actually, I think I was on *that* beach." I pointed to the painting that hung against the living room wall. "The one I've used as a metaphor for my channeling. And I was dressed in white, as were my mothers, and many other people I didn't recognize. It felt like they were my family—the coven my mothers belonged to—who helped them escape when those dark forces came for me when I was still in the womb."

Daelon's face was suspiciously impassive, but I thought I saw a flash of shock in his eyes.

"They were chanting, I think for my healing and protection. My mothers told me they loved me, and that I had friends where I least expected them. They told me to stop blaming myself for their deaths, and that there was a greater purpose for that tragedy and other events, too. It's all connected in a way I can't see yet, but will eventually," I finished. Something made me want to stop talking about this aloud, like it was too intimate or sacred.

"Did they say anything else?" he asked, his eyes searching mine intently.

I found his reaction slightly off-putting. "No."

"I'm glad you had that experience," Daelon said. "I think we all long to see our loved ones again. I know I do."

I remembered Daelon had a similar start to life, and I immediately softened my composure. I reached for his hand. "I'm not sure normal will ever really be an option for us, will it?"

He chuckled, but the smile didn't reach his eyes. "No, I don't think it will."

By the time the moon replaced the sun in the sky, Daelon and I had retreated under his duvet to beat the cold. Our night of normal was a relative success, but we knew it was a futile effort. There was far too much subtext to ignore. Unanswered questions and suppressed truths hung over us like a dark storm cloud. I felt it even now as I lay in his arms, but I tried to focus on the sound of his heartbeat instead. Its steady, rhythmic beating beneath my ear was soothing.

"Go to sleep," he whispered.

"How did you know I wasn't?"

"Because you just answered me," he laughed softly.

He kissed the top of my head, and I rolled off of him and onto my side. It was colder over here. Almost immediately Daelon shifted to lay against my back, warmth radiating off his chest like my own personal space heater. Part of me almost didn't want to sleep. Here in this quiet, this stillness, so close to someone who made me feel things I'd never felt before, I had a familiar desire creep up.

I wanted to pause time and stay in this moment forever. I wanted to avoid the truths my mothers instilled in me: everything changes, everyone grows old, everyone dies, and not even magick can stop the natural course of fate. I wanted to fight the idea they'd planted—that sometimes terrible things had to happen for a greater good.

I closed my eyes, resigned to commit every detail of this moment to memory. I focused on Daelon's breathing, the comforting heat from his body, his arm around my waist, the near darkness except for the faint trickle of moonlight from the far windows, and the way my body tingled and my stomach lurched every time I thought of this afternoon.

I drifted off thinking about what Daelon wanted from me, and how much a part of me wanted to give him everything.

I was back on the beach with multicolored sand. The sky was a gorgeous shade of deep blue, and the water was tranquil and waves docile. I walked around in search of my mothers and the people in white, but I was alone.

A din of whispers started to rise from higher on the beach, over the dunes in the distance. I had never ventured onto the mainland, and the slopes were too high to see anything on the other side. I began to walk toward the soft voices, but as I moved closer my feet sunk deeper and deeper into the sand. When I reached the dunes, the sand was rising to my knees with each step. I couldn't go further without becoming completely submerged.

The whispers swirled all around, as if coming from all different directions. Then they combusted with a screech that led into an eerie silence. If that wasn't warning enough, a sudden change in the energetic environment raised the hair on the back of my neck.

I knew immediately who the intruder was.

I quickly backtracked, scrambling toward the ocean where the sand was more stable. I whipped my head around to look right and left as I went but saw no one. Fog began to roll over the sand, making it impossible to see very far in either direction. I stood with my back to the waves, my feet rooted in the more solid, damp earth.

The sky darkened, similar to the white candle when I learned someone was using magick against me. The blackness crept out over the blue until it had been completely obscured. I turned to the water, which had become murky and clouded. The waves grew violent and erratic.

Face me. The voice boomed.

I knew whom it belonged to, and I felt his ice-cold energy snake around me. His presence was suffocating, as if it ran contrary to my very existence. I resisted his command, my hands balling into fists at my side, but this turned his energy wild and volatile. A force reached out for me, compelling me to turn against my will.

There he stood, again shrouded in black to conceal his true appearance.

Coward.

He hovered back in the mist at first. When he stepped forward, so did a crowd of fifteen or so others dressed in black uniform. They did not conceal their faces, which appeared human rather than the demon-like glamour their leader had used before. I couldn't make out specific features, but most were men, relatively young and in good shape. They all stood just a step behind the man who hid from me —the man who reeked of death and decay.

What do you want from me? I asked him telepathically.

I took a step back and cried out when boiling hot water lapped at my heels. I jumped forward, casting back a glance at the water that was now waveless and bubbling. My power erratically danced all around, preparing for a fight.

I want you to know your place, he answered.

I glowered. I would not be intimidated. *Fuck you.*

He was quiet for a moment, then burst into laughter. The others were silent, looking to him for a moment before joining in, sneering at me.

"You are alone. Do you see anyone here on your side?" he said aloud, breaking the telepathy I had grown accustomed to in dream and meditative states.

I realized it must've been because the people backing him up couldn't hear us speak to each other in that way. I stayed silent, reaching for the power that rose up within and around my body. I focused on everything opposite of his energy—on the natural, the calm, the bright, the good—and used it to fortify my energy field as Daelon had taught me. I needed to shield myself from potential attack.

The group looked up at the sky, and my eyes followed. The blue had resurfaced and began to ripple out over the dark in a silent battle for supremacy. I looked back to the crowd and couldn't help but feel the corners of my lips turn up at their confusion and shock. They looked to their leader for guidance on how to react.

It didn't seem like he was used to being challenged, and he dropped his shroud of darkness to reveal the devilish face beneath. His lips contorted into a snarl. I knew his festering skin and demonic features were merely a glamour, but I couldn't deny it was effective in making my stomach drop. It was creepy as hell.

The group looked less intimidating now that the sky was lighter, and I noticed their formation was asymmetric in an otherwise completely orderly layout. While they all stood behind the leader, the man closest to him on the left side stood a step above the rest. He had dirty blond hair and an angular nose. There was a gap on the leader's right side.

"Cute trick," he snarled. "Is that the best you can do?"

He bent down to touch the earth, and with a crack, the sand began to diverge and pour into the center of the separation. The crevice shot toward me, deepening as it went. I took a deep breath to release my fear, and I bent down to touch the earth as he had, my palms melding into the warm, damp sand.

Halt, I spelled to the earth.

The crevice stopped, sand still tumbling into the divide. I stared at my attacker over the valley, our eyes locking and something dangerous passing between us. His people were silent, averting their eyes as he took a step forward.

"Do you see this?" he asked, gesturing to the space on his right. "Who do you think belongs here?"

Surely, he didn't mean *me*. Puzzled, the intensity of my gaze faltered. I wasn't sure what game he was playing, but it felt sinister. It seemed his end goal was to shake my trust in my own judgement and conception of reality. He wanted me to feel weak and alone.

Something about his dark energy held an emptiness, something thirsty and unnatural. Maybe he thought he could use my power for his own gain, somehow, like an energy vampire. Whatever he wanted, I knew it was evil. And if he was indeed the enemy, then there was no doubt he was connected to my mothers' deaths. My anger rose from that cavernous wound, the tide of my power flooding in and threatening to consume us all.

It was at this moment I realized I'd lost control of my protective barrier, and he used that as his opportunity.

You're unfocused, and you lack control. That makes you easy to manipulate, little witch.

The use of Daelon's pet name drove me over the edge, and my power went spinning in every direction at the heat of my rage. I pushed a burst of whatever I could grab onto out at the formation, my intent murky but seething. I yelled as it flowed through me, hot and volatile like a tropical storm.

It sent all but the faux devil flying backward into the sand. He smiled, revealing his pointy, jagged teeth.

Hungry for round two, are we?

With a flick of the wrist, he sent me levitating above the ground, where I thrashed around midair, struggling against his icy magick. Suddenly I couldn't move, and I realized in a panic that I'd let him win with my lack of control over my emotions, yet again, just as Daelon had warned. I felt pressure on the sides of my neck, and soon I lost my ability to breathe.

I bet it was better when Daelon did it, hmm?

I watched as his people rose up beside him as my vision blurred. In that moment, I knew he reveled in my humiliation. In my pain. In my struggle. He wanted to show off to his followers that I meant nothing. That I *was* nothing.

A new voice broke through my haze as the darkness descended. *It's just a dream, Áine.*

Daelon.

My body went limp.

CHAPTER 12

Daelon's voice pulled me back into his bedroom, where I lay in a cold sweat, my heartbeat deafening and erratic as it boomed in my ears. I sucked in air and then coughed, grasping the sheets. Dizzy and disoriented, the face of the devil was still imprinted in my mind's eye.

"Áine," Daelon murmured, kissing my knuckles. "Come back. You're safe now, little witch."

I pushed myself up, those words reminding me of the fury I had just felt throughout every inch of my being. "It wasn't just a dream. It was *real*, on some level. I felt it all."

Upon waking from normal dreams, it was easy to tell I had been dreaming, regardless of how real they felt when I was inside them. But with some of these nightmares, reality seemed to follow me from here into the dreamscape. I remembered suddenly what the mystic said in the mysterious castle. I never really found the opportunity to tell Daelon about that experience since he'd been so angry about my solo venture outside the house. Plus, it was just too strange to put into words.

"What's astral projection?" I asked.

Daelon looked pensive as he turned on the bedside lamp and pulled me into his lap, running his hands through my hair. "It's when your consciousness leaves your physical body and travels elsewhere. It's quite difficult to do, and it can be dangerous." he explained. "Where did you hear of it?"

"When I escaped to the woods to meditate, I somehow got pulled from my ocean and into this castle. It was a place I'd seen before in my nightmares. There was this old man who seemed to sense I was there but couldn't see me, and he said I was astral projecting. I had to find my way back to my body," I said.

"Why didn't you tell me about this before?" Daelon asked, his voice terse.

I paused. What was with that tone? "You were so mad at me for going off on my own. I didn't really get a chance to... and I didn't think it was that important. I mean it was a medieval castle for god's sake, so I thought it was some sort of weird metaphor from my subconscious." I paused to look up at Daelon's face, which was contorted with tension but quickly went blank and detached under my gaze. "Was it a real place then?"

"What happened tonight?" he asked, ignoring my question.

"I was on the same beach as before when I saw my mothers, but this time the man who pretends to be the Devil was there. He brought others, too—to intimidate me and to amplify the feeling that I was on my own. I was trying not to provoke him like last time and just work on my defensive magick, but he kept egging me on and... well... he attacked me."

Daelon stopped moving his fingers through my hair, and I felt him stiffen.

"I lost control of my focus because I got so angry," I admitted, feeling like I'd failed. It turned out I wasn't as ready as I thought I was. "He got the upper-hand and..." I trailed off. I knew Daelon would take it hard.

"And *what* Áine?" he asked through gritted teeth.

I could nearly feel Daelon's anger through his shielded aura. "He just... took control of me. He pulled a Darth Vader," I mumbled, knowing he wouldn't understand the reference.

"Explain. *Now*."

I sighed. "Just some levitation and more asphyxiation. His favorite move, I guess," I said quietly, bracing myself.

Daelon took a sharp intake of breath. He carefully moved me off his lap and climbed out of the bed. His muscles flexed as he balled his fists at his side, his back to me. He walked to the far wall and in one swift motion, punched a hole right through it.

"Kind of a Chad move," I said, laughing nervously.

"This isn't something to joke about, Áine," he hissed.

Okay, now he was starting to genuinely piss me off. "Listen, I'm the one who keeps getting fucking attacked, so I don't know why you're taking out your anger on me... or that wall, actually... instead of explaining what the hell is going on," I yelled, my voice faltering. I meant to sound a lot harsher than I actually did, with all of my frustration and confusion getting the better of me. Instead, I felt hot tears well up in my eyes.

Daelon's eyes softened, and he uncurled his fists.

"It feels like I'm fighting a battle while wearing a blindfold," I said, struggling to rein in the brimming tears. "Which may excite *you*, but they aren't very practical for outside the bedroom," I said, unable to stop myself.

Daelon rolled his eyes, but I could tell a smile played at his lips. He walked back toward me, and I met him halfway to sit on the edge of the bed. I reached out for his right hand, which was red and bruised. I brought it to my lips as I looked up at him.

"I'm sorry," he said. "Of course, I'm not mad at you. I'm mad at the people who hurt you, and I want to destroy them." He looked away for a beat. "I feel like I'm failing you."

"You're not failing me. But I do need to know more."

He sat down on the bed next to me, burying his head in his hands. "Okay."

My heart rate picked up.

"I think you're right about the astral projection. It can be triggered unintentionally when you're in an altered state of consciousness, such as while sleeping or in a deep meditation. It's rare for most people, but others have a natural gift for traveling between dimensions. Or they just hold a lot of power or trained intensively for a long time to be able to. I think this last time though, you probably were summoned into the astral realm while you slept by Lucius, the man who has been attacking you."

Okay, so we finally have a name. We were making progress.

"Who is he? Why is he so powerful?"

"There are some things I wish I could tell you, but I literally, physically, cannot. I know how frustrating that must be. I'm trying my best, but there are magickal barriers at play," he said warily, staring forward. He lowered his voice. "I don't know why he's so powerful, but he sees you as a threat. He's the enemy, Áine."

I sucked in a breath. *The enemy. Lucius.* I mulled over Daelon's words, grateful to finally receive some of the truth but annoyed with these supposed magickal barriers.

"The astral realm? Is it like the witch realm?" I asked.

"No. It's not as solid. It's much closer in makeup to Aradia than Aradia is to Earth, if that makes sense. It's not somewhere you can get to in your physical body. It's a realm of pure consciousness. You can see things that are based in physical reality, but you can also see things that aren't—or at least, they don't exist in the human or witch realms. Everything in the astral realm is influenced by energy, beliefs, and thoughts. It's a tricky place, and there's still so much we don't know and can't explain," he said, struggling for the right words. My brain already hurt. "The astral realm's rules are hard to understand because they are constantly in flux, to a much greater degree than the lower realms. You can travel in your astral form to the Eiffel Tower, but you could also conceivably travel to the Christian conception of Hell or to a planet that someone else dreamed up."

"Right. That is very... confusing." What did that mean for the things I'd seen? What did that mean for literally everything I thought I understood about the fabric of reality? Yep, my brain really did ache right now.

"I know."

"So, you can't tell me more about Lucius because you

physically can't? Or because you don't want me to go on a warpath, like you originally said?"

I stared at him, and he pursed his lips and moved off the bed again. He ran his hands through his hair. When he turned to face me again it looked like he was concentrating very hard on something.

"Stop using his name, please," he said. "It's complicated. Insanely, indescribably complicated. It takes a lot of my own power to shield us from him." His voice strained. I could see the effort written all over his tense features. I had no idea that protecting me required him to use his gift on a constant basis.

"He knows when he's being talked about?" I murmured, lowering my own voice. I hated seeing Daelon in pain.

He nodded. "It's a real possibility. That's how powerful he is. I don't lie to you, Áine. I did, and still do, worry about you finding out the whole truth about our enemies and your purpose. You saw how he used both your emotions and your lapse in focus against you tonight. It could've been much, much worse. But I also want you to have all the answers you need, when the time is right. I'll help with that in any way I can. Above all, I want you to be prepared for everything you have to face once we leave here."

This was a lot to process. I had never seen Daelon this... out of control. And despite the guise of anger, I saw flashes of fear in his eyes. He stared at me for several seconds in silence, and I watched as his features hardened back into a more determined and guarded appearance.

He moved closer to me. "I will not let anything happen to you." He stroked my cheek, brushing his thumb over my lips before dropping his hand back to his side. "You're already up, so let's get to work."

Despite my exhaustion from poor sleep and astral battles, Daelon had me doing exercises all morning to work through my anger and keep learning defensive strategies. He hadn't calmed down from earlier, and his intensity was overbearing, to say the least.

"Again, Áine. I feel how erratic your power still is. What if he were to kill me?"

"Stop, Daelon," I spat, opening my eyes. The fire beside us roared, the flames spitting and furious. "I don't want to—"

"You need to be prepared for the worst," he insisted. "You need to learn to use your emotions constructively. Just think about the possibility and try to light this candle."

"I am not going to think about your death!"

We carried on like this for a while. Daelon provoked me and then asked me to channel my energy into far too simple of tasks. So far, I had scorched the carpet, exploded two apples, and sent Daelon across the room, which I had to admit, was mildly entertaining. He'd deserved it.

However, I did see notable progress, in spite of his questionable methods. I was beginning to tap into my ocean of power quicker and more easily—to access different forces and frequencies without getting completely lost in my mind. I was detaching more and more from my impulses. I was uncovering my own methods for magick that worked with the source energy.

I was learning how to separate my emotions from my magick so that I could finally stop closing myself off to the limitless possibilities at my fingertips. I contained so much, and my ego only got in the way. I was slowly but surely beginning to open up—to find the faith my mothers needed me to have in my purpose—the purpose I knew would save witches from the evil of this realm like Lucius and his companions.

Lucius wanted to make me feel like I was alone, but in each burst of magick I felt my mothers, my people, and sometimes, I even felt everyone all at once. Daelon might have refused to tell me more about this enemy, but I could sense that Lucius's powers were unnatural, cold, and lifeless. It was as though everything he had was stolen.

It was he who was truly alone.

"Daelon. I'm tired," I said, after I was pretty sure I made it snow at least a foot.

"I know, baby." His eyes softened slightly. "But I have more planned."

"Damn this is a lot of snow," Daelon muttered. He side-eyed me, an impressed smile on his lips. His hand was clasped in mine, which would've been endearing if he wasn't practically dragging me along through the forest.

I was thankful I had my black snow boots from last winter handy, as my magickal tantrum had snow up to my knees. I wore a chic red cape-like coat that Rena had talked me into, which she insisted gave me a 'sexy, red-riding hood vibe.' She was right.

"I like this," Daelon said, pulling at the fabric.

I knew he would. "What are we doing, Daelon?" I groaned, still exhausted from this morning's intense sessions. Not to mention my battle in the astral realm.

"It's a surprise." He led me toward the clearing where he practiced magick, and a chill ran down my spine at my last memory of the place. "I'm teaching you offensive magick now."

We headed into the center of the circle of trees, but Daelon suddenly halted and let out a frustrated sigh. "I tire of this. Can you melt it?" he asked, nearly pouting.

I laughed. "Okay." I let go of his hand and moved a few steps ahead.

I reached out as if to clear a path for us, but instead turned on my heel, channeled a gust of wind, and hurled a wave of snow at him. I couldn't contain my laughter as the burst of white powder rammed into his chest, some of it ricocheting into his face.

Confusion quickly turned into annoyance as he lunged for me. I couldn't stop giggling as he wrapped his arms around me in a mock hold and pulled my back up to his chest. "You think that's funny?" he asked into my ear. He attempted to sound menacing, but I could tell he was trying not to laugh with me. His forearm was tight under my chin.

"No, no, not funny," I laughed, gripping at his arm. "Hilarious."

He let go of me, spinning me around to face him. I looked up into his eyes, dizzy from the movement and laughter. He looked flustered for a moment, but he soon melted into pure adoration. His hands encircled my waist, and I looked to his lips. I thought he was going to kiss me, but he pulled me into his chest instead, his hand on the back of my head. I breathed in his clean, woodsy scent, content to skip out on the rest of training to be held by him instead.

He let go and clasped his hands on either side of my face. He leaned down and finally pressed his lips, which were soft and tasted of cold and snow, to mine. I responded to him hungrily, tilting my head and reaching up to tangle my fingers in his hair. He groaned softly, feeling his way along my curves and grabbing my ass.

We lost ourselves in each other, my head spinning with desire, pent up emotion, and intensity that needed an outlet. He bit my bottom lip lightly, deepening the kiss until I couldn't figure out why we ever did anything else.

He pulled back, resting his forehead against mine. "As enticing a distraction as you are," he said, "we have work to do." He pulled his head back.

I huffed. "Sounds boring." Tired and longing for him—all of him, I changed tactics. "And I *want you*," I said softly, putting all of my yearning into my gaze up at him. I reached my hand out slowly, curling a finger through one of his belt loops beneath his coat, lightly pulling him toward me.

He shook his head, grinning. "No, Áine. But an admirable effort, truly."

I glared at him. "I know you want to," I said, feeling bold.

He chuckled. "Of course I do. But I need you safe most of all, and I think I know something that will help."

I sighed in defeat, pulling back to cross my arms. I turned on my heel and continued to the center. When we got there, I faced an amused Daelon.

"We're going somewhere," he said, a glimmer of excitement in his eyes. "I thought you'd appreciate that, at least."

This *was* an interesting development, I had to admit. "Aw, at least my kidnapper is kind enough to take me out every once in a while."

He shot me a warning look. "Stop that."

I raised my hands up. "Kidding!"

"I'm going to need to channel you to make the leap, if that's all right. Nothing like last time, of course." We both paled at the memory.

"Maybe if you tell me where we are going."

He nodded, though I could tell my pushback made him edgy. "Have you ever been to any Nordic countries?"

I shook my head. "Are we going to Earth?"

"Similar to there, but here in Aradia. It's remote enough to avoid any prying eyes, and I know you like the snow," he said with a shrug. "Plus, I'm hoping we can catch a glimpse of the aurora borealis."

I grinned. "That's been on my bucket list. I'm down for witchy Norway." I furrowed my brows, remembering his intentions for this session. "Wait, why are we traveling to use offensive magick?"

"When we get there, I'll explain what I have in mind." He gave me a reassuring smile, but something darker flashed in his eyes.

I swallowed. I didn't know how much more action I could take today. "What do I do?"

"I need you to act as a battery again so we can make the jump."

He held out his hands. Reluctantly, I placed my hands in his, making sure to give him a warning look. I would not channel that dark power from last time ever again. It felt eerily similar to Lucius's energy... I wondered what that meant about Daelon's spell.

In that moment, my hands began to tingle, and I felt myself pulling in power from the world around me. I was pleased to feel the familiar head high as it flowed through me, like a rush of euphoria. Just as energy sharing had been, this process felt intimate. I couldn't imagine someone channeling through me without my consent, or anyone but Daelon, for that matter. It was like I was giving him access to the entire Universe.

The impression from this energy was that of travel and movement, and I could catch glimpses of our destination as it flowed. I could see the snow, the monstrous evergreens, and the magickal night sky.

"How does this w—"

Before I could finish the thought, a loud whirring sound filled my head as if we were being sucked through a cosmic tunnel of space and time. Almost instantly the scenery shifted, and in the dizziness of the transition I fell forward into Daelon.

CHAPTER 13

"You all right?" he asked as he caught me.

I steadied myself. "Yeah. Motion sickness, I guess."

"Teleportation is weird the first couple times. Like airplanes, I would imagine."

"This is much more eco-friendly," I joked as I spun slowly, in awe of our surroundings. It was like a winter wonderland.

Daelon was right, the landscape was very remote. Nothing but snow and trees in all directions. I looked to the sky and broke out in a grin at the swirling green, blue, violet and pink hues shimmering above. It was even more breathtaking than what I'd seen in pictures or videos. The air was fresh, crisp, and woodsy. Daelon moved to stand behind me, wrapping his arms around me and kissing my neck.

Then he pulled away and knelt to the ground next to me, chanting something unintelligible. His forehead creased in concentration.

"What are you doing?" I asked. I felt an almost undetectable shift in the energetic field around us, like I was suddenly exposed. I frowned, scanning the dim environment. "Is something wrong?"

He stood, now all business again. "We can only do so many mental exercises, Áine. You need some low-stakes real experience."

"What does that mean?" My voice turned icy, and I narrowed my gaze. "What did you do?"

"Sent out a bit of a broadcast," he said, and my stomach dropped. "Only to some local lowlifes. Remember when I told you about energy vampires? Witches who syphon energy and magick from unwilling victims?"

He said they were like moths to a flame, and that my flame burned brighter than most.

"You want me to *fight* them?" I asked, incredulous. "What if I don't want to?"

He sighed, exasperated. "They're terrible witches, Áine. They abuse other witches and humans, often killing them, eventually, for power or fleeting pleasure. They are probably abusing people right now in order to syphon enough energy to make the jump to us. When they sense your power, they will want to do the same to you." His features were stony, his voice commanding. "I need you to be able to defend yourself."

I gaped, a million thoughts racing through my mind. I knew this was one of the moments Daelon wanted my submission. He wanted me to blindly accept that he knew what was best for me. I wasn't sure if his methods were as solid as his intentions, or if I was ready to give over so much control.

"Daelon, I—" I paused. "You said you wanted my consent for all things."

"I do," Daelon scoffed, his face contorting as if I'd offended him. "You agreed to learning offensive magick. You say you want to hurt people who hurt others—to avenge the downtrodden. This is your first opportunity. We can't stay in that cabin forever, and you need to be able to fight off even greater evils."

A flash of Lucius masked as the Devil entered my mind. I shuddered, pressing my lips together. Daelon was right, mostly, but he still hadn't adequately prepared me for this. He'd made the decision for me, and I didn't agree to that kind of power exchange.

"You can be angry at me. We can discuss it in detail later, but we don't have much time now."

"How long?" I asked curtly, barely looking at him.

"A couple minutes, probably. You'll do fine. I'll be here for backup in case something goes wrong. I'll coach you through it."

"Do I have a choice?"

"No."

I took a deep breath, blowing the air out slowly from my mouth. Daelon seemed to ignore my displeasure. He'd been hellbent on pushing my limits all day long.

"A few things to remember: Focus on reining in your emotions, like we've been practicing. Be very direct and intentional. You have a lot more power than they will ever taste, which obviously gives you the upper hand. But, as we've seen, you can get lost in its depth and forget how to channel it into more simple, practical moves. This is what you will need to fight them."

"How many?" I refused to meet his eyes.

"Whoever was in about a thirty-mile radius. There's a camp of them near here. I wouldn't guess more than a handful would show up. I didn't let them sense all of what you are."

My pulse quickened. I *really* didn't want to do this. It was one thing to defend myself from attack, but this felt different. We were luring these people into a deathtrap. Did their crimes fit the punishment? Daelon seemed to think so, but who was he to decide? I didn't think he understood why I took issue with this at all. What did that say about him? Or did it say something about me? Maybe I was just scared to face reality and leave our bubble, like he insinuated.

The time for careful analysis was over as a series of whooshing sounds erupted in the distance. I counted as a group of witches appeared, dressed in ratty, tattered clothing with haggard features and grown out facial hair. There were seven of them as of now.

Daelon grasped the back of my neck in a move of dominance, whispering, *"You were made for this*. Let them approach us, and then give them hell."

I closed my eyes and took one last deep breath as they approached, excited as they eyed us with wild curiosity. They stopped about ten yards in front of us, some cocking their heads to the side, looking at each other in mild confusion.

They were close enough now that I could read their auras, and as Daelon warned, the energy they emanated was disturbing. It was devoid of color, light, or warmth, its hunger overwhelming, like an addict in the depths of withdrawals. It hit me like a foul smell in a dark alley, and I could sense the remnants of their victims hanging on to their auras like ghosts. I could feel their pain and desperation as these witches had drained them, used them, or even killed them.

My blood boiled at what I gleaned, and my palms began to tingle. My nostrils flared as I watched the energy vamps huddle together. I sensed how badly they wanted me to be their next victim.

A man with a red beard and a scar below his left eye spoke up. "The power comes from the girl," he spoke, his tone as if he was answering a question. One of his eyes was unfocused, the other darting between Daelon and me.

"It does," Daelon answered.

"What is this? Does she belong to you?" another hissed, his eyes narrowing as he shivered in the cold.

I glanced at Daelon, who smiled slightly in a way that was deadly.

"You're outnumbered. I think we can take her off your hands and all get back to our business, okay?" the red-haired man said, his strange accent lilting.

Daelon stiffened, but an easy grin spread across his face. "You may try."

It only took a couple seconds before the red-haired man's hand made the slightest of movements at his side, and I felt a pull on my body like an invisible riptide. I smiled coolly, which seemed to unnerve him. I could tell he thought this move would be enough to send me flying toward him, but to me it felt like a small child's attempt at magick.

With a flick of my wrist, I intercepted this force and sent it hurdling back at him, colliding with his body in a violent jolt. His fall backward sent the others deeper into their frenzy.

The only woman of the group licked her lips. "She's strong. She's going to taste delicious."

Um, ew.

I wrinkled my nose in disgust. Her words seemed to excite them, and I wondered how long it would take for that excitement to transform into fear.

She chanted something under her breath, and a jolt of fiery electricity shot through the air in a crackling white orb.

In that instant, Daelon's words flashed in my mind: *You were made for this.*

They triggered something deep within me, like the flip of a switch, and I tuned into my power in a way I'd never done before. I entered a deeply natural, instinctive state, and time seemed to slow down as I connected all of my experiences together. They lay out before me like a web, each a connecting thread of who I was. I felt the guidance of my mothers, the elements, the oceans' tides, all witches who had come before me, the oppressed and the suffering, and even Daelon, all of this intertwining to weave a tapestry of who I was and why I was here.

I didn't need spells for my magick. I *was* magick.

I held out my hands and absorbed the orb sent to hurt me, neutralizing its aggression and carrying it into my palms. I watched the incredulity pass over the energy vampires' faces, scrambling to make sense of this action. I strained as the electricity bubbled over my skin, yelling out as I hurled it back at them.

It slammed into a short man next to the woman, sending him into a fit of spasms as it stunned and then electrocuted him, like a military grade taser. I stepped toward the group, and they began to hurl their attacks.

But I could feel their fear now. It tasted raw and wild like a cornered animal facing a predator.

I deflected what they sent my way, moving on autopilot in this heightened state of alignment. A man with a bag over his shoulder stepped forward and hurled what seemed to be a dagger my way, and at the same time the woman cast another ball of electricity. I heard Daelon utter a low growl from behind me. I caught the dagger in front of my face, where it hung suspended, and then sent a gust of wind to deflect the orb into the snow where it crackled and snuffed out. I frowned at the dagger, realizing it was charmed somehow. I could nearly taste the torture it had inflicted on others as it dropped to the ground. The thought of all those victims' suffering sent me into a fury.

This was almost too easy. Whatever power they'd stolen from others was no match for mine.

"End them, Áine."

I hesitated. I knew I could, easily. I glared at the man who threw the dagger, lifting him up into the air and throwing him sideways. He landed awkwardly on the snow and his body stilled. The bag he'd been carrying spilled out its contents, which appeared to be shackles. I could sense their painful, stifling magick from here.

"Were those for me?" I asked sweetly, cocking my head at the girl, who was now backing away.

The red-headed man ran forward to his fallen friend, grasping his arm just before they both vanished. I submitted to the power that coursed through my veins, sending a jolt at the woman who stayed to attack me. She screamed as I sent her flying into a nearby tree with a loud crack.

"Good, Áine. Use the anger constructively."

The other four started chanting, and soon a high-pitched wailing overwhelmed my eardrums. I cried out in pain, momentarily stunned. I couldn't concentrate. Daelon doubled over next to me, also overcome by the assault.

Seeing his face contort in pain sent me straight back into my power. I shouted out again as I channeled an intense force of natural chaos, moving through me like a storm. The snow in front of me lifted off the ground and formed a shimmering white cyclone, and on my command, it moved to attack. I heard screams as it drew bodies into the tempest, jerking them in all directions before throwing them back out onto the earth.

Daelon stared at me in awe, and as the arctic wind dispersed, I could make out a lone vampire remaining. He knelt on the ground with his hands planted firmly into the earth. He'd somehow avoided the cyclone.

When he rose, he looked ravenous. "You've deceived us," he snarled. "Are you the one they speak of only in whispers?"

I had no idea what the hell that meant, but considering everything, the answer was probably *yes*. Before I could respond I felt a force sneaking toward me, catching me off guard. It blew into me like the wind, knocking the air out of me. I tumbled back onto my backside, gasping for breath. In this lapse of concentration, he sent what appeared to be a storm of glass shards toward us.

In a panic I went off instinct, leaping to my feet to stand firmly in front of Daelon. I channeled fire, feeling its heat rush through my blood. The shards melted above us, showering us with warm water. It was ice, not glass, which my power intuitively understood on a level my conscious mind couldn't.

I let the fire continue to move through me, and a burst of crackling flames spread out along the earth from me to the man, who scrambled back. But the fire was too fast, engulfing his body within seconds. I watched him roll around in the snow, steam and smoke rising from his body. I frowned, realizing this would kill him. I looked back to Daelon, who looked fierce and determined. The flames in front of us reflected in his eyes.

I turned back to the man who was yelling out in agony, feeling the fear rolling off his body. I shuddered, and in a split decision I waved away the flames.

"No, Áine. Finish him."

I walked forward, following the trail of charred earth. I stopped to hover over the man as he writhed around on the ground, his skin badly burned. A lump grew in my throat, and I recoiled from the smell of burning flesh.

He stared at me in both terror and rabid rage. "He won't allow you to live," he spat.

I heard Daelon approach. He reached for the base of my neck again, his grasp firm.

"You'll get what's coming to you, you crazy bitch," the burned man screeched. "He will eat you alive."

"That's enough of that," Daelon said, revealing the cursed dagger that had been hurled at my face. In one swift movement he brought it down into the man's chest, where it sunk down into him and glowed black. The skin around it festered and turned gray.

I looked away. I felt like I was going to be sick. The power was still teeming in my periphery, waiting on my next direction. I sent it away, and a wave of exhaustion followed.

Daelon caught me as I swayed. "I need you for just one more minute, little witch. We have to get back."

I steadied myself wordlessly, letting him intertwine his fingers through mine.

In one last flow of magick the world around us melted away and transformed into familiar scenery.

CHAPTER 14

I was suddenly cold and empty, having lost the euphoria and sense of purpose my power had given me in battle. The sky was back to its normal appearance; the sun had freshly disappeared below the horizon. I was dizzy and disoriented, glancing around at the clearing as my head pounded.

Daelon studied me, concern etching his features. He reached a hand to my face. I flinched at the movement unconsciously, still hyperalert. He frowned, dropping his hand to his side. "Are you okay? Talk to me."

"I'm overwhelmed," I said, and my voice felt detached from myself. I was reacclimating to normal existence—coming back down to earth after a trip to the cosmos. "It's as if I became someone else for a moment. Or a different version of myself. I don't know—it's hard to put into words. It was like I became one with what I channeled, not separate."

Tears welled up in my eyes. I could still smell the rot of burning flesh.

"I can't begin to understand how you're feeling," Daelon said, his features finally softening. "You're incredible, Áine. Watching you was like nothing I'd ever seen before."

"Who am I, Daelon? Why do I feel everything all at once?" I looked away, willing myself not to cry. "I'm not alone in this magick. I feel the guidance of so many others..." I trailed off, shaking my head.

"I wish I had more answers for you," he murmured. "The truth is I only know vaguely about why you were born. I don't know why you feel the way you do. Or how exactly all of your power works. I can only speculate."

I clenched my fists in frustration. Part of me thought Daelon would eventually make everything clear—that he would one day answer all of my questions, and I could finally carry out whatever purpose I was designed for.

"It has something to do with *him*," I ventured, watching Daelon's features closely. Lucius. "And righting a wrong." I furrowed my brows, quickly reaching my emotional and mental limits. I was so drained.

"Yes. You're right," he said, but his face was far more impassive than I would've liked. "I'm going to help you find all the answers, Áine, I promise you. You did amazing today."

My mind quickly flashed back to the fight with the energy vampires, the images of bodies flying through the air and a man nearly burnt to a crisp still vivid. I looked away, shivering in the cold night air. "I can't believe you did that," I said. He started to speak but I cut him off. "Why? Why would you force me into that situation without any warning?"

Daelon faltered, seeming to weigh his words carefully. "I can't lose you Áine. I needed to make sure you could defend yourself without me, and that required realistic practice."

I crossed my arms over my chest, my breath billowing out in a white cloud in front of me. "That's not an apology."

He hesitated, which was enough to earn my narrowed gaze. "I'm sorry. I shouldn't have left you out of the decision. I just thought you might..."

"Refuse?" I finished. "That's kind of the whole point of giving someone a choice."

He nodded. "Come. Let's get you inside."

He reached for me, but I shrugged him off. Then I turned and headed off toward the house, leaving Daelon to follow behind me. With barely any effort, I cleared the snow away from the path as we went. I tried to focus on this task instead of the horrible, gut-wrenching energy of the vampires and their many victims, or the way I practically reveled in their destruction—up until I sent the fire away. But my efforts were in vain. One thing I couldn't shake was the realization that no matter how evil the vampires' auras, they paled in comparison to the suffering and darkness of Lucius's.

And that begged the question: What had *he* done?

My emotions and exhaustion had overcome me by the time we made it inside. There was too much to analyze, too many secrets and monsters lurking in the dark.

Daelon sighed, watching me wipe a hot tear from my cheek. "Come here."

He pulled me into his arms, and I eventually relaxed into

his embrace, clinging to the comfort the solid shield of his aura provided me. I breathed in deeply as I pressed my cheek into his chest. He pulled away, moving his hand down to intertwine with mine. As much as I wanted to resist him, to hold him at arm's length until I knew all of what he hid, I couldn't deny the power he had over me. I wanted Daelon to quiet the chaos of my mind. I wanted to let go—to trust in him the way he wanted me to. I wanted to trust him so badly it hurt.

He wordlessly pulled me down the hall to my room, stopping in front of the bed. "Sit here a moment," he commanded softly.

I watched as he disappeared into the bathroom. Soon after, I heard the sound of running water. I stared out the window, barely noticing when Daelon returned.

"I'm running you a bath," he murmured, still regarding me with concern.

I rose from the bed, and after a moment of hesitation, I allowed him to undress me. He removed my red jacket, laying it neatly on the bed. I lifted my arms as he pulled the sweater over my head. We paused to look at each other for a moment, and he fixed strands of my hair that had gone awry. He knelt to the ground to remove my snow boots, pulling them from my feet and placing them off to the side. Next, he lent me his arm as I pulled off my pants and leggings underneath.

The cold air formed goosebumps along my bare skin. Now in merely a pink bralette and panties, he scanned the length of my body. It was nothing like how he looked at me the previous night, but his eyes still held the same air of possession.

Tonight, he looked at me as though he cherished me—like I was something to be in awe of. "You're shivering," he said softly. He trailed his fingers along my arm until they encircled my wrist, then turned and led me to the bath.

When he let go, my body felt the absence of his touch. He stooped down to feel the temperature of the water in this grand, white bathtub, and then turned the faucets off. I slipped out of my panties and bra, casting them to the tile floor. When he turned to look at me all I could see in his features were devotion. A lump formed in my throat.

"You're so beautiful, Áine," he said.

He crossed the bathroom and grabbed a hair tie from the vanity. When he returned, he stood behind me and kissed my neck softly, then carefully swept my hair into a bun high on my head. Grabbing my hand, he steadied me as I stepped into the warm water, which was brimming with bubbles and smelled subtly of perfume.

Something about the way Daelon was taking care of me in such an intimate way, with that undeniable look of adoration, nearly brought me to tears again. I should've felt exposed, as I lay naked before him and he knelt beside the tub fully clothed, but all I felt was security, warmth, and gratitude.

He brushed a wayward strand of hair behind my ear. "Would you like to be alone?"

"No," I said quietly, leaning my head back against the tub, tilted to hold his gaze.

He nodded, stroking the side of my face. He looked like he was mentally working through a puzzle.

"What is it?"

"I just—don't understand you sometimes," he said.

"You say you want to avenge your mothers. You want to stop people from inflicting harm. You heal wounded animals. Yet you stopped. You couldn't kill that murderer."

I inhaled deeply, drawing my brows together. "There is no contradiction. I hate violence. But it seems I must use violence to stop violence."

He was silent for a moment. "I see. I've also had to do a lot of things in my life that I hated for the greater good. A lot of terrible things."

He seemed to retreat to a dark corner of his mind. I reached out a soapy hand to his face to bring him back, and he leaned into my touch. He grabbed it and kissed my knuckles. "I know that I'm here for something greater than myself," I said. "Even without knowing exactly what it is, I'm terrified that I'll fail. It feels like people are counting on me—like without me, it all falls apart."

"No. I will make sure that you don't fail, Áine. I will help you every step of the way." He sighed. "I'm here for a reason, too. It's how I found you. I know my purpose is to protect and guide you by any means necessary."

I swallowed, suddenly feeling brave. "When will your past no longer be off-limits? When will you tell me everything you know? Everything I *need* to know, not just what you want to tell me?"

Daelon's eyes hardened, jaw tense. "When I've done all I could do to prepare you—when we run out of time."

I flashed back to the spell Daelon did in the clearing, when he channeled something dark, and my body rejected it. *A spell for more time.*

"When will that be?" I asked. My stomach churned. I

was terrified that whatever was coming for us would steal Daelon away from me.

"I don't want to think about it, Áine," he pleaded.

He was scared. I closed my eyes in defeat, relishing the soothing warmth from the water. I breathed in the aromatic floral and fruity notes of the bubble bath. The stress from this long, arduous day began to fade away. I hadn't even had a chance to think about last night, when Daelon and I had finally given in to our desires.

I became more aware of how exposed I was as I recalled those moments—the feeling of his hands on me, his hips moving against mine, the way he made me want to obey his every command and submit all of myself to him... I still wasn't entirely convinced he hadn't spelled me somehow. What else could explain all that I felt for him? Even as he hid so much.

"What are you thinking about?"

I knew my cheeks flushed bright red. I kept my eyes closed, nearly flinching again as his fingers grazed my cheek.

"Ah. I see," he said, humor leaking into his voice.

I opened my eyes to squint at him, unable to stop the smile tugging at my lips. "Shut up," I muttered, closing them again.

As I lay submerged in the water, I heard rustling—Daelon's clothes dropping to the floor. My breath hitched, and I waited silently until I felt the water rise, nearly to my chin.

This time when I opened my eyes, I was met with the breathtaking sight of a naked Daelon sitting opposite me. His legs touched mine under the water. He cocked his head, motioning with his fingers for me to come to him. I shook my head, challenging him. He lifted a brow, his eyes shifting into something more primal.

He lurched forward, grabbing me at my torso. I laughed in surprise, water splashing up out of the tub and splattering onto the tile below. I let him spin me around so that my back was to him. His arms snaked around my body in a tight grip.

"So defiant," he growled near my ear.

"But you already knew that," I said, breathless. "If compliant is what you want, then I'm not the one for you," I joked, but as soon as it left my mouth, I regretted my phrasing.

Daelon took a breath. "*You're* what I want."

The room was too silent for a moment as the energy shifted into something more serious. I swallowed. I wanted a lot of things, and Daelon was definitely one of them. He also felt like something that I needed. He was my protector and guide. I knew that despite it all, he was devoted to me. I wished I could just let go completely, and tell him everything he wanted to hear, but something in my gut held me back.

I could at least ignore that nagging feeling for now. "I'm scared how much I care for you." It was the most honest thing I could say.

"I'm scared, too," he whispered, tickling my ear.

I remembered what one of the energy vampires said to us in the clearing. He had asked if I belonged to Daelon.

"I just can't let go completely," I said, quieter now.

"I know. I wish things were different." He intertwined his fingers with mine, then raised them to his lips. He kissed my knuckles lightly. "I can wait. Until after you know everything about me."

"You think that will change my mind," I said, more as a statement than a question.

Daelon stilled. "I don't know. I don't know how this will all play out." He paused. "I just need you to know that whatever happens, I am and always will be on your side. That will never change."

I frowned, frustrated at all of the vague foreshadowing. "I know, Daelon. I've felt it." What could I possibly find out that would change that? Energy couldn't lie.

He relaxed. "Good."

We sat there for a while longer, Daelon silently trailing soft touches along my skin and delivering kisses to my hair, my neck, and then my lips. I lost myself in him, pushing aside everything else until all that was left was my body and his.

After we left the bath, he lifted me into his arms and carried me to his bed. His commands started to feel like gospel, and his touch like worship.

"Hold still," he whispered, and I stilled.

He gazed down at my body, placing his palm on my chest where my heart was. I wanted to reach for his hand, but I kept my arms above my head. Something passed from his palm to me, another feeling that he wanted so desperately for me to know he felt.

This energy was more complex. There was an underlying darkness that was constantly being resisted and eluded. It seemed to be a glimpse into how much Daelon strained each day to protect me. There was so much torment here, like every breath was an act of resistance. I saw a flash of myself from his eyes as I lay in the bathtub, and I felt Daelon yearn to tell me something but being almost physically unable. It felt torturous.

I grimaced, gazing into Daelon's stony, dark eyes. He moved his palm from my chest to my cheek, and a more pleasurable energy enveloped me. I held my breath, searching his eyes. It was a feeling neither of us could say aloud. It was too risky, too vulnerable, too soon...

As quickly as this flash of energy breached my detection it disappeared, making me wonder if I had even felt it at all. All I knew was that he hopelessly adored me, his feelings genuine and pure, just as mine were for him. What we felt ran deeper than either of us understood, and definitely deeper than what either of us could own up to.

Daelon balanced just above me, melding his lips with mine. I quelled the urge to reach for him again. I hungrily moved my lips against his, and he tugged on my bottom lip with his teeth. His fingers trailed along my torso as he kissed me, and when they reached between my thighs, I lifted my hips slightly to meet him.

He swatted my inner thigh, and I gasped at the slight sting.

Lifting off my lips, he narrowed his eyes. "What did I say about moving?"

"Not to?" I laughed at the sudden surge of adrenaline.

"I know you can follow directions, baby," he whispered, and in a quick movement he slipped his fingers inside of me.

I moaned against his mouth as pleasure rippled through my whole body. He moved his fingers expertly, rendering me incapable of a single intelligible thought. Trying not to move was beginning to feel impossible. I looked up at Daelon in a silent beg but was only met with a small smile and eyes that swam with dominance and control.

"Please," I begged.

"Please what?"

He suddenly upped the intensity, and I nearly cried out. "Daelon," I breathed.

He kissed me again, and when he stopped, he said, "You can move now."

I tangled my hands through his hair, sighing in relief. As he continued his relentless torment of my body, driving me to the edge of release over and over again, I couldn't help but feel as though he was showing me just how deeply I already belonged to him, no matter how much I consciously resisted.

On this deeper, subconscious, physical level, I had already made up my mind. There was no denying it.

As if he could read my thoughts, Daelon, now inside of me as my legs wrapped around him, moved his hand to the base of my neck. His fingers rested on either side of my throat, not daring to deliver any pressure. The gesture alone was evocative of his possession.

"You're mine, Áine," he said.

I placed my hand over his. "I know."

We could say these things right now, when the world of the physical trumped all logic and reason. This space between reality and fantasy was safe from whatever waited for us beyond this bed. We both knew these unspoken rules. We knew that there existed an undeniable, underlying magnetism between us. It was something that couldn't quite be put into words. Maybe it was why Daelon could find me and speak to me telepathically when I totaled that taxi, or why he seemed to know my body as well as his own. Despite my tendency for the skeptical, these things were beyond the explainable.

He felt like home.

This was the energy that I could feel throughout the room. Like magick, whatever was between Daelon and me was natural and immutable.

"You're mine," he repeated later, this time from behind me as he held my back to his chest.

We lay on our sides under the duvet. I was curled against him, and his arm reached around me, grasping my hand in his. He nuzzled my neck, and I inhaled in surprise as he bit down lightly into my skin. He moved to grasp my shoulder now, growling low next to my ear.

I wasn't sure how much more I could take as my body submitted to his over and over again in different ways. We complemented each other's actions and desires so perfectly.

When we finished, I lay on his chest with his arm draped around me, drawing circles on my back. He pulled my body as close to his as it could possibly be, but it still didn't feel close enough.

"You must be exhausted," he murmured.

I sighed. "Very."

"Sleep now. And please try not to get into trouble in your dreams."

I closed my eyes, and in no time, I fell asleep in Daelon's arms.

CHAPTER 15

I woke with a start at the sound of a voice.

Áine, the voice called, sounding like hundreds of voices in one.

I opened my eyes to darkness, cemented into my body, unable to move. I began to vibrate as if jolted by waves of electricity. Popping noises erupted in my ears. I floated up above the bed, suspended in midair.

Áine, the voice called again. This time it was the voices of my mothers.

I slowly turned to face the bed, my heart leaping from my chest as I came face to face with... *myself.* I cocked my head, staring down at my body as it lay next to Daelon's. He lay on his side, his arm still draped over me. I watched as my own chest rose and fell.

Well, at least I'm not dead, I thought. I was astral projecting again. Somehow, this didn't scare me. So much for not getting into trouble in my dreams, though.

I continued to ascend, farther away from my physical

form. I passed through the ceiling and then the roof, shifting myself so that I was more vertical. I gazed down at the modern architecture of the cabin, admiring its sleek and open design.

As I rose higher, I noticed a circle of light amongst the trees, shimmering white energy that moved around the perimeter of the property. I knew the border was a part of Daelon's magickal workings. There was also a hub of iridescence gathered in a smaller circle, and I recognized it as the clearing Daelon used for rituals.

I was delighted by my ability to see these energies here in the astral plane, but the most captivating of all was the shimmering white light collecting at a focal point in the center of the roof. It's ever-moving rays of pure energy shone up through the air and far above me into the night sky.

I knew it came from me. This is what Daelon had to conceal each day.

I flew through the air to admire its brightness, drawn like an insect to a streetlight. It was warm and inviting like the soft rays of a summer morning. As I reached a hand into the swirling shimmers, I suddenly flew upward.

Áine, a voice called again. This time it was my own voice.

I soared through the air so quickly that it was uncomfortable, the rushing sound of wind assaulting my eardrums. The house became a blip and then disappeared, and soon I knew I was far above the atmosphere. I was moving too fast to see anything now.

There was a *pop* as my movement came to an abrupt stop. I was dizzy with whiplash. It felt like I was wading through a pool, but when my vision finally came into focus, I gasped at the sight of a giant blue mass below me.

It was Earth, but it was also Aradia—like two overlapping dimensions existing in the same space.

I gazed all around at the twinkling stars forming constellations, and as I did, entire galaxies took shape in the darkness like ethereal landscapes—shimmering blues, purples, reds, and yellows that spread out before me. I grew lost in this celestial showcase, forgetting who I was or how I got here.

Here among the stars, I was everything again. I was Magick itself.

Áine, the hundreds of voices called, and like the flip of a switch I was back in my own consciousness.

The galaxies and constellations dimmed until there was just nothing but darkness and the bright blue sphere of a planet below. I felt a tugging sensation, stronger than gravity, and soon I was plummeting back down into the atmosphere like a meteor.

I passed through clouds in a haze of white, and in the distance, I could vaguely make out a towering castle. Below me lay scores of trees, barren and blackened as if burned. This was my trajectory. Moving too quickly, I flailed my arms in any attempt to slow my descent.

Stop, I yelled to anyone who was listening.

Just before I collided with the hard dirt, I halted, my face mere inches from the ground. From there, I reached out my hands, dug my fingers into the soil, and then fell to the barren ground.

After a moment to catch my breath, I pushed myself up and stood. The trees around me were tall and dark, with long, curving branches. The few leaves they held were black and shriveled. The ground was largely devoid of life, muddy and abysmal, and the plants that did exist were adorned with dead and rotting foliage. Thorny vines crept over the soil and up the trunks of the barren trees. The air smelled of death.

The energy here was as unbearable as Lucius's, or like what Daelon channeled through me in the clearing. It was unnatural—it didn't belong in this realm or any other.

"Áine," I heard outside my mind, coming from my left. It was my mothers' again.

I walked quickly in that direction, trying my hardest to block out the unnerving energy of this lifeless forest. I started picking up on a din of whispers, wincing as the energy only got stronger around me the closer I got.

A mist began to spread out over the land, obscuring my vision. A shiver crept down the length of my spine, and I began to feel like I was in a horror movie.

Maybe it was time to go back to my body... especially since I wasn't sure it was my mothers I was hearing at all.

My heart leapt out of my chest as I stumbled into a circular clearing, surrounded by a natural barrier of tall trees with branches that wrapped around each other to form a wall. I watched as a tree sprung up at my point of entry, branches growing rapidly out of its sides to connect to the others.

"What are you doing here?"

I jumped. My heart pounded harder, sounding loud inside my ears.

I spun around to see the old man from the castle standing in the middle of the circle, just in front of a large slab of stone. The earth was scorched from its center.

The energy of this place leapt up and assaulted my

senses, bringing pain to my every nerve. I fell to my knees, crying out. "Where am I?" I called to him.

"Somewhere neither of us should be, I'm afraid," he responded, regarding me with renewed interest.

I took a deep breath, drawing up my defensive wall as Daelon had taught me. My clairsentience was far more of a hindrance than an aid right now.

The discomfort subsided, and I got back to my feet. I walked closer to the peculiar formation of stone.

"I'm so glad I can see you now. I was wondering when I finally would," he said, his body outlined by a nearly translucent bluish glow.

So, we were both astral projecting. *But why? Why here?*

He smiled at me, his eyes crinkling. I let down my guard for a moment to find that his energy was serene... and far from threatening.

"Who are you? Were you calling to me?" I asked. Was this all some sort of trick? A trap?

"I'm Amos." He stroked his beard. "And no. How peculiar..." He was looking *at* me and *through* me at the same time.

"Is this an altar?" But my intuition knew the answer from the dark shadows of magick that breathed through the stone.

He raised a finger to his lips. "We shouldn't be here. *You* especially, I'd imagine."

"Because of him?" I asked, careful not to say his name.

He sighed, turning from me and trailing his fingers along the stone. He hummed something, low enough that I could barely make it out, and the tune was so familiar, so sacred, that it sent a wave of chills over my entire being. It sounded like home.

He turned back to me, a sad smile on his lips. "I think I will see you again soon. Very soon. Leave here quickly."

In a flash he was gone, as if he had never been there at all. Against my better judgement, I crept toward the stone altar, holding my breath as to avoid its putrid magick. As I focused my gaze, a dark, polluted energy began to shine out from it into the air. It was thick like smoke, as pitch black as the night sky without stars.

When I stood just before the structure, a deep sadness washed over me, like nothing I had ever felt before. I heard screaming, crying, shrieking, from the thick aura, and I knew that this place told a story of utter destruction. It sang of horrors that language could never do justice.

Áine, the voices said again, strong and clear. *Remember this.*

I recalled what my mothers said during the meditation after Daelon and I fought, and as I did their voices played in my mind as if they were here now:

You will avenge us all, but not as an act of vengeance. As an act of salvation. You are made up of everything good in the world.

You are hope embodied—the hope of thousands—the hope of this world and all the rest. You will deliver us. You will restore this realm to its former state of balance and goodness. Trust your intuition. It will guide you always, sweet girl.

Something rustled from behind the wall of trees, and I wasn't in the mood to figure out what it was. I closed my eyes, envisioning my physical body in Daelon's bed.

I snapped back into my body like the flick of a rubber band. A sweat broke out across my forehead. I gasped, reconnecting with the room around me, feeling the weight of Daelon's arm across my chest as I'd seen from above.

I slipped carefully out from under his arm, admiring his peaceful features as sleep washed away his usual mask of strength and control. I set off to the kitchen to grab some water, still reeling from my astral journey.

Who was calling me to that altar and why? What atrocity had happened there that left that kind of disturbing, mournful energetic imprint? What did it have to do with my purpose or a supposed wrong that needed to be righted, a balance that needed to be restored? What was this Amos character's role in all of this? Or Lucius's?

I shook my head as I sipped on water in the dimly lit kitchen. It felt like I was running blindly through a multidimensional, cosmic maze. My mothers wanted me to have faith, but I was only growing more and more restless with my confusion and ignorance.

I stood over the pale purple candle that sat on the marble island, absent-mindedly setting it alight and playing with the flickering flame. I watched as it danced wildly and then stilled, influenced by my every silent command. I felt a sort of comradery with this bit of fire. I knew how it felt to be under someone else's spell.

I heard footsteps approach, but I stayed mesmerized by the flickering light. I set my water down on the counter.

A hand swept my hair over my shoulders, its gentle trail

across my exposed skin sending a shiver down my spine before resting on the back of my neck.

With a whoosh, the candle snuffed out. I frowned, but before I could wonder what caused it, Daelon grabbed my waist and spun me around. I squealed in surprise as he dipped me as if we were dancing, holding me suspended below him and his devilish crooked grin. He leaned down and kissed my neck, and I let out a small sigh.

"You're coming back to bed," he said, pulling me back upright.

Breathless and disoriented, I nodded.

"Yes, sir," I said teasingly.

He narrowed his eyes, but a smirk played at his lips. He kissed my forehead. "Good girl," he whispered.

In a quick movement he lifted me into his arms bridal style.

"Daelon," I protested, but he ignored me, of course.

He brought me back to his bed, laying me down slowly before crawling in after me. "No bad dreams or astral projections?" he asked, stroking my cheek.

"Nothing bad," I said, only half a lie. I didn't know why, but I had the compulsion to keep all that I saw to myself for now. Maybe because I knew Daelon was doing the same.

Instead, I turned on my side to face him, reaching my fingers to trail across his defined chest.

He inhaled, catching my hand. "You need more rest."

"What if I don't want more rest?" I asked, batting my eyelashes.

"Then that would be unfortunate, but irrelevant," he sighed. "Your needs come first to me."

I could take care of myself just fine. Well, most of the time.

"Don't roll your eyes at me," he warned.

I smiled, feigning innocence as I turned away from him. He pulled me close to his chest, biting at my ear. I giggled involuntarily at the tickling sensation.

"Go to sleep."

"You aren't exactly making that seem like the appealing choice, right now."

"Good thing you don't have a choice," he growled.

I wanted to talk back again, but I also knew he was right. I needed far more rest after the day that felt like many days in one. I could already feel exhaustion rolling back over me like a thick cloud, and I couldn't fight the security I felt in Daelon's arms.

Or how safe I felt without any choices to make. So, I relaxed into him, and as I did, his body relaxed against mine.

CHAPTER 16

The next time I awoke, bright rays of sunlight cast shapes on the wood flooring of Daelon's bedroom. I'd managed to sleep dreamlessly the rest of the night, and for that, my body and mind were thankful.

When I rolled over to face Daelon, I found him wide awake, clothed, and staring at me as he leaned against the headboard. A book rested in his lap.

"Finally," he murmured.

I narrowed my eyes, stifling a yawn. "Contrary to what human pop culture would have you believe, staring at me while I sleep is far more creepy than it is endearing."

"I sensed you wake," he said nonchalantly, shrugging. "But I'll keep that in mind."

His gaze was unwavering, his jaw set. His demeanor had shifted right back into its usual business-like, perfectly controlled self. It was striking how off-putting I used to find this because it felt like a challenge to my own independence.

Now that I understood him better, I knew that it was something else entirely.

"Does it bother you that I'm so much more powerful than you?" I asked.

He laughed. "No." He reached down to grasp my chin, brushing his thumb over my bottom lip. "It only makes it all the more thrilling."

I knew now that his tension was due to the lengths he went to protect me and conceal my power, and his façade of control was teeming with fear of losing me. Daelon wanted me to be my strongest, most powerful self. His dominance comforted me, and it quieted my indecisiveness, my doubts, and the overwhelming nature of my power.

It was also exciting.

He looked down at me still, moving his book from his lap without breaking his gaze. I watched something dangerous flash in his eyes, and I knew the suggestion of my power had excited him. Holding my breath, I braced as he climbed over me.

His dark hair was slightly tousled, falling lazily on his forehead. Stubble lined his sharp jaw. He regarded me hungrily, and I could tell he enjoyed when I didn't know what was coming next.

In a swift movement, he grabbed my wrists and slid them up along the silk sheets until they were parallel with my head. "How powerful are you now, baby?" he teased. "Push me off."

I hesitated. He did know that I could still send him flying through a wall, right?

I decided to go with my physical strength, which was

abysmal compared to his. I struggled underneath his grasp, pushing all of my muscular force through my arms.

"You're not trying your hardest, are you?" He cocked his head, drawing his brows in.

I scoffed. "That's actually so rude," I said, feigning offense. I stifled a giggle as he stared at me incredulously.

"Looks like physical training will be our next endeavor," he muttered.

I glared at him indignantly. "Whatever. You know I could make a Daelon-sized hole in the wall if I really wanted to."

"Then do it," he growled, fighting back a smile as he bent his head down to kiss my neck. His weight was still holding me in place.

Everything inside me stirred at his soft touches, juxtaposed with the way I lay helpless beneath him. As soon as I shifted attention to those universal forces, that power stirred —questioning, lying in wait—but Daelon and I both knew I would never unleash it on him like that. *At least not on purpose*, I amended, remembering the few times I may have accidentally knocked him on his ass.

There was something oddly poetic about this philosophical truth, that Daelon had articulated to me from the beginning. Power was far more about how it was wielded than its tangible reality.

I relaxed under him, and he shifted his weight off my wrists.

"That's what I thought." He smirked as he leaned down and touched his lips to mine in far too short of a kiss.

I couldn't help but pout as he rolled off of me.

"You slept for like fourteen hours," he said. "You need to eat."

My eyes widened slightly. I didn't think I'd ever slept that long, except for when Daelon first brought me here. The look he gave me held a certain finality, so I sighed and slipped out from under the warm covers.

We sat at the dining room table, where we ate in a comfortable silence. My mind was still heady with a pleasurable afterglow from the experience yesterday of becoming one with my magick. But like a smoky haze, Lucius's darkness lingered and taunted, reminding me that our cozy stay in this secluded cabin had an expiration date.

"I really am sorry about yesterday," Daelon said suddenly.

I swallowed my food, surprised. "Which part?" I wasn't sure I would ever get a full apology, since Daelon seemed dead set that his methods were the only way he could protect me.

"The parts that caused you pain," he said. A grimace played at his lips. "But also, the way I went behind your back. I wasn't thinking clearly."

I nodded, sipping my coffee. I could tell this was hard for him, which made me wonder again what he did as a so-called *witch trainer* before all of this. He clearly wasn't used to being questioned or having to apologize for his decisions. He'd also been pretty ruthless in his command during the fight, and I couldn't help but question what kind of *terrible things* he'd had to do for a greater good.

"I'm just having a hard time..." he paused, searching for words. "It's hard for me to come to terms with the fact that I can't protect you from everything, everywhere, at all times."

I sighed. "Well of course you can't. You can't hold yourself responsible for such unrealistic expectations. That's just insane."

A flash of anger passed through his eyes, but I wasn't sure where it was directed. "Well, it's what I want," he snapped.

He wanted control of the uncontrollable. Daelon found the same comfort in his drive to control as I did to cede my power to him and take a break from it all... it was a complementary coping strategy, but it was one that was impossible to maintain in this world.

"You're used to getting what you want, aren't you?" I said, my tone aching to lighten his mood. I was only met with exasperation.

"Yes," he said, looking away. "In some ways, I guess I am. In other ways I'm used to getting exactly the opposite." He looked back to me. "Knowing you were attacked while lying right next to me just set me off. I want you to be able to protect yourself when I cannot." He paused for a moment, closing his eyes as he took in a breath. When he reopened them, they held my gaze with a level of solemnity that scared me. "No," he said. "It's not a matter of my want. You must learn to protect yourself when I'm not around."

"Sometimes you talk as if you're dying," I said quietly. "You're not, are you?"

"No, Áine, I'm not dying," he sighed, softening his voice. "Just trying to set *realistic expectations*."

He was annoyed, and even though I knew it wasn't

directed at me, it still felt like it was. I didn't like the way it made me feel—almost like I was failing at something. "I can protect myself. You saw that I can," I said. "Isn't that sort of the whole point of being a mysteriously powerful witch?"

Daelon was impassive. "Possibly." He crossed his arms. "But there are some evil, unnatural forces coming for you. Much more powerful than a group of energy vamps," he said, his voice low and conspiratorial like other times he alluded to our enemies.

"You don't think I'm stronger than them? Or *him*?"

"Not now. But you will be. I'm going to make sure of it."

I frowned. Ouch.

Daelon got up suddenly, making me jump. He strode across the room to the window, appearing to fight off another urge to punch a hole through a wall. I wanted to joke about that but thought better of it.

I pushed up from the table, far more deliberately than he had, and approached him. He stiffened when he sensed me behind him. One of his hands was pressed above him to lean on the wall, his other balled at his side. I reached for his fist.

He straightened out his fingers at my touch.

I tugged on his arm. His features were hardened as he regarded me, his jaw tight. He still let me lead him to the couch, a smile breaking through as I tried in vain to push him onto it. His body was like a brick wall. He humored me, letting out a breath as he sat down.

I climbed into his lap, snaking my hands around his neck. His glare finally melted under my gaze, and his arms encircled my waist. I concentrated, allowing what I felt to pass from me to him.

It was a flood of warm hues of my energy—my desire to soothe him, my gratitude for the position he's put himself in to constantly ward off the darkness, and my uncontrollable adoration of him. It was a tapestry of lightness and strength, forged against all odds during our short time together.

His hands moved upward to wrap around my back, pulling me tight to his chest. I rested my head in the crook of his neck.

We stayed like this for a while, each tentatively sharing the feelings we already knew we shared—the feelings we still were unable to say aloud for reasons we both concealed. I feared this unpredictable, fiery relationship wasn't just built on shaky grounds; it was built on no grounds at all.

We were free falling, and I wasn't sure where we would land. Or if we ever would.

When I finally lifted my head, his grip around me tightened.

"I'm not going anywhere," I whispered to reassure him.

His dark eyes were so vulnerable now that the anger had melted, offering a rare glimpse into an emotion he so carefully hid: fear. "I know you aren't," he said, the corners of his lips quirking up. "Because I'm not letting you."

He looked like he wanted to say something more, but I sensed it was something that we only said through energy sharing.

"I want you to know that I've never felt this way about someone before," he said. "I need you to know that."

"Because you've only had kinky sexual relationships before?" I ventured, remembering things he'd hinted to in the past, then I quickly shook my head. "Nope! Never mind. Don't need to know. Forget I asked that."

He narrowed his eyes as if to gauge what I was feeling. A playful grin spread across his lips. "You're jealous," he said, somewhere between question and a statement.

I scoffed, trying to move off of him, but he held me firmly in place. He was enjoying this far too much. "I am not," I said, unconvincingly. I glowered at him. What had begun as a tender, vulnerable moment had quickly devolved into our usual games.

He laughed, which only made me more flustered.

"You'd be jealous too," I taunted. "Believe it or not, you were not my first."

"Oh, I've gathered," he said.

My mouth gaped. I swatted at him, and he caught both my wrists. In one swift movement he had me pinned underneath him, my head resting at one end of the couch.

I searched his eyes, pleased to see that his façade of the unbothered and unthreatened wasn't as strong now. Now it was my turn to smile.

"You're right. Thinking about you with others does make me jealous," he started. "So I need to ensure that you know you're mine now."

I was stunned to silence, suddenly aware of every place on my body he currently touched. His thumbs stroked my hands from his hold on my wrists, and his hips rested on mine. He moved one hand to travel down the length of my body, stopping between my thighs where it teased and tormented.

After far too short of a time he pushed himself off of me to stand. I sat up, shooting him a look of confusion.

"Stand," he instructed.

So, I did, and something about the way his voice and

demeanor shifted like it always did when he took full control sent me deep into an altogether different headspace. The more he exercised his dominant role the more I relaxed into my submissive one. He wanted to hold on, and I wanted to let go. He wanted to feel more powerful than whatever he hid from me, and I wanted to surrender to the magnetism between us that felt just as natural and transcendent as my magick.

He gestured with his hand for me to follow him to stand behind the couch, facing the fireplace. "Turn around," he said, making the movement with his hand as well.

I faced away from him, a shiver running down my spine. Without the ability to see him physically or to read his aura, I was left completely in the dark, tethered only by his commands.

"Take them off."

He didn't need to say what for me to understand. I was wearing an off the shoulder sweater dress, so it was easy for me to complete this task. I reached down and slid the thong down my legs, casting it to the side with my bare foot.

I waited in a frenzied anticipation for my next instruction, but instead I felt him move closer to me. He dragged his hands down the sides of my body, and then his right hand bent me over, so that I had to grab the back of the couch for support. I gasped as his left hand moved to where my underwear had been.

This position left me feeling utterly exposed, especially now that he was touching me in this way, his fingers moving expertly. I moaned softly, my fingers digging into the fabric. Suddenly he slipped two fingers inside me, stroking my hair momentarily with his free hand. The contrast between these soft, endearing gestures and the rougher, domineering ones was entrancing, and I felt myself fall once again under his spell.

After bringing me to the edge, he withdrew, leaving me breathless and back in my anticipatory state. I heard the rustle of clothes.

I pushed off the couch, and as soon as I did Daelon engulfed me, reaching from behind to grasp lightly at my throat, his arms holding me tight against him. He lowered his head so that his mouth was close to my ear. I could tell he was almost completely naked now.

"Did I tell you that you could move, little witch?"

"No."

He let me go, bending me over more forcefully this time.

My breathing rapid, I fought the urge to look back at him. I wanted to see all of him—to admire the way his muscles flexed as he moved, the way his eyes consumed me possessively, hungrily—each time feeling as though it was his first.

When he finally touched me again, I calmed, unaware of how tense I had become with anticipation. His hand made featherlight touches through my hair, down my back, and finally coming to rest on my hip. I held my breath, realizing what was coming.

His first thrust was slow, and a moan escaped my lips. "You feel so good," he cooed.

I inhaled sharply, his next movement anything but light. I didn't need to read energy or body language to interpret this message, as he grasped my hips, moving forcefully, deeply, over and over as my legs began to shake. I heard his message loud and clear.

I gripped the couch, overwhelmed by pleasure and intensity. Soon there was no room to think about anything at all but the present moment. There were no more doubts, fears, questions, or really any thought at all.

There was only Daelon marking his territory.

My perception of time melted away, so I wasn't sure how long it had been when he finally released me. He pulled my dress back down, gently guided me up to face him.

"Are you okay?" he asked, his eyes softer than I expected them to be.

"Uh, yes," I stuttered. My mind felt cloudy, my skin flushed, and my body still shaking slightly. Finally able to see Daelon's chiseled body, I couldn't help but stare.

He narrowed his eyes, studying me for a moment. A smile spread across his lips.

"Good," he murmured. He scooped me into his arms effortlessly and carried me to his bedroom.

"I can walk." I gave him an indignant look.

"I'm not so sure," he chuckled.

I felt my cheeks redden even more. He set me down on the edge of the bed, his eyes soft and adoring for a moment.

"Take off your dress," he commanded, so I stood and pulled it over my head.

I smoothed my hair, unable to keep my eyes off him.

He seemed incapable of the same. "You're so lovely, Áine," he said, holding my chin in his hand. "Now get on the bed."

I returned his slight grin before doing as I was told.

"Hands above your head. Don't move," he instructed. "Or speak. Which I know is hard for you."

I shot him a glare but obeyed. I took this opportunity to

catch my breath, but soon Daelon moved over me. My heart skipped a beat, but there was also a wave of intense calm that spread over me when he was close—so strong it was hard to believe it wasn't magick.

He was safe. I didn't believe that whatever he hid from me could ever alter that fact.

"You're the most beautiful person I've ever met," he said, surprising me. He rested a hand over my heart. "Everything you do amazes me. You give me hope, Áine. You're going to give so many others hope, too. You remind me of where—who—I come from," he faltered, a sadness passing through his eyes.

I wanted to speak, but I felt myself compelled to do what I was told. Noticing my hesitation, he placed a finger on my lips.

"And I don't want you to ever change. Or to lose your heart."

His words hit somewhere deep, and I realized it was because they mirrored things my mothers told me. They said I was here to give people hope. They told me to never lose my heart.

I could tell he wanted to say more, but he leaned in to kiss me instead. At first soft and coaxing, the kiss quickly deepened into something more impassioned and forceful. This constant contrast nearly gave me whiplash, but I didn't want Daelon any other way.

He pulled away. "I'm not done with you yet."

I longed to reach out and touch his chest. He met my gaze, his lips curving into a slow smile.

"You give up power so well for someone with so much,"

he said nonchalantly, trailing kisses along my throat, past my collarbone, and to my breasts.

His next destination challenged my ability to keep still, my hips struggling not to move upward. He grasped my thighs in either hand, spreading them apart. His grip tight, teetering on the edge of pleasure and pain—*as usual*.

I dug my fingernails into the sheets above my head, feeling the pleasure build. There was no teasing this time, no stopping or slowing. I let go, falling deeper into Daelon's pervasive hold over every part of me as I did. My body tensed all at once as the pleasure overtook me, and then I stilled.

Daelon stopped, moving back up to hover over me.

"Did I give you permission for that?" he asked, a hard edge in his voice that didn't match his grin.

I shook my head, knowing full well that he had set me up. This game was unwinnable.

"You can move and speak now. Not that you'll be able to do much of either." He entered me, grasping my wrists and holding me in place.

I wasn't sure how much more I could take, understanding now that this was just as much of a punishment as it was a reward. Everything was more intense this time, and Daelon was relentless.

He moved one hand to my cheek as the other trailed down my torso. "Whose body is this?"

"*Yours.*"

CHAPTER 17

I lay facing Daelon, my hair still wet from our shower—where he had insisted again on delicately washing my hair and running soap over my skin. Just as before, he seemed unable to keep his hands off me for too long, preferring me close to him. I wasn't about to complain.

"Just so you know," I said, my heart rate picking up. "I've never felt this way about anyone either."

He didn't say anything at first, letting my words hang in the air between us.

No relationship I'd ever had could match this—not that I'd ever made it past a couple months with someone on Earth. It just wasn't something I thought was possible, at least not with the men I'd met. I had too much baggage, too much I couldn't say, too much they could never understand. The trauma from my mothers' deaths and multiple placements in foster care sure didn't help, nor did the negative beliefs about myself and the haunting inevitability of loss, change, and impermanence. I wore intimacy issues like adornments, and aside from my three best friends, it was hard for me to ever relate to anyone at all.

Basically, I wasn't relationship material. And no amount of therapy could help with that. The whole my-mothers-told-me-I-would-someday-return-to-the-witch-realm part of my trauma couldn't even be discussed without being stuck with a psychosis label.

I'd spent a decade in a realm that made me feel hollow, misunderstood, and forgotten. But Daelon understood me completely, more than any of my human friends were even capable of.

"Lucky me," Daelon said, pulling me back from my reflection. His smile didn't reach his eyes.

"What is it?"

He shook his head slightly, moving his hand over mine where it rested on his heart.

"It's okay. I've accepted that we can't pretend that we're normal for very long," I said, forcing a smile. I wasn't sure if it was convincing.

"I just don't like the feeling of running out of time. Especially with you."

"Are you sure you're not dying?"

He rolled his eyes. "Yes."

"It's him, isn't it? You think he's going to find me soon?" I asked.

It was the only explanation that made sense. Daelon's mysterious spell in the clearing had channeled power that matched Lucius's, so I assumed that meant the spell was an attack against him.

We were far too intimate for secrets now. I willed him to finally give me just this one straight answer.

He hesitated. "Stop," he said, pained. "I can't."

My mood soured instantly. I couldn't make sense of his off-limits topics or keep track of all of them. I had already met Lucius, after all. What more could there possibly be to hide? It was hard to believe that he still feared I would run off without him on a revenge path.

Daelon closed his eyes for a moment, his forehead creasing. Was he shielding us from Lucius's magick now? The thought of that terrified me.

"Well, I guess I'll find out when he's on our doorstep," I snapped.

Daelon's eyes flew open, so fiery and sharp that I gulped, the hairs on the back of my neck pricking up.

"You can't stop, can you?" he said, his tone cutting. "You can't just enjoy the time we have. You have to go and ask questions that I've told you so many times I can't answer."

"Can't? Or *won't?*"

I recoiled from him, and I could tell the act wounded him as a flash of hurt passed through his eyes. I shrugged off his attempts to stop me as I pushed myself up and out of the bed. I faced him, and I felt raw power calling to me from all directions.

"We're close enough for you to have just been inside me as you made me say I was yours, but not close enough for you to be completely honest with me. You ask for the impossible, Daelon."

He jerked back as if I'd just slapped him, his face falling and his anger melting completely away.

I turned away from him, but I was unable to erase the image of his wounded features from my mind as I left, the door slamming shut on its own behind me. The afternoon light illuminated the hallway, and I walked to my room in silence, wearing nothing but one of his shirts.

I was quick to tear it off me as I entered my room, putting on some warm sweatpants and a thick turtleneck and scarf. I grabbed a jacket from my closet and slipped on the snow boots that Daelon had removed from my feet so carefully last night. Each day felt like a week here.

I sighed, biting back frustrated tears. I needed to go somewhere I could think. That shift from safety to danger had come too quickly, reminding me just how tumultuous our arrangement truly was. And this latest reminder of just how much effort he put into keeping me in the dark was maddening.

When I opened the door, I found Daelon on the other side. He was quick to look me up and down. A flash of panic moved through his features.

"What are you doing?" He stiffened, blocking my path.

"I just need some space," I said, exasperated. "I'm only going to the circle. Just to meditate and think. Nothing to worry about."

As annoying as it was to have to spell it out to him, I knew in the logical side of my brain that it was sort of in his DNA to protect me. However, my power was frantic as my emotions spun out of control, so I wasn't keen on logic currently.

"Please—let me come with you."

"I don't think you understand the concept of *space*," I said, crossing my arms.

"And I don't think you understand the concept of safety," he said. "You're a danger magnet, Áine. You get into trouble while you sleep, let alone your astral adventures while you meditate. Need I remind you how much more vulnerable you are in this kind of emotional state?"

"I am not in an *emotional state*," I hissed, and the sound of a fireplace roaring to life from one—or maybe both—of the living rooms erupted. A kettle wailed in the kitchen.

Not cool, I spoke to the forces around me.

Daelon lifted his eyebrows.

"I said no," I said. I wasn't going to budge on this. "I'll cast a protective circle. I'll use every single defensive tool you've taught me. I just need to be alone for one single moment, and I don't think that's too much to ask."

I watched as Daelon visibly cycled through emotions, from hurt to angry to desperate and back again. It was the hurt look that gave me pause.

"I just need to think," I repeated. "I'm not going to think my way out of feeling the way I do for you," I added, quieter this time. "But I need some time alone."

I noticed his shoulders relax slightly, and with a sigh he moved out of my way. I exited out the glass door, grabbing a blanket from the couch on my way, and descended down the winding wooden staircase. The snow had melted down to a couple inches now, and it crunched beneath my feet as I headed off on the beaten path. Being out in nature instantly soothed me, and my connection to myself and my power strengthened. As I homed in, I could sense the energetic imprint of the circle call out to me from the east.

At the sound of the glass door shutting again I turned back toward the house, where Daelon stood on the balcony.

I hesitated, my free hand balling into a fist and then opening out again at my side, but after a few seconds, I turned back toward the path.

I slowed my breathing, concentrating only on energy. It was hard to squash the thoughts that rose up, taunting me, calling me foolish for how far I'd fallen for Daelon—but I knew that in order to cast a decent circle of protection I needed to have a clear mind. As if on cue I felt him reach out to the corners of my psyche, his energetic imprint unmistakably guarded, strong, and assertive.

What? I asked him telepathically, tuning in to him. I turned off the path at the familiar formation of trees, pushing into the clearing.

Remember to reach out like this if you need help. And also that you need a clear head when you cast the circle. Holding on to negative emotions will make it ineffective, and possibly even more d—

I know! I interrupted him. *Stop worrying, please.*

I'm never going to stop worrying about you.

I lay down the blanket in the center of the clearing and sat down with a sigh. I mentally cut off our connection, sort of like hanging up the psychic telephone.

I heard the faint chirping of birds, and I breathed in the earthen, woodsy air of the forest, which was tinged with the faint, but unmistakable scent of snow and cold. I practiced the technique Daelon taught me where I locked away my racing thoughts for later, envisioning them disappearing into a locked safe.

I began calling on the raw power that sat in wait, feeling it rush toward my body and send tingles along my skin. Wind whipped in circular movements around me as I channeled, thinking of all things safe, all things stable and impenetrable, all things warm and light and good. I made a circular motion with my fingers, and when I opened my eyes a bright white fire had moved along the perimeter of the clearing, just as Daelon had likely done many times before.

I scanned the area, tuning in to its energies, and when I was satisfied that it was stable, I closed my eyes again and dove inward. I opened the safe, unleashing all of my thoughts once more.

At some point during my trance-like state I'd entered my psychic ocean of energy, feeling the water lap around me as if I were really there. It wasn't quite on the level of reality as astral projection, as I knew I was still within my own mind, but in some ways, it was hard to tell the difference. Reality as I knew it on Earth simply could not account for how things worked in Aradia. Honestly, if I thought about it too hard my head hurt.

I lay on my back, reaching my hand toward the sky to shift its enchanting, deep blue, into a breathtakingly clear night sky. Now, under the sparkling stars and the varied hues of the Milky Way, I could finally think. I was grounded in the deepest core of myself, the part of myself that felt eternal, connected to people I'd never met and places I'd never seen.

Who am I?

I gave into the pull at my back, letting my body fall below the surface. The stars above distorted and blurred as I was pulled deeper underwater. I reminded myself I could breathe, and I stilled as I gazed around at the murky blue surrounding me.

The energy answered my question, but not in words. It answered in its usual storytelling style of esoteric glimpses into the beyond—all that lay outside of my own personal knowledge and experience. It was the energetic pool of all of existence, and it was unfocused and hard to discern.

Visions of my mothers began to play out in front of me in hazy projections. Momma Celeste clutched her pregnant stomach, and Momma Jane kissed her cheek. As the imagery panned out, I saw others surrounding them, all dressed in white. They were the same people I saw before during my near-death experience. They were chanting in a foreign tongue, a language I knew was connected to the intrinsic fibers of my being.

One of them stepped toward my mothers. Her gaze was focused beyond them, her eyes glassy and white. She looked entranced, and I couldn't shake the feeling that she was staring straight at me.

"You will be our salvation from the greed and cruelty of witches disconnected from themselves, so that we may have hope, so that we may preserve the natural power and fabric of this realm, the one below and the ones above, so that we may once again live in peace on our sacred lands, so that we may honor the Goddess, representing balance, compassion, truth, and unity—our guiding light through the darkness and the essential wholeness of the Universe."

Her voice trailed off. The more I tried to hold on to the vision, the quicker it disappeared. A cascade of chills ran over my body. This was another piece of the puzzle of who I was, and I couldn't shake the warmth and serenity that radiated out from these people—*my people*. My heart ached knowing that they were all most likely dead, slaughtered by the forces that led my mothers to flee to Earth.

I wondered if the woman was referencing Lucius and his people when she mentioned witches who were *disconnected from themselves*. The cruelty sure met the description, and

Daelon seemed to imply he was at least as powerful as I was, if not more. Was I the Universe's way of maintaining balance, just as my mothers said? Just as Daelon hinted at? But then how did Lucius disrupt that balance, and how was I to restore it?

There were just so many questions. I needed to learn who my people were, where they came from, and what happened to them. I knew this was key to unlocking my fate. I wouldn't let anyone get in the way of fulfilling the purpose they'd instilled in me, not even Daelon.

But I didn't want to consider the idea that Daelon was somehow keeping me from this grand plan. Not yet. It was far too painful. I wanted to believe his intentions were honorable until he gave me a reason not to, consequences be damned.

In an act of desperation, hoping that my power would once again confirm that Daelon was who he appeared to be, I asked: *Who is Daelon? Can I trust him?*

I sent my intention out into the water, then watched as an image began to take shape. I just hoped it was something helpful.

The projection that emerged was of a young boy running through the streets of a vaguely European-style village, ashes falling all around him like snow. The buildings were scorched and crumbling as if rampaged by a great fire or an explosion.

"Mom!" the boy screamed, his voice hoarse. His face was covered in soot, his clothing tattered.

At this point I knew it was a young Daelon, and the image broke my heart.

He frantically searched and called for his mother. Tears

streamed down his face. He couldn't have been more than eight years old.

"Hello there," a woman's voice called.

I watched as the boy halted and turned around, but I couldn't see who he was looking at. He looked petrified, backing up slowly with his eyes wide.

"I think they killed my dad," he said, sniffling. "Who are you? Will you help me find my mom?"

A second voice spoke, but it was warped and distorted. The vision went black suddenly, and a strong force pushed me back toward the sky.

In my confusion I breathed in some water, spluttering and coughing when I breached the surface. I sucked in fresh air, centering myself.

I wasn't sure what the Universe was trying to show me with that vision, other than a glimpse into what appeared to be a traumatic childhood. Hot tears slid down my cheeks as I was overwhelmed with sadness for him. I almost felt guilty for intruding on something so private, so tragic, that he himself wasn't able to tell me. Then again, it wasn't like I consciously went looking for it. Something beyond my understanding wanted me to see this memory fragment.

I looked back up at the stars, feeling so conflicted that I physically felt pulled in all different directions—and it was excruciating. Even in my universal ocean, that which connected me to everyone and everything, I felt utterly alone.

CHAPTER 18

When I snapped back into the present moment, the sun was just starting to descend in the sky. Dried tears stained my cheeks, and my fingers were numb, even inside my gloves.

I wasn't sure how to approach Daelon after all that I had just seen. Did I tell him about the uncovered piece of his childhood? I figured considering the lengths he went to avoid talking about it, combined with our current tension, it was best to leave it be for now.

While I hadn't received the clarity I needed, my inward journey had at least grounded me in a reminder of the bigger picture. Daelon and I were connected. And seeing him in those heartbreaking moments only cemented that fact. I surmised from my vision and given his talk of parallel pasts and common enemies, that his parents were likely killed by the same people that mine were. He told me in bed that I gave him hope, and that I reminded him of where and who he came from. That was just too similar to all that I'd seen in visions and had been told by my mothers about my purpose. He was a part of this overarching puzzle. I just had to figure out how.

I decided that despite my lingering frustrations, I wanted to give him the benefit of the doubt for as long as I could.

I only hoped that this was the right course of action, and my judgement wasn't being clouded by my feelings for him. All I had right now was the mysterious, murky guidance of my universal power. I needed to listen to what my mothers always told me:

Trust your intuition, Áine.

At this point, my intuition leaned in Daelon's favor.

I pressed my hands down on either side of the soft, plaid blanket, releasing the energy of the protective circle. I watched as the white fire extinguished gradually along the perimeter, leaving a trail of smoke in its wake.

I got up slowly, dizzy from all the psychic exertion. It was like I was walking on a cloud, not quite reacclimated back to physical reality.

As I walked back to the house, I ran through a hundred different scenarios of what to say to Daelon, but none of them seemed right. My feelings for him were overshadowed by something bigger than us both. After all I had just seen, I couldn't help but feel the decisive force of fate resting on my shoulders—like I was a cog in the machine of a grand plan I had yet to uncover.

When I made it up the stairs, I found him sitting back in one of the patio chairs, facing a lit firepit. His body relaxed as I approached and took a seat next to him, my stomach fluttering as he set his intense gaze on me.

"Any transformative insights?" he asked, his features guarded.

You don't even know the half of it.

"Yes, actually," I said, considering my next words carefully. "I saw more about who I am, in that ocean, and I... There's something so much bigger than us at play."

"I know," he said, staring off at the setting sun.

I watched him carefully, but his features were still unreadable. "I know that something happened to my mothers' people—to *my* people—and I know it's connected to what happened to my mothers, and to why I was born. I know that I was born from magick. Powerful magick," I said, speaking aloud the web of truth I already knew.

Daelon stared at me fiercely as something unknown flashed in his eyes.

"They hid me on Earth until the time was right for me to return. They hid me from *him*, I assume, and whoever else took part in the cruelty that cast a shadow over this realm."

I faltered, remembering the scared young Daelon running through the streets. I saw a brief flicker of that fear in his eyes now.

"And even though I still don't know how or what I'm going to do to fulfill my purpose, I know that *I will fulfill it*. No matter what it takes." I kept my voice level and strong. The fire beside us rose higher in the air.

"I will do whatever I can to help," Daelon said. "Even if you don't understand my methods," he added, almost wistfully.

Well, he was right about that. "I will believe you until you give me a reason not to, at which point I will figure everything out myself," I said, an edge to my voice now.

I knew the threatening tone would bother Daelon, anger passing through his features right on cue. I didn't want to challenge him. *But I had to.*

He regained his composure quickly, but I didn't miss the moment of anxiety swimming in his dark brown eyes. I didn't need clairsentience to tell me what he was afraid of.

I sighed, but then pushed up and crawled into his lap. It caught him off guard, his body stiffening at first before snaking his arms around me.

"I don't want to lose you," he said as a rare vulnerability seeped into his words.

"I don't want to lose you either."

He kissed my forehead then brushed a strand of hair from my face.

Nothing lasts, I thought, and a lump formed in my throat. The natural state of all things was change. This was what my mothers taught me.

I buried my face in his sweater, breathing his scent in deeply to commit it to memory. He held the back of my head in one hand, his other arm holding me tight to his chest. The warmth from the fire was hot against my back.

My mind flashed to how I felt floating in the ocean, staring up at the Milky Way. I realized with a great sadness that even here in Daelon's arms, I still couldn't let go of that deep, pervasive sense of loneliness.

As we ate dinner, we both failed at our favorite game of pretending to be normal. The energy between us had definitely shifted. There was a desperation now, like we were running from inevitability and hiding from fate.

"You're barely eating," Daelon said, pulling me from my daze. He shot me a disapproving look across the dining table. We sat facing each other at the end, closest to the wall with the ocean painting.

I couldn't stop glancing up at it, getting lost in the blue brushstrokes of the waves and the dotting of multi-colored sand. I remembered both of my mothers' individual stories of this place—where they said magick lived and danced in the salty wind and washed away the badness in its tide. And as I envisioned these crashing waves, the loneliness began to lose its hold on my psyche.

"Sorry," I mumbled, shifting my gaze back to him.

He cocked his head, his brows drawn together. "You don't need to apologize. I just want to make sure you're staying strong," he murmured.

I actually hadn't meant to apologize; I just wasn't paying attention. I kept that to myself, though.

"I told you I would take you there," he said, glancing up at the painting himself. "If you still want to go."

"I've been there a million times," I said quietly, almost to myself. I lost myself in the brushstrokes, feeling an unshakable calling, a pull stronger than the gravity that tethered me to the earth.

There was something there I needed to see.

Daelon frowned. "Áine, look at me," he said.

It was nearly painful to pull my eyes from the painting back to him. I wasn't sure what had come over me.

"Are you okay?"

I shook my head slightly, tucking my hair behind my ear.

"Yeah. I just had a weird... witch feeling. I don't know." I felt compelled to speak again, this time more certain. "But yes, I would love to go."

"It's been a long few days. Well, weeks, really. You need rest," he said, still eyeing me with concern. He muttered something lower, unintelligible, but it almost sounded like *while you still can.*

I nodded. I was still pretty tired from yesterday, and Daelon's comment was accurate. I had a feeling there wouldn't be much time to rest when I had evil witches to fight and whatever else I was magickally conceived to do.

"We can go in a couple days—when you're feeling more recharged."

"Just an energy battery to you, huh?" I asked demurely, my humor unsurprisingly lost on him.

His eyes darkened. "Only because all my power goes to protecting you."

"Daelon, it was a joke. Trust me, I've seen it," I said.

"Seen what?"

"Your magick. I saw it in the astral realm, around the property's perimeter. It was very bright and shiny." I smiled reassuringly. I knew how much he strained to keep me safe.

He once again looked perplexed. "Interesting. Did you see your own power?"

"Yes. It was... a lot," I said, recalling the heavenly spotlight that shone from the roof to the stars.

Daelon steepled his fingers in front of his face. A smile played at the corners of his lips. "Yes, it is."

"How literal is what I see in the astrals?" I asked. "Like I can obviously experience real places and see real people... but what about the more dreamlike aspects?"

I thought back to the strange scene with the altar in the forest of dead trees, and once again wondered what was being revealed to me there—and by whom?

"The astrals are easily influenced by our thoughts and emotions, much like magick, and to a lesser extent the witch realm. Not everything *there* is a direct reflection of reality *here*, which can be very tricky. Here in the physical, our consciousness is separated from physical reality to a greater extent because it's limited to our bodies—aside from magick—but in the astral realm, consciousness flows more fluidly from the perceiver to the perceived and vice versa. It's not separate." He tapped his fingers absently on the table, his brows drawing together as he mused. "The astral realm is a fluid, tangible representation of the collective consciousness of all of existence—human, witch, animal, and all the rest. Dreams, visions, goals, and art... it's all there, just as real as what we call physical reality. It affects us and we affect it, like a perfect circle of balance. Just like magick."

I leaned back in my chair, trying to glean any semblance of coherence from Daelon's words. Things were a lot less complicated on Earth; the laws of witches weren't exactly accessible. From what I gathered, it seemed like this was because on the scale of magickal malleability, Earth was at the bottom—thus more rooted in the physical—and then came Aradia, and at the top was the astrals. This hierarchy made my mothers' escape to Earth a smart move and explained why they stuck me in the least natural place in the human realm: New York City. My ties to magick were literally at their lowest point, just as they wanted for me until I was ready to return.

"I know it's hard to understand," Daelon said. "Even the

most seasoned witches struggle to explain how exactly the astrals work. Or magick for that matter."

"Or me?"

Daelon chuckled. "You would definitely fall into the category of the Universe's greatest mysteries."

"Great," I muttered, my brow still creased in concentration. I took a moment to try to relax, massaging my temples.

Daelon inhaled, his eyes softening. "We're going to figure it out. I promise."

I nodded, stealing one last glance at the beach painting. I had an undeniable feeling that our trip there would help me to do just that.

※

At some point in the night my mind stirred while my body stayed in sleep paralysis, and I was overcome by the familiar energetic vibrations of my astral body detaching from the physical.

I'm tired. Just let me sleep, I groaned telepathically to whatever mysterious forces were afoot. Popping noises erupted in my ears right on cue, and my arms began to float upward.

Seriously. I'm not in the mood for cryptic astral road trips to creepy castles and forests.

I began to float up toward the ceiling, and as soon as I realized my energetic field had been breached somehow, it was too late to block the intruder from my mind.

Not even for me? a familiar voice answered.

In a panic, I opened my eyes, and I realized I was no longer in Daelon's bedroom. I was lying in the same field as my previous encounters with Lucius, tall golden grass blowing in the wind all around me. The sky above was overcast and darkening.

I pushed myself to stand, looking all around for any sign of my enemy. I quickly grounded myself, building up my defensive barrier and decisively shoving him out of my head.

"What do you want now?" I asked, annoyed as ever that he'd summoned me from my sleep for more cruel games.

In a burst of thick, black smoke, a man appeared. He appeared to be in his late twenties or early thirties, with jet black hair that had a loose curl to it, striking, light blue eyes, and fair skin with angular cheekbones. He was dressed in a dramatic black jacket and pants with golden accents, blending the modern and archaic. He also wore an intricate, golden crown.

"Always with the theatrics," I muttered under my breath. So, this was really what Lucius looked like. He was finally done concealing himself.

His energy was undeniably dark, thick, and deadly, and I instantly recoiled, taking a step back. I breathed in deeply, blocking it from my perception.

"Now what's this about my castle?" he asked, his voice no longer distorted. It was deep, clear, and surprisingly humored. "Not to your taste?"

I faltered. *His* castle?

I narrowed my eyes, trying to erase what I could only imagine was dumbfounded shock from my face. "No longer hiding, I see."

When he took a step forward, I took one back, determined to keep a good twelve feet of distance between us.

"And no posse. Feeling brave?" I feigned warmth in my

smile. I refused to give him the satisfaction of thinking his intimidation tactics had worked.

He laughed, again surprising me. We mirrored each other's demeanors and movements, like some sort of strange, ritualized dance.

"I have no need to conceal myself any longer," he sneered. "You'll be seeing me in the flesh soon enough."

I tried not to let the dread seep into my disposition, even if his words brought every ounce of it into my body. I chose to ignore the comment, pretending it didn't faze me. "See yourself as a king, do you?" I nodded to the silly golden crown perched on his head.

He glared. "Your king, foolish girl," he spat. "The king of every witch."

I racked my brain for any mention of him in my mothers' stories but came up blank. They never spoke of any monarchy, or any ruling hierarchy for that matter. Daelon had never mentioned any kings or castles either, which was even more strange. As usual, I was fighting a war wearing a blindfold, and it was increasingly frustrating.

"You just have no idea," Lucius chuckled, his anger quick to dissipate. "About *anything*. It's adorable, really."

I clenched my fist at my side. Yes, I was well aware that after over a month in Aradia, I still had no idea what the hell was going on.

"Has Daelon not been forthcoming?" He smiled, goading me.

I clenched my jaw, my power awakening and shifting to the offensive. I knew Lucius's game was to intimidate and confuse me. He tried to shake my trust in my protector before, and I nearly shuddered at the memory of Daelon's grip around my throat.

It made sense that Lucius would want to drive me away from Daelon and his shielding. How else would he be able to find me? He wanted me vulnerable for attack back in the physical—because he saw me as a threat to whatever power he had here, a power that I knew in my gut was inherently unnatural and stolen.

"I've hit a nerve," Lucius purred. He stepped closer, his light blue eyes dancing with a malevolent humor.

"How could you when I don't believe a single syllable that comes out of your mouth?" I fired back. My palms tingled with electricity.

"You should." His lips curled upward, his eyes alight. It was like I was the punchline of a joke I wasn't privy to. "*I wouldn't lie to you.*"

I couldn't help but let out a dry laugh. His energy didn't lie, that was for sure. It was so dark and suffocating that I couldn't tolerate reading it for more than a couple seconds.

"He will betray you," he said, quiet and insistent, watching me closely.

My stomach dropped at those words, my greatest fear and most haunting doubt. I tried to maintain impassivity, but I knew I'd failed when Lucius smiled again.

He looked confident now, staring at me with his head slightly to the side. "Has he seduced you yet, little witch?"

I couldn't hold back any longer, wind whipping all around us. Lucius reveled in my unraveling, and I was unable to stop myself from unleashing a shockwave of energy out from my body. It spread out over the tall grass and slammed into Lucius, and I watched as he struggled against the force.

He stumbled backward but caught himself, a flash of shock quickly transforming back into his menacing grin.

"Well, that's surprising," he called out, still toying with me.

Why did he act like he knew Daelon? Dread swam in my gut, threatening to take control over my power. I fought against it, reminding myself that this was all a game to him. He probably saw Daelon's thoughts when he possessed him, and now he was using them as ammunition.

This realization soothed me, and I held fast to the trust I had just placed in Daelon hours ago. I wouldn't let Lucius's lies change that, especially after seeing the pure, white energy field surrounding our little house in the woods, after feeling how much Daelon worried and cared for me—no, I would not let Lucius pollute these facts.

"Why are you so threatened by me?" I asked, throwing him off guard. I watched his eyes darken.

"I think I've proved on multiple occasions that I have no reason to be threatened by *you*," he spat.

"Then why am I here?" I raised my voice, planting myself firmly in the soil. I sensed the earth's energy beneath my feet, strong and grounding. I closed my eyes, picturing my body in Daelon's bed, feeling the warmth of his body wrapped around mine, the silkiness of the sheets, the pressure of the comforter...

Don't say I didn't warn you. I'll see you soon, foolish girl, he said telepathically as I snapped back into my body.

CHAPTER 19

My return to my physical body was jolting but welcomed. I was still fuming, enraged at Lucius's attempts to drive a wedge between Daelon and me.

Has he seduced you yet, little witch?

Those words somehow stung even more than the promise that Daelon would betray me. My stomach soured, and I rolled over on my side into a fetal position. I breathed in deeply in an attempt to self-soothe. I failed to block out the frenzied, dark thoughts that rolled in like a storm cloud.

Daelon stirred at my shift in position, moving onto his side so that his chest was to my back. "Are you okay?" he asked, brushing his fingers through my hair.

I leaned into the pleasurable tingles along my scalp, and I allowed myself to melt into the safety of his body so close to mine.

"Bad dream," was all I said, and much to my relief, he didn't ask for elaboration.

He just wrapped his arm around me and kissed me above my ear. I wanted to ask him if he knew Lucius more than he had let on. I wanted to ask him about kings and castles.

I wanted to ask him if he was going to betray me.

But I didn't.

The next couple of days were uneventful, and I welcomed the reprieve. Daelon helped me cast circles around the bed at night to ward off unwanted astral summoning. I kept my mouth shut about my recent encounter with Lucius, content to bury it in the back of my mind until I was forced to confront it again.

Daelon and I carried on our potentially disastrous affair in between training sessions, and I fell deeper for him despite it all. There was a sense of naturalness and inevitability between us, like we each reflected our desires back to each other. We reminded each other of where we came from, and that meant something that was hard to put into words. It was sacred.

Today I watched the sunrise with a cup of coffee in hand, curled up on a couch on the back deck. With the snap of my fingers, I lit the firepit, and because I was alone, I couldn't help but smile with childlike glee. That would never get old.

I leaned back into my oversized sweater, my hands warming against the hot mug. Daelon was inside working out, refusing to let me watch like I'd very much wanted to—because apparently that would have been *distracting*.

The snow had melted, but its smell lingered in the air.

The atmosphere was sharp and frosty, and because of Lucius's threat of *seeing me soon*, I scanned the surrounding energy for anything out of the ordinary. As usual, I came up blank. All I could sense was the strong energetic wall around the property's perimeter—along with the wall of a human being that was Daelon in the next room.

The sun had risen over the distant mountains by the time my mug was empty. I thought of my mothers in the stillness of the morning, remembering their soft-spoken prayers in the early hours each day. I now understood they were also magickally charged spells.

Goddess protect us, they had said.

And when I came into my power, they said: *Reveal to us the right path to keep Áine safe.*

My heart was heavy at the thought of this prayer, as I knew now that the path required their death. If Lucius had something to do with their murder, then let him come.

I would destroy him.

"Áine?"

Daelon pulled me from my inner diatribe, and I turned to look at him as he stepped onto the porch. His skin shone with sweat in the soft morning rays, his dark hair tousled and clinging to his forehead. He spotted me and his face visibly relaxed.

I smiled, waving my hand over the firepit to extinguish the leaping flames before walking over.

"Hey," I said, stealing a very long glance at his chiseled frame. The veins in his arms protruded as they coiled around his muscles.

He shot me a sly grin. "Ready for your workout?"

I gazed at him quizzically, raising a brow. "What workout?"

I squealed as he lunged at me, throwing me over his shoulder in one swift movement.

"Ew. Put me down. You're sweaty," I protested, squirming against him.

He swatted my ass playfully. "You didn't seem to have a problem with that when you were just undressing me with your eyes."

"Okay. Fair enough."

He set me upright, and I steadied myself against him after a wave of dizziness. I ran my hands along his chest, looking up to meet his heated, possessive gaze.

"Take off your clothes," he commanded.

And I obeyed.

"Okay, now we really should go. I want to get there soon so we can be back before dark," Daelon said, slightly out of breath.

His hand cupped the side of my face, both of us nude on the carpet in front of the fire. We had barely made it out of the shower and into the kitchen before we ended up getting tangled in each other once more. Over the past few days, our escapades had only gotten even more intense and all-consuming, if that was even possible. Daelon seemed desperate to make sure I knew I belonged to him.

And I was desperate to believe him.

I groaned, unwilling to peel myself away from him. But I was quick to rise when I remembered our destination, and the same mysterious pull from before arose in my gut. We were finally going to visit the ocean my mothers told me about in bedtime stories—the ocean I used as a metaphor to make sense of the vast, infinite pool of energy that lay at my fingertips.

"Your excitement is quite endearing, as usual," Daelon chuckled, picking up my clothes from the floor and handing them to me.

He stooped to lock his lips with mine, moving slower now, less urgent. He moved his hand to rest at the side of my neck, his thumb softly stroking the sensitive skin of my throat. It was a move of subtle authority, and I felt myself still and calm under his touch.

He smiled down at me, dropping his hand and kissing my forehead. "Get dressed."

I hurried back into my sweater, slipping away to the bathroom to fix my mess of hair. After trying in vain to make my long, tangled hair cooperate, I threw it into a messy braid instead.

"It's not a warm beach, right?" I asked as I emerged from the bathroom. I realized I'd never really paid attention to its temperature in the astrals. It was always just sort of pleasant.

"No. It's northern, so it's mild all year long," he said. "You're dressed fine. You can take your jacket off once we make the jump."

I frowned at his demeanor, which had shifted decisively in the last few minutes to the more moody, guarded, and stressed Daelon I knew all too well.

"What's wrong?"

He hesitated. "It's just a... complicated place. In terms of its history," he said. "And while we should be in the clear, it makes me nervous to leave here. We will be a lot more vulnerable. I think it's important for you to see the place that has called to you so strongly, but at the first hint of foreign energy we're out of there, okay?"

I nodded. "What happened there?"

He shook his head, giving me the familiar look that meant a topic was off-limits. I knew in my gut that it was something I needed to find out. There had to be a reason I was so drawn to this place—why my mothers spoke of it so often, why I used it as my metaphor, why I kept ending up there in the astrals—and most importantly, why Daelon couldn't talk about it.

"Fine," I muttered indignantly. "Let's go. Stop worrying. You have an ultrapowerful witch on your side, after all."

Daelon laughed dryly, leading me to the door built into the glass paneling. "*You* are exactly what worries me."

As we walked to the clearing, I watched Daelon's tension build. He didn't seem as sure of himself as usual, nor as present with me as he had been this morning. He was distracted, and as I cast glances in his direction, he often looked strained—like he was fighting a battle I couldn't see.

"Daelon," I said, grabbing his arm just as we reached the circle of trees.

"What?" he snapped, his jaw tight and forehead creased.

I flinched, dropping my arm back to my side.

Like he was pulled from a daze, his features softened. "I'm sorry. I didn't mean to talk to you like that."

"I would hope not," I muttered, frowning as he reached for my hand, intertwining is fingers through mine.

"I'm sorry," he said again. "I was... lost in thought."

"I just want to make you feel better and I don't know how," I said. *Because you won't tell me anything.*

He forced a smile, snaking his arm around my waist. He kissed my forehead, visibly releasing some of the tension he carried in his facial muscles.

"You make me feel better about everything all the time," he said softly.

I smiled, feeling self-conscious under the weight of his words. "And you me."

A sadness passed through his eyes, almost undetectable.

"You still don't feel like you deserve me," I said. I was getting better at reading Daelon without my gift.

"I'm not sure anyone could deserve you," he said, deflecting my call for vulnerability.

I opened my mouth to try again, but he released my waist and started toward the center of the clearing. I decided to drop it.

"What's this place called again?" I asked, struggling to remember what my mothers had told me.

"It used to be called something that loosely translates to the Beach of the Nameless and Formless. It's not really called anything now," he said, his shoulders slumping as if burdened by some mournful truth.

The name stirred something within me. Nameless and formless was precisely how it felt, even in my astral travels—like a current of something transcendent ran through its waters and blew over its sand. It complimented my own power seamlessly. But why wasn't it called anything anymore? The thought of no one knowing this place triggered a pang in my heart.

"Because something bad happened there," I guessed.

Something *cruel* perhaps? Something that had to do with my mothers' coven and Lucius's unnatural reign.

"A lot of good happened there, too," Daelon said, quieter now. His eyes darted around the clearing. "Are you ready?"

I nodded, offering my hands. Daelon took them in his, his touch delicate as he closed his eyes in concentration.

"You can do it this time. You have a connection, after all," he said. "It should be relatively easy for you. Visualize, concentrate, and channel enough power to take us there."

"Okay."

I closed my eyes, then took in a long breath as I conjured up the familiar imagery of the Beach of the Nameless and Formless. The name itself seemed to hold an energy of its own—a connection, a certainty—like it was magickally spelled. I moved through this current of power, channeling it through the crown of my head, and connected it to Daelon through my fingers. A sense of deep serenity enveloped us where we stood.

Then, I felt the spray of seawater on my cheeks, the soft sand beneath the balls of my feet, and I tasted the faint essence of salt on my tongue. My ears popped, and I felt my body jolt through space.

After a shrill burst of static and a moment of disorientation, I opened my eyes to find the world stable once more. The sky above was a soft blue, and the ocean roared to my right.

"Good job, Áine." Daelon leaned in and kissed my forehead. He rubbed his thumb across my hand before releasing it.

I looked down at the shimmering, multi-colored sand.

Everything here was teeming with magick. It was also rife with connection—to who I was, who my mothers were, and possibly even who Daelon was...

"You've been here before?" I asked, trying to sound casual but desperate to uncover these connections.

He nodded absently, scanning our surroundings like a secret service agent sweeping an area in advance of a president's arrival. Well, I guessed he sort of *was* my own personal bodyguard, after all. The beach was clear in both directions. I reached out for any sign of foreign energy but came up blank.

"There's no one here," I murmured.

He nodded again, but he barely relaxed.

"Want to swim?" I quirked a brow, unable to keep the glee from my smile.

Daelon melted a little, rolling his eyes. "The water's freezing."

"Pretty sure magick can fix that." I raised my palms in illustration, which now gave off subtle waves of heat that moved translucently above my skin.

He cocked his head, a smile playing at the corners of his lips. His eyes darkened as I threw my jacket to the sand, proceeding to pull my top over my head next. I maintained our locked gaze as I pulled off my pants, leaving me clad in a bra and panties. He looked around the beach again.

"No one is here!" I laughed, stepping closer to him.

He looked back down at me. "That's good, considering if someone was, I'd have to blind them."

I gulped. "Well, that's a bit dramatic." I bit my lip, pulling up on his shirt in an attempt to undress him.

He gave in, pulling it off the rest of the way. He grabbed

my chin, his stare intense and electric. A flash of dominance passed through his eyes. "You think I'd allow anyone else to look at you like this?"

"Doesn't seem like you," I said, holding my breath. I felt caught in an invisible rip tide—one that began and ended with Daelon.

He smiled, kissing me briefly before releasing my chin. He took off his pants, stripping down to his boxers.

"Let's swim."

CHAPTER 20

As soon as I stepped into the water it was like two worlds had collided. My inner reality and my outer reality merged into one, and I was in awe of how much power swam alongside Daelon and me. It was an overwhelming bath of electricity and infinite possibility.

"What does it feel like for you?" Daelon asked, watching as I waded in front of him.

We were well out from the shore now, but still a safe distance. I was struggling not to get lost in the formless as it pulled at me from all directions. I wasn't sure how to put the feeling into words that would make sense to him.

"You know how when you're young and learning about the phases of matter, and you're taught that liquids take the shape of their container?"

"Sure," he said, his tone skeptical. Maybe that wasn't a lesson at witch school.

"Well, normally, the power I have available to me feels outside of myself for the most part. And it's so great, so vast, that it expands limitlessly. It's nowhere and everywhere at the same time. No beginning and no end. But here, it feels as though the ocean has become a container for this power. It's taken its shape."

I reached for his hand. "I want to see if I can let you feel it too."

I concentrated, searching for a means to let Daelon in. I wanted him to experience what I experienced. It was just too beautiful not to share.

"Whoa," he said, faltering.

I watched as he grimaced at first, his eyes widening. As I let him in, he shifted into a dumbstruck awe. Suddenly his shielded aura shone through the cracks, like a blinding white light. But soon I realized it wasn't only his—it was mine, reflected in him—and it was breathtaking.

"I—" he stuttered, his brows pulling together. He muttered something in a language I didn't know but felt familiar. "This isn't witch," he said, his tone grave. "This is literally divine, Áine."

"I know, right?" I said, excited that someone else could finally feel it too.

"No, I mean seriously. I—I'm not very religious, but this is something *more*." He frowned. "I don't know what."

You are a gift from the Goddess, my mothers had said. To them, the Goddess seemed like more of a representation of the Universe, embodied in a conceptualized deity. They gave form to the formless, just as the infinite landscape of magick took shape in these waters and inside of me. This gift I'd been given meant something bigger than any of us. It was indescribable, inexplicable.

"I don't know either," I said. "But I will find out."

Daelon reached out for me, running the back of his hand across my cheek. The way he looked at me made me falter from self-consciousness—like now that he'd seen the depths of my power, he couldn't see anything else.

I wanted to remind him I was still me, and contrary to what this magick would have him believe, I was still very much mortal, but before I could open my mouth something pulled me underwater.

I thrashed against this force, and in doing so sucked in a mouthful of water that burned its way through my lungs. The more I struggled the deeper I was pulled. So, I gave in.

I opened my eyes, relaxing my body so that I could concentrate on forming a pocket of air to extend past my mouth and nostrils. I coughed up water, breathing in the oxygen I'd spawned.

I looked up, confused to see that the surface was nowhere in sight. All around me was clear blue. I was unable to detect any energy pollution, which meant whatever had pulled me under had come from the ocean itself. I floated, waiting, and after a few long seconds a vision began to take shape.

It was of my mothers again, dressed in white and standing on this very beach. The waves crashed into them as they held hands chanting, tears streaming down their cheeks.

Let us be of service, they said, the meaning translating seamlessly in my mind from their native tongue.

Show us a way to return balance to the realms. We dedicate our lives to this end. We dedicate our hearts not to revenge, but to salvation, to goodness, light, and truth. In return, we ask for hope.

Goddess bring us hope.

They walked further into the water, disappearing into the waves, and the vision turned hazy. A disturbance in my surroundings made me spin around, my heart leaping out of my chest as I saw the younger versions of my mothers swim toward me.

They looked like angels, their white dresses floating around them among the currents. Momma Celeste's golden hair flowed around her like silk, and Momma Jane's pale skin was clear and heavenly. As I looked at them, a lump formed in my throat as they stared back, smiles on their lips.

In my stupor I lost my hold over my magick, and water broke through the air bubble and into my open mouth.

Oh, bloody hell. Not this again.

My lungs heaved and burned as they rejected the salty water. My mothers vanished, and I gathered up all my strength to propel myself toward the surface as my oxygen level plummeted.

I shot upward, my vision blurring as I breached the open air. My limbs thrashed as I forced more water from my lungs.

I felt a presence at my back, grabbing my torso and pulling me toward the shore.

"Shit, Áine, where the hell did you go?"

I continued choking up water, my body weak from all the exertion. I was grateful for Daelon's support as he dragged me back to shallow water.

He released me once we could stand, and I turned to face him. I was just finally starting to breathe in pure, unadulterated air. The taste of salt in my mouth was pungent.

"You're okay." He rubbed my shoulders. "I couldn't see you anywhere. And you were gone for so long," he said, panic still lingering in his tone.

"I found a way to breathe. I don't know what happened. Sometimes those unknowable forces want to show me things in the water," I was struggling to explain, my brain not working at its usual capacity.

"Like what?"

Daelon's lips were blue, and I realized that I was shivering as well. My warmth magick must've been snuffed out in the panic.

"Like... my mothers. Praying or doing magick—it's hard to tell the difference. I think it was the spell they cast to conceive me."

Daelon reached for my hand, his eyes still carrying the wonder and awe that they had when I let him into my power. It was reverent and... unnerving.

We walked back ashore to where our clothes lay, both shaking in the cool air. The sun was starting to descend in the sky.

"Sit," Daelon ordered, laying out his shirt on the sand for me. He closed his eyes, chanting something under his breath.

I knew instinctively that it had something to do with fire, and right on cue flames sprung up on the piece of driftwood to our right. They were golden and mesmerizing, their energetic imprint a reflection of Daelon's protective energy.

I sat down on the shirt, the sand warm on my skin from soaking up heat from the sun.

Daelon pulled on his jeans and reached for my jacket, kneeling to drape it over my shoulders before sitting down beside me.

"I feel like the waves are telling me a story," I said, still staring at the flames, even as Daelon pulled me into his lap and held me close to his chest. I reveled in the soothing heat from his body. "But it's so fragmented, that it's impossible to see the whole picture. I think because magick doesn't seem bound by linear time, or by any sort of order at all."

"Timeless," Daelon murmured.

"Timeless and nameless and formless," I echoed, suddenly feeling as though we were speaking in a secret language, one that we understood on a level deeper than could be vocalized.

"I have a dear friend who speaks often of these things—the mystical. You two would have a lot to discuss," Daelon said unexpectedly.

My heart sped up a bit. Daelon *never* talked about anyone he knew, or his past. Thinking about how much of a mystery he still was led me right back into my persistent doubts and confusion about whether I could fully trust him. So, instead, I drew no attention to it in the hopes he would divulge more.

"So, you *do* have some good friends," I tried, pulling some humor into my voice in an attempt to disarm him.

He stiffened slightly. "This is true."

Oh, come on.

Just when I thought he wasn't going to say anything more, he clasped my hand and started again.

"We can never be normal, and I can't express enough how sorry I am for that. But I vow to you that no matter what our lives look like, I will never lie to you. I will never stop protecting you and fighting for you... as long as you still want me to. I will never stop—caring for you." He faltered, and I wondered if he wanted to say something more but stopped himself.

My heart beat wildly in my chest, but I felt a wave of calm wash over me. It was like he knew exactly what I needed to hear in this moment.

I knew what I wanted to say—what he no doubt wanted to hear—but I wasn't going to say it. I leaned into him, breathing deeply. "I hope I never want you to stop," was all I could manage for now.

He sighed, kissing the top of my head. We sat in silence for a while, but it was a comfortable stillness—the kind shared between two people who were always destined to be here in this moment. There was never any other outcome.

"I'm glad we're here for the sunset. It's the most beautiful in the realm—well, anywhere, I'd say," Daelon said.

"That's what my mothers said."

As the sun began to descend, the sky's deep blue slowly transformed into a swirl of delicate purples, pinks, and oranges over the rolling waves. The sand sparkled and the water shimmered. There was so much magick here. I could see now why Momma Celeste said the waves washed the badness away.

This land felt like Daelon did. It felt like home.

Here in his arms, I'd never felt closer to him. The loneliness I'd felt before dissipated, replaced by a profound sense of connection. I was glad he was a part of this cosmic story with me.

I shifted around to straddle him, snaking my arms around his neck.

"You're so beautiful," he said, smiling.

"No, you," I said, leaning forward to meet his lips. I was desperate to be as close to him as possible—for this moment to be even more perfect than it already was. I wanted to say with a kiss what I couldn't with my voice.

He met my intensity, his hands trailing down to rest low on my back. Our lips moved hungrily, devotedly, getting lost in each other. Soon there was nothing but us. Everything else faded away.

We were so absorbed in each other, in fact, that I almost didn't notice the atmosphere shift with the presence of foreign energy. I pulled away.

"What's wrong?" Daelon asked, stroking my cheek.

"I—I thought I felt something," I said.

Daelon stiffened. "Fuck."

My eyes darted all around, my stomach lurching when I saw a figure off in the distance among the dunes.

Daelon all but threw me off of him as he leapt to his feet. I reached out to feel the figure's energy, which I immediately discerned as sinister, but nothing close to Lucius's distinctive presence. He just stood there, watching us.

"I need you to do as I say, now more than ever before," Daelon said, his tone sharp as a blade. In an instant, he'd shifted into someone entirely different than the man who'd just held me in his arms.

I pulled my jacket closed over my exposed body, still clad in underwear.

"Zip up that jacket, put on your pants, and do not move from here," he ordered, his tone like ice.

"But—" I needed to tell him about the man's energy.

He cut me off with his glare. "Do not follow me, Áine."

He was seething, cursing under his breath as he began to walk toward the figure, leaving me reeling behind him.

The hairs on the back of my neck stood up as I rose and

slipped into my jeans. I felt vulnerable, and at the tone of Daelon's voice paired with the intruder's voyeurism, ashamed. Why didn't he want me to come with him? What if he needed me?

I watched Daelon approach the threat, who also moved closer to meet him. He was dressed in dark clothing and appeared to be young and athletically built. He had sandy blond hair, and his energy was sneaky and teeming with ego. The aura slithered toward me like a wriggling snake, hued bright red, grayish, and black.

My pulse quickened, and Daelon didn't stop until he was only a couple feet apart from the man—who grinned as he crossed his arms.

Did they know each other? I wished I could hear them, but the ocean was loud in my ears.

The hairs on my neck stood up again at the recognition of another presence—this time on the outskirts of my mind rather than here in the physical. I knew it was Lucius trying to communicate with me, and in my frustration with Daelon's imposed helplessness, I let him.

You could hear them, if you so desired... he purred.

I watched as the man wagged his finger at Daelon, and I could tell now that he was sneering more than smiling.

Don't you want to?

I pursed my lips, clenching and unclenching my fist at my side. How the hell did Lucius know what was happening? Did that mean he knew where we were?

Yes, I answered, surprising myself. I told Daelon I would trust him. But that didn't mean I would allow him to hide things from me right in front of my face. Not when I could so easily get at least some semblance of answers...

After a moment's hesitation I closed my eyes, concentrating as I projected my hearing outward.

Good.

Unsettled by Lucius's sudden mental presence, I shut down our telepathic connection. I concentrated only on Daelon and the stranger.

"He knew?" Daelon asked, his voice hushed.

"Suspected."

"You think you can use this to your advantage."

The man shrugged. "I have no idea what you mean. I don't see how it's my fault that while I was busy putting out fires you were fucking the—"

Daelon lunged, punching the man square in the face. He stumbled backward, catching himself in a dune.

"You've dug your grave," he spat, wiping blood from his nose. "Man of *honor*." He laughed—an ugly, cruel sound.

"Oh I doubt that, Nathaniel." Daelon's voice was surprisingly cool and collected given he'd just assaulted someone. "We both know this changes nothing. You've never been anything more than aggressively mediocre and unimpressive."

They sounded like quarreling brothers, surprisingly petty even as they hinted at a deeper conflict, one that I was desperate to unravel. In a flash, the stranger—Nathaniel— shot out a dark bolt of energy, which slammed into Daelon and sent him flying backward.

I cut off my audio channeling and flew into action, forgetting all about Daelon's command to stay put. Without stopping to wonder if it was possible, I jumped through space rather than waste time running.

In a rush of wind and disorientation, I appeared in the

sand next to Daelon, which stunned both men into momentary pause.

"I told you not to follow me," Daelon growled through clenched teeth, pushing himself back to his feet.

I took a purposeful step forward, placing myself in between the two men. Nathaniel eyed me up and down, and I was glad to be wearing clothes again. Humor danced in his hazel eyes.

I stiffened, narrowing my eyes at the instigator as my palms tingled in anticipation. "I saw that you boys weren't playing nice," I said without meeting Daelon's gaze, which I could only assume was deadly right about now.

"Marvelous," Nathaniel mused, spitting blood in the sand to his left. Something about his face looked very familiar to me, but I couldn't quite place it. "Here I thought Daelon turned you into his pet," he laughed.

I bristled, feeling power swarm us. *What the* fuck *did that mean?*

Daelon stepped forward to be level with me, letting out a sharp breath. "I think we'll be going now. Always a pleasure, Nathaniel."

Before Daelon could turn away, Nathaniel stepped forward. "Oh, come now, Daelon. Don't be selfish."

I watched as Daelon's jaw clenched, his eyes fiery. The tension was palpable, and my anger at this stranger and his arrogance bubbled up, threatening to spill over. If he came any closer, I couldn't be held responsible for what happened to him next.

"You try it, and I'll cut off your hands," Daelon spat. It was like I missed a portion of their dialogue.

Nathaniel grinned. "You're going to cause a lot of

trouble for yourself, you know that? I think you've forgotten yourself."

"You have it all wrong. Goodbye, Nathaniel."

Daelon grabbed my arm, but before either of us could begin to channel, Nathaniel unleashed another attack with the flick of his wrist. It was a dark, aggressive energy that flew at us, as sharp as a dagger and as chilling as the energy I'd felt radiating off of Lucius. It was the frequency that my body rejected.

Failing to brace myself, it knocked the air out of me and sent Daelon and me in opposite directions. The sinister magick slithered in my blood like paralytic venom, leaving me immobile as I lay on my back in the cool sand.

Panic began to set in as Nathaniel strode over to where I lay, crouching down next to my helpless form. He looked completely unbothered, curiosity dancing in his eyes.

"Don't worry. I just want a taste."

I glared, searching for my power as I fought in vain against his insidious spell. Every command to my body to move my limbs, to run far away, was thwarted. I felt unbearably cold, shivering as I did that day in the clearing. This magick was corrupted, polluted, dirty...

It was evil.

He reached for my arm, just above my wrist, and began to syphon like the energy vampire had done weeks ago. It was so invasive, and I was so *cold*.

"Ah. It's true, then," Nathaniel said, still pulling from my power as he grinned, appearing to be in pure ecstasy. "I've never felt anything like it." He licked his lips as his eyes grew wide, and the tugging feeling grew more and more uncomfortable as the biting cold hollowed me to my core.

Help, I called out, digging deep into my psyche for my source of connection—all of the forces that seemed to be guiding me, revealing a cosmic story piece by piece. I needed them *now*.

"I will fucking kill you, Nathaniel. Get away from her," I heard Daelon bellow from a few feet away.

"What's wrong with her?" Nathaniel asked, staring down at my shuddering, cold body pensively.

I closed my eyes, moving beneath the cold, the dark, the ugly—following the voices of my mothers, the songs in an ancient tongue, the sound of the ocean roaring in the distance, and even the magick that seeped through the land beneath me—and I found my footing again.

In a surge of strength fortified by thousands of witches, I began to channel.

"Ow, shit," Nathaniel cursed.

My eyes flew open to see him clutching the hand he had grabbed me with, which was red and blistered now, as if he'd touched it to a hot stove.

I sat up and reached out an arm, my palm pointed toward him. I lifted him up into the air with little effort.

"Wait, Áine, stop," I heard Daelon say, but it barely registered. I was too immersed in my magick now.

I held Nathaniel midair as he flailed, his nostrils flaring and his glare sharp.

I smiled sweetly. "Doesn't feel very good now, does it?"

"You stupid bitch. Do you have any idea who I am?" he spat. "You'd do well to do as you're told. Or you will regret it."

"I don't think so," I said coolly, my voice sounding

slightly detached from myself. I didn't care who he was. I wanted him to feel as helpless as I had just felt.

I let my hold over him travel up to his throat and squeeze at his airway. That was enough to finally wipe the smug arrogance from his features. He held his hands at his neck, wrestling with a force that eluded him. His eyes turned from dark to pleading as he struggled.

It was funny to me how cruel men cared so little about empathy until they needed to evoke it to save themselves.

Out of the corner of my vision I saw that Daelon had been freed from the paralysis, jumping to his feet and moving toward me. He stepped between me and Nathaniel, who was choking and sputtering.

"Enough."

I am not your pet, I hissed telepathically.

"I know," Daelon said with a roll of his eyes. "But we both know you don't want to kill him. Because you're better than him."

I considered his words, reminded that I was pulling a page from Lucius's playbook with this move. Daelon was right; I wasn't him. I snapped out of my warpath and eased up on my attacker's throat, and with a sigh I released him and let him fall to the ground in a heap.

Nathaniel pushed himself up, dusting sand off his front as he fumed. "Consider whatever *this* is," he spat, rubbing his throat with one hand and gesturing to Daelon and me with the other, "over."

And with a rush of wind, he disappeared.

CHAPTER 21

Daelon offered me a hand, his eyes wild and features stricken with unfathomable anger. I took it and let him pull me to my feet. He turned away from me, running his hands through his hair before clasping them behind his head. He kicked the sand at his feet, sending the grains flying in the wind in their multi-colored shimmers.

I furrowed my brows, attempting to reel in my racing heart and erratic breathing. Every fiber of my being was still teeming with electricity and limitless potential. It was hard to make sense of the strange, rapidly escalated series of events I'd just bore witness to.

"How did you know him? And what did he mean by *consider this over*?" If he was indicative of the *wrong crowd* of Daelon's past, then I understood why he wanted to conceal it from me.

"It means we've run out of time."

My heart dropped. The conversation between Daelon

and Nathaniel played on a loop in my head as I struggled to make sense of the conflict. "What does that mean? And how did he find us?" I sucked in a breath, remembering how Lucius had found me somehow, too, at least mentally. How had he known what was happening? Did that mean we were in danger of him showing up now, too?

I paled, looking around the vacant beach. Daelon turned back to face me, his features stony now.

"Probably because of whatever happened in the ocean, when I lost you for a moment. I don't know, maybe wherever you went was out of reach of my magick."

We've run out of time. The words sent me into a tailspin, my gaze warping into tunnel vision as I stared at Daelon.

Something wasn't adding up. Actually, a *lot* of things weren't adding up. How powerful was Nathaniel that even after Daelon threatened his life, he also still stopped me when my grip was around his throat? And how was he able to end our time together?

"*What aren't you telling me?*" I asked, for what felt like the thousandth time, my voice strained. All of my pent-up frustration was rising up again. I was blind, and I wanted to rip the damned blindfold off.

I took a step toward a motionless Daelon, a thousand emotions cycling through his dark brown eyes.

"I—"

"What are the rumors about me? Why am I such a threat to Lucius, who by the way, is apparently a *king*? Whatever that means."

Daelon looked momentarily stunned, but stayed silent, watching me unravel with an infuriating impassive expression.

"Also, he knows where we are. Yet he isn't here, which I find strange considering he wanted so desperately to elude your protection and find me."

Daelon's forehead creased. "How do you—"

"No!" I held a hand up. "*I'm* asking the questions. *Who are you?*" I was still chilled to the bone from Nathaniel's magick. A shudder passed through me as I stood planted before the man I felt so connected to just moments ago.

His eyes softened. "You're freezing. And justifiably emotional. Let's go home."

That place isn't my home.

I narrowed my eyes, tensing as he reached for me. I begrudgingly let him pull me into an embrace, still holding tightly to the questions he refused to answer.

"I'm so sorry," he consoled. "I want him dead for touching you."

I let out a ragged breath, still refusing to relax into Daelon's hold.

"I know you do." *But you didn't want me to actually kill him.* "You could've stopped him from doing whatever he's about to do—however he's going to blow up our bubble. Why'd you let him go?" I pulled back, needing to see Daelon's eyes as he spoke.

He reached for my hands like he wanted to teleport, but I flinched, pulling back. He stared at me wearily, a desperation setting in. "You don't understand, Áine. Killing him only would've made matters worse. It was already in motion. Nothing I could've done would have stopped it. I just wish he hadn't seen..."

"Us? Together?" I asked, the wheels of my mind turning.

Daelon resisted our magnetism from day one. He said over and over that he couldn't be with me.

I crossed my arms over my chest, trying to generate warmth. I still felt the magick's residual darkness like a storm cloud over my power.

"I—Áine, please. Let me get you home and we can talk more. It's safer there," he said, urging me, nearly pleading. It wasn't a disposition I was used to on my supposed fearless protector, but it was one that was becoming more and more frequent.

I cast a glance back at the ocean, wondering why I had been called here. I thought something important would be revealed to me—like everything would finally fall into place. Instead, I was attacked and violated.

At least I got to see my mothers again, before the chaos ensued. They even seemed to see me, somehow, through means by which I was only beginning to comprehend. I watched as dark clouds began to form in the sky, my stomach sinking. Daelon was right about Aradia being so easily influenced.

Maybe things *were* starting to fall together. Maybe the problem was that the pieces weren't completing the puzzle I'd once imagined—one where I finally found the connection I so desperately chased since my mothers passed, one where I finally felt complete and my purpose was clear, one with a happy ending after the fight, one with triumph, hope, and light. Maybe the puzzle taking shape was something else entirely.

The low roar of thunder rumbled in the distance, and the atmosphere shifted decisively.

Daelon followed my gaze toward the now turbulent waters, paling at the sight. "It almost never storms here."

We stared at each other for a moment, and Daelon reached for my hands again.

I hesitated before finally giving in. "Fine. Let's go."

Hot water cascaded over me as I stared straight ahead through the steamy glass, moving on autopilot as I washed the last traces of ocean from my skin. I couldn't even remember the few words I mumbled to Daelon after I left him in the clearing and retreated to the cabin without him.

All things change. The fundamental truth of existence was impermanence and transience. I was naïve for thinking that I—we—could defy the very nature of reality. Whatever was coming for us was always destined to come.

I wrapped myself in a soft white towel, studying my face in the mirror. My eyes looked frighteningly empty, my appearance far less vibrant than it had been this morning.

"Áine. Are you all right?" Daelon called from beyond the closed bathroom door.

No.

I stepped away from the mirror, and with a sigh I stepped out into my bedroom, where Daelon sat on my bed in wait.

He glanced over my body. "Are you okay?" he repeated.

"I'm fine."

He studied me skeptically, his dark eyes probing.

We've run out of time. I couldn't shake the words away. They clung to me like the sticky strands of a spiderweb.

I swallowed, turning from him to rifle through my dresser for clothes. "How much time do we have?" I asked, my tone flat. I grabbed some leggings and a sweater, not really concerned with what I wore at the moment.

"I don't really know," Daelon sighed. He crept closer to me, concern in his eyes. "What are you thinking?"

I dropped my towel, watching as his eyes traveled my exposed body, flashing something intense before returning to mine. I pretended not to notice the change in his breathing as I dressed myself.

"I'm thinking that I don't know what to think. Because how could I when I don't even know what's happening right now?" I snapped.

Daelon strained, fighting an internal battle that I wasn't privy too. He let out a breath, his jaw unclenching.

"I can't protect you from him much longer."

Lucius. "Why?"

Daelon hesitated. "He's too powerful. I was always meant to train you for as long as I could. Until you'd have to face him."

"What does Nathaniel have to do with it? Or us being together, for that matter?"

Daelon shook his head, his eyes burning with anger. "You were right, Áine. You're a threat. And we were in a place with a lot of complicated history. You are so... powerful. I knew you were incredible, but feeling it in the ocean..." he trailed off, averting his gaze. "It was bound to set things into motion. To force Lucius to make his move."

I slammed my dresser drawers shut with my magick, which made Daelon startle. His anger had dissipated into something more mournful.

"You're saying that *I* caused this? By simply existing, I guess," I muttered. "And now Lucius is going to come and kill us, I presume?"

Daelon was unreadable now. "I will never allow him to hurt you."

I nearly asked what he'd do about it if Lucius was that much more powerful than him, but I knew that those words would hurt Daelon more than anything else. By the look on his face, he was probably already thinking it.

Suddenly all the times he'd allowed me to read his energy came rushing back, and it was as if I was currently reading him all over again. The soft golden and pink hues of care, devotion, and awe swam around me, reminding me of the man I knew he was—underneath all the secrecy and front of perfect control.

"What *will* happen when he comes, Daelon?" I asked. "Why are you still hiding so much when you said you'd tell me everything when the time came? The time has come, so *tell me*."

I begged with my eyes, pleading for him to earn my trust. I didn't want to lose him. I didn't want to believe Lucius's whispers of betrayal. More than anything, I didn't want to be *out of time*.

"I don't know what's going to happen. But I will be by your side, and we will survive whatever comes. I can promise you that. Because what we've been building toward these past weeks is so much bigger than all of this. I don't know where our path leads, but I know you were destined for something great. Something that will change the course of history and restore this realm to what it once was. I promise that every single thing I have concealed has been for the greater good. I know that's impossible to believe right now, but it's true. All that I do is for you," he said, the expression in his eyes so pure I couldn't help but be melted by it. "Always," he finished, softer now. And even though it was just a single word, it seemed like a promise forged by magick and fate.

I crumbled just enough to let him back in, though I knew rationally that we would never be the same. He was right. It was impossible to ask me to believe in him fully. Not now. Maybe not ever—and that thought was crushing.

With an impending battle on the horizon, I refused to squander these last moments on fear and anger. As foolish as it might've been, I walked to him, and I let him pull me into his chest. He relaxed as I did, and he rested his chin on my head.

"I will not let anything happen to you," he repeated softly.

"Because I'm your *pet*?"

After a beat he laughed, the sound welcome to my ears after the day we'd had. "Of course, that's what bothered you most after all of that," he chuckled, kissing the top of my head.

"I wouldn't say *most*," I said, unable to match his laughter as I faced the impending storm.

He lifted me into his arms, and in a flash of movement managed to throw me on the bed and pin me under him.

"However, you *are* mine," he growled, grabbing my face in his hands.

I nodded, breathless and so close to losing myself in his possessive eyes. But I didn't.

I couldn't.

He rested his head against mine. "But I am also yours."

I was strangely devoid of the anxiety I knew I should've had, knowing that at any moment Daelon's defenses could be breached by some cruel, power-hungry witch king. The thing about inevitability was that it was going to happen whether I was anxious or not. I refused to waste my energy on what I couldn't control.

Let Lucius come. Let our world come crashing down. Like those who came before me—whose strength flowed through my magick, whose whispers reminded me I was a part of something much bigger than myself—I would fight.

Daelon had been on high alert the rest of the night, wrapping his arms around me possessively once we retired to bed. So when his body twitched next to mine signaling he'd fallen asleep, I was more than surprised. I figured he'd continue his hypervigilance until the early hours of the morning given the circumstances.

I frowned, listening to his slowed breathing. I couldn't fall asleep without at least making a lap around the perimeter, and lucky for me, I knew just how to do that without leaving Daelon's arms.

I relaxed each muscle in my body one by one, envisioning the other times I'd floated up out of my body as I breathed deeply. After a while I began to feel the familiar tingling, which turned into more violent vibrations as I leaned into them. The usual popping and ambient sounds filled my eardrums, and I heard someone call my name. I began to detach, floating upward at my own accord this time.

When I opened my eyes, I was midair between the bed and the ceiling, casting a glance back at my body eclipsed by Daelon's before rising up past the roof. I followed the light that shone from my physical body up into the sky. Once I was high above the house, I searched for Daelon's protective barrier. It was just as bright as before, encircling the forest around the house.

I swooped down toward the outskirts of the property, flying past the tops of trees and coming to a halt just above the ground. I tentatively touched down to the earth, digging my feet into the snow. The magickal force field resembled more of a wall from this perspective, rising as tall as the evergreens. It shimmered a whitish glow, opaque enough for me not to be able to see through.

I reached a hand to it, yelping when it shocked me. It felt decisively solid and impenetrable. I took a step back, satisfied with its energetic sturdiness. Snow had begun to fall, dusting the ground in a thin layer of powdery white.

The hairs on the back of my neck suddenly bristled, and a chill ran down my body. I got the distinct sense that I was being watched, but I couldn't see through the barrier. I backed up, concentrating on seeing past the wall of energy into the forest beyond. Just as the beyond came into vision, revealing nothing but moonlit evergreens and brush, I heard whispering from behind me. The voice was low and masculine.

I spun around, peering into the darkness to see a man kneeling in the dirt with his eyes closed. I crept closer, the wind biting as it carried the now heavy fall of snow. My heart beat violently in my chest, and dread pooled in my gut. I became aware of two things instantaneously as the moon illuminated this intruder: It was Lucius, and he was not in his astral form.

I held my breath, staring straight at him as he rose to stand. He'd stopped whispering, and a slow smile lifted the corners of his lips. His eyes darted all around, and I remembered he couldn't see me.

"I know you're here," he said. He was dressed in regal gold and black attire, his hair in perfect, loose, black curls peeking out from beneath his golden crown. "I feel your presence."

How did you get past the barrier? I asked him, trying to sound strong. Somehow, I knew I could only communicate telepathically cross-dimensionally.

I watched Lucius stand in the snow in utter horror, his energy somehow even more crippling and violent in the flesh. The black smoke of his aura held the screams of thousands, and it whispered tales of utter destruction from mass death, torture, and suffering.

Daelon's voice sounded in my mind from memory: *We've run out of time.*

Lucius laughed. "What barrier?"

I breathed erratically, a lump forming in my throat. Something was wrong. Something was terribly wrong. This didn't make any sense. My astral body started to feel heavy, burdened by a sudden, overwhelming desire to sleep.

What are you doing?

"*I'm* not doing anything," he said, pacing around me, his eyes still unable to pinpoint my location. "What I would be concerned about, however, is what's happening to your physical body."

I felt my eyes begin to droop, feet cemented in place. I didn't understand, but I knew I had to get back to warn Daelon. I thought back to my body in his arms, praying that whatever Lucius was doing hadn't affected him yet.

CHAPTER 22

I snapped back into my body, still fighting off impending sluggishness that threatened to pull me into its unconscious depths. I fought to open my eyes, and when the dark room came into focus, I found Daelon standing over me, chanting something with his hand on my shoulder.

My face contorting in confusion, I pushed his hand away. He was the one who was using magick against me. His eyes snapped open as if pulled from a trance.

"Daelon, what are you doing?" I sat up, crawling away from him.

He didn't look like himself, a deep pain shimmering in his glassy eyes. My mind flashed to Lucius's whispers in the woods.

"Áine, I need you to trust me," he pleaded.

"He's controlling you again," I said. Fury rose within me. I built up my defenses, putting a psychic wall between us.

"I don't want to hurt you," I said, my voice shaking. "But I'm going to need you to keep your distance."

I rolled over to the other side of the bed, quickly moving to my feet as I shook off the last remnants of whatever magick Daelon was using at Lucius's will.

He held up his hands as if to placate me. "You don't understand."

"Then explain it to me, damn it."

I kept the distance between us as I weighed my options. Daelon stood next to the door, which meant I would need to find a way to subdue him, so I could find Lucius and break whatever hold he had over him.

He ran a hand through his hair. "I know you think the way out of this is to fight him. But you can't win, Áine. Not right now, at least. You aren't meant to yet."

"What are you even saying? You want me to just let him kill us?"

I eyed the door, and Daelon stiffened, his features darkening.

"He's not going to kill you. He wants you to go with him."

I scoffed. "Go with him *where*? You're not making any sense. He's literally evil, Daelon. He probably killed my mothers and my people, and your parents too." I remembered seeing Daelon as a little boy, stricken with fear after watching someone kill his father.

He seethed, his jaw clenching. He moved away from the bed slowly, blocking the door from view. He shook his head, straining as if fighting an invisible force.

He was fighting Lucius.

"You said you were going to trust me. He's not making

me do anything right now. I know that it doesn't make sense to you at the moment, but you know I would never let anyone hurt you."

"Get away from the door," I said. This didn't feel right. Daelon would never tell me not to fight. What else had we been training for all this time?

"Áine," Daelon said, slowly and deliberately. "I won't let you fight him. This is your best chance of finding out who you are and fulfilling your purpose."

I felt my power rise up all around me, ready to be used for its most important task to date.

"I've done all I could to prepare you in what little time we've had," Daelon said quietly. "Hold on to it all. I've never lied to you."

"I think it's my turn to protect *you* now," I whispered, preparing myself for what I had to do next.

I wasn't sure what lies he'd been fed or spell he'd fallen under, but Daelon wasn't on my side right now, and I knew in my body and soul that Lucius wasn't someone to be trusted. He was the evil my people rose up against.

I started to channel.

"Don't do this. Just stay with me," Daelon pleaded one last time. "I love you."

I stopped, momentarily stunned. These were not words we'd said aloud. Tears welled in my eyes as I studied him, watching his chest rise and fall rapidly as he begged with his eyes for me not to fight.

My heart physically ached as I shook my head in confusion. I took a determined step forward as I wiped the stray tear from my cheek. "I—I'm sorry," I choked out.

Daelon took in a deep breath, his body stiffening. His

forehead creased, his gaze traveling off into the distance like he wasn't in this room with me any longer.

I recalled the time I'd heard voices in Daelon's room, the lump in my throat growing. "You're talking to him right now," I realized aloud. Had they been communicating this whole time?

I stepped forward again and felt the atmosphere between us grow thick and heavy like an invisible wall. I gasped.

"You let him in," I said in an accusatory whisper, sending my power out to dissolve the defenses Daelon was constructing.

He didn't answer me, his face contorting in exertion. His magick shattered like glass into millions of shimmering pieces. He was no match for me.

I bit my lip. I didn't want to do this, but I had no other choice. He wasn't going to move unless I made him.

I reached out through space and pulled him from the door, crying out as he fought against me with his own power. He'd never used magick against me like this before.

Had he told me he loved me as a way to manipulate me? Just thinking it broke my heart.

In a sudden burst of anger, I sent him flying into the wall to my right, next to the bathroom's double doors. He crashed hard with a thud then fell to the floor in a motionless heap, and it took every ounce of my emotional strength to leave him there as I rushed through the door.

I quickly slid into some sneakers I'd left in the living room and pushed through the glass paneled door to the back deck. A couple inches of snow had gathered on the ground now, coating the patio in a delicate blanket of white. I started down the stairs before realizing I had a more efficient form of transportation.

I hesitated. I had said that if Daelon wasn't who he said he was then I would go off on my own. I could try to find what was left of my people. I could figure out who I was on the run. But could I outrun Lucius?

I sighed in frustration. I couldn't bring myself to abandon Daelon. Not when I didn't know the extent of Lucius's hold over him. Not when—even if I couldn't say it—I loved him, too.

I balled my hand into a fist, my lips pressed together in a hard line. I needed to find this evil so-called king and end him. He clearly would never leave me alone until I did.

I reached out with my mind, searching around for his energy. An image of him leaning against a tree flashed through my head. A haunting smile played at his lips. I gripped the handrail and willed myself there, the scenery around me blurring and then refocusing in less than a second.

"Isn't this a surprising turn of events," Lucius said, moving his hands as he spoke. It seemed that everything was some sort of performance to him.

"Get out of his head," I snarled. "And I will consider doing what you ask. Just leave him alone." That was a lie, but I would've said anything to get him to stop.

Lucius shook his head, looking at me with distinct pity. It only made me angrier. "You poor thing. I almost feel sorry for you. It takes a special sort of... *weakness* to believe in a false sense of reality so fervently." He smiled, stepping closer to me. "To be so blind."

The blood in my veins turned fiery, the warmth from my

magick protecting me from the biting wind against my thin sweater.

"I'm not in Daelon's mind," he said, as if he was spelling out a simple concept for a child. "That's a hard thing to do, given the whole *shielding* business."

"You've done it before," I said, trying to sound unbothered even as he made me question everything.

"Ah yes, that was quite amusing." Lucius looked off into space, chuckling to himself like it was a pleasant childhood memory.

I had to block out the dark energy that radiated from him once more. It was too distracting—sour and reeking of death as it slithered into my perception.

"You're going to be difficult about this, aren't you?"

I opened my mouth and then closed it. Why was he so cavalier about finally finding me after all this time?

"You should just be happy I decided not to kill you. Because I could have. And I still could if you try my patience." He paused, a sickly smile taking place. "Though, maybe a little fighting back before you submit wouldn't be the worst thing. Your pain is the most delicious of all."

I wrinkled my nose in disgust. I didn't know what to say. My head was spinning, and my chest was weighed down with a sense of understanding I didn't want to accept. "I'm not going anywhere with you," I settled on, planting my feet firmly in the ground.

Lucius studied me, his eyes narrowing. "Well, yes you are. And so is Daelon once he brushes himself off." He glanced down at his watch as if he had somewhere more interesting to be.

I backed away, beginning to channel the forces around

me. They were turbulent and wild in Lucius's presence, spitting and hissing like a host of scorned spirits. This power was angry. It recognized who he was and what he'd done, and it recoiled against the sheer unnaturalness of his power.

I flashed back to what Daelon had said about the magick that my body rejected—how he suspected that it had to do with my very existence. I wondered what that meant about Lucius's existence, and how he had access to so much destructive, corrupted power.

"I think it takes a special kind of weakness to be so insecure about your own strength," I said. "We will not be going with you." My power seemed to agree with me, even as Lucius bared his teeth, and his eyes turned deadly.

"I don't think Daelon did an adequate job teaching you of your place," he said, looking me over like I was something to be assessed and judged. "But I'm more than willing to fill in the gaps."

I bristled. My power began to take over like it had when I fought the energy vampires or Nathaniel. I started to feel the familiar head high, like I was walking on air—not tied to my body or bound to the earth any longer. The strength I borrowed from the people who came before me yearned to see Lucius fall.

When Lucius made his first strike it was in a burst of black fire, leaping out at me through the snowy air as it crackled and hissed. It was a spell that sought to cause excruciating pain.

I countered it with a force of my own, a natural reflection of the connection I could feel but could not see, and as I watched my magick neutralize the spitting black curse I realized yet again that *I was not the one who was alone.*

The fire dissipated into cloudy mist, but Lucius snarled and came back harder, sending another cruel blast through the space between us. I held his gaze as I let the magick nearly reach me before countering it at the last moment. It dissipated up into the air in charcoal smoke, screaming like the cries of fallen innocents and gruesome torture. I grimaced, barely holding back a gag.

Lucius paused, his anger melting. "Sorry, hold on a moment. What is that face you keep making?" Lucius asked, bemused as he raised his brows. "You made it in the astral realm, too."

I faltered, incredulous. We were literally in the middle of a battle in which I fully intended to kill him, and he was asking about my *facial expressions*?

"Your energy," I hissed. "It's putrid."

He cocked his head, the corners of his mouth turning up in amusement as he narrowed his gaze. "You're an energy reader," he said. "Bet that doesn't work on Daelon. Or else I don't think we'd have made it this far."

We? Who was *we*? I felt so far out of the loop that he might as well have been speaking a different language. In my confusion I let my protection slip, and Lucius took his opportunity to force my body forward, my feet dragging in the snow as I struggled against the pull toward him.

With a motion from my fingers a deafening crack erupted as a tree to our right split at its base, falling toward Lucius and breaking his link to my body. As it toppled over, he rolled out of the way just in time, a cloud of snow and the ripe scent of pine billowing out from the crash. My eyes darted around, losing sight of where he ended up.

I swallowed, backing up. I inhaled sharply as I stumbled

back into a body, and when a hand closed over my throat, I knew it wasn't Daelon joining the fight. Lucius's skin was like ice, and he squeezed around my airway. I could feel an insidious magick beginning to slide through my barriers, seeping into my skin like suffocating black ooze.

I grabbed at his hand, channeling fire and attempting to force Lucius to loosen his hold.

"Ow," he muttered, releasing his grip and the curse along with it. "That actually sort of hurt," he marveled, as if surprised by something unexpectedly delightful. His ambivalence was unnerving. Was he normally immune to pain?

I took hold of a current of power reaching out for me, and in a rush, I was transported to the other side of the fallen tree. I coughed, glaring at Lucius as he shook out his singed hand. I could feel his red-hot anger, and it only mixed with and inflamed my own.

"You're less erratic now," he said. "More focused." He narrowed his eyes as if he were asking a question.

I opened my mouth to say something about Daelon but thought better of it. Lucius had told me Daelon would betray me. He wanted me to believe it so I'd lose control, and I would not provide him with that ammunition. Whatever magick he'd worked on Daelon could be broken. I just needed to find it within myself to pull the trigger.

"You think you're going to kill me, don't you? I can see it in your eyes." He seemed amused by this, not an ounce of fear in his aura. "You will never be strong enough for that, little witch."

I didn't answer, focusing on raising energy. I thought back to Daelon's teachings about invocations, intent, and aggressive magick. I knew that the power I had at my disposal wanted Lucius dead as much as I did. I recited silent prayers like my mothers had done before me.

Momma Celeste, Momma Jane, I call upon you and our people for protection for Daelon and me. I call upon your strength so that I may defeat this evil and be free to discover my purpose.

I homed in on the currents of power reaching to me from all directions, my mind flashing to all of those swims in the ocean, where I was connected to all of the energies of nature, uninhibited and unweighted by the fabric of physical reality.

Time halted as flashes of visions ran through my mind's eye like memories that didn't belong to me—of Lucius and men tied to him committing atrocities, murders, and torture in the name of power, in the name of supremacy, and in the name of cruelty. I saw Lucius on that altar in the forest, convulsing as he inhaled dark shadows, his eyes completely white. I saw my mothers murdered from their perspective. I saw Daelon running through the street as a young boy, buildings and homes crumbling into ash all around him. I saw myself murdered by men who saw me as a threat over and over again in different ways in different places. It wasn't *me*, but I took the place of the fallen as I relived their last moments.

I was seeing the darkest part of the story, and though it was more fragmented than seamless, with no clear context, I knew that these images were what made Lucius's energy so dark. He was empowered by the pain of others.

I lost myself, my ego stripping away until I was no longer separate from my power. I *was* power. With a scream that felt detached and foreign even as it left my own lips, I let go. I was vaguely aware that my feet were no longer planted on the ground, my vision overwhelmed with a white light emanating and pouring down from my palms.

Lucius braced himself back on the ground below, raising his hands above his head as the brightest, most fiery energy I'd ever seen collided with him. It crashed into an invisible shield he'd constructed around his body, and I heard him strain and fight as it permeated, then broke through his defenses.

Paralyze.

I may have gotten something useful out of our run-in with the mysterious Nathaniel after all. As Lucius convulsed in the snow, my spell took over his body, and I dropped from the air back to my feet. I took my time making my way over the fallen tree, still riding my power high. I watched as Lucius reacted to my energy in the same way I reacted to his, shivering and shuddering in the moonlight.

He glared up at me, and in his aura, I finally detected fear. It looked like the defensive paranoia of a cornered animal.

I knelt down beside his body. "What was that about showing me my place?" I asked sweetly, my voice strong as I reacclimated with my own ego again. "I'm going to need some answers while I think about whether or not to kill you." *I was definitely going to kill him.*

I ran through all of the mysteries I so desperately needed solved, but the only question that sprung to mind for several moments was: Where was Daelon? Shouldn't he be here by now?

"Who am I? Why are you so afraid of me?"

I compelled him to speak, admittedly reveling in his helplessness after all of his attempts to make me feel the same.

"I'm not afraid of *you*," he spat. "I don't know who you are any more than you do, though I suspect that your existence is mostly to annoy me."

I pursed my lips, feeling the anger turn over in my stomach. He wasn't being honest with me even as he faced death. "You killed my mothers, didn't you?"

He smiled, no doubt hoping to provoke my weaknesses to get him out of this situation. I was prepared for that, thanks to Daelon. Nothing he could say would make me falter.

"Not personally." His eyes flashed disdain. "They were working against their new king. They were traitors and heretics."

Yes, I was going to kill him. But not yet. I channeled my anger into my paralytic hold over him. "What were your plans for Daelon and me?"

"My plans were, and still are, to take you back to my *creepy* castle, as you put it. It's the only way I can figure out what to do with you. Although, a part of me sort of wants to end you now," he spat. "As for Daelon, he'll be free to go back to doing whatever he wants."

I faltered. There was a glint in Lucius's eyes now that ran contrary to his current predicament—even as he lay at my complete disposal, he looked at me as if he'd won the fight. I felt my power slipping as he pushed against it, and I knew I was running out of time. Daelon was right. Ultimately, Lucius was stronger than me... which meant I needed to kill him soon.

"What do you mean whatever he wants? You're not going to kill him?"

Lucius laughed like I'd just told him the most glorious joke. I gathered that *I* was the punchline. "How many times do I have to spell it out for you? I would never hurt Daelon." He said the words slowly, his eyes so steady that they nearly revealed boredom.

I started to feel physically ill, a wave of nausea overwhelming my perception. My hold over Lucius dimmed. I recalled in horror that astral encounter in which Lucius had gestured to the place next to him and asked me who I thought belonged there. At the time, I thought he meant me.

Daelon's off-handed remarks about his friends, his past, his pleads for me to trust him—*the wall that Lucius could get through without issue but that shocked me to the touch.*

"No," I whispered to myself, my power spinning out of control.

But he was like me—I saw it in the ocean, I saw it in his energy—all I *had* was my intuition. There was no way that it had led me so far astray, over and over again. He told me he loved me, one of few to say those words since my mothers' deaths. As I reminded myself of all the times Daelon had proved himself to be on my side, to truly care for me and yearn to shield me from the darkness, I felt Lucius push back stronger than ever before. His sickening energy began to reach out to me like a thick fog.

It was as if he was syphoning the energy of my pain.

"You're messing with my head," I hissed, trying to gain back control over my power as I saw Lucius beginning to flex his fingers.

I took all that was left of my channeling capabilities, using more power than I'd ever used before, and I balled it into a single, lethal weapon. Cool steel materialized in my hand, my eyes widening at the dagger I'd manifested from thin air. *That was an interesting new development.*

I saw the moonlit blade reflected in Lucius's glare as he clenched his teeth. His ice blue eyes were rimmed with hatred, but as I brought my hands up above my head, eyeing his heart beneath his rising and falling chest, Lucius smiled. I hesitated, feeling a shift in the atmosphere around us.

"Took you long enough," Lucius said casually, like he was in the middle of watching a movie rather than paralyzed under a magickal dagger of death.

My breath hitched, and I knew Daelon had found us. I felt time slow down, the forest all too quiet aside from the sound of my labored breathing, the whistle of wind, and the crunch of approaching footsteps.

I was out of time.

The forces around me broke through the stillness, calling upon me to act. They were a cacophony of lyrical notes, of song and loud whispers. With a decisive exhale, I brought down the blade, a visceral sound escaping my throat.

In the same second, I was grabbed from behind, pulled away from Lucius as my only chance to kill him was torn from my grasp. The voices faded from my ears until I could only hear my heartbeat. I struggled against Daelon as he twisted the dagger from my grasp and held me in place.

My hold over Lucius had dissipated, along with every last bit of the power I'd channeled. I was fading quickly as I fought against Daelon.

"Let me go!" I yelled, watching Lucius rise from his

place in the snow. I looked into Daelon's eyes and saw nothingness.

It couldn't all be true. *It couldn't.*

My limbs grew heavy, and my vision turned hazy. As unconsciousness reached for me, all I could focus on was Lucius's triumphant smile. He wasn't looking at me, though, his gaze focused on the space above me.

He was smiling at Daelon.

"*Sleep now,*" Daelon whispered in my ear, just as he had the night we first met.

CHAPTER 23

From an empty darkness I was thrust back into reality, my heart sinking as soon as I regained consciousness.

"Glad to be back?"

"Of course."

"How long is she going to be out?"

"Last time it was nearly a full day."

Realizing I had awakened much earlier than my captors expected, I kept my eyes closed. I felt softness beneath me, as if I was on a bed or couch of some sort. The room smelled of roses and chamomile.

"You missed so much," Lucius exclaimed. "Like I had to interrogate half the court because Amos convinced me one of them was behind this whole Armageddon business. Full on plague, locusts, water to blood... it was a whole ordeal."

Amos. I knew him. His energy was pure.

It took everything within me not to cry, not to fight, not

to let them know that I was awake and was going to destroy them both.

"What have you learned?"

Daelon cleared his throat. "Not as much as we'd hoped. Her mothers channeled the dark magick of their own murders to conceal her for so long. They cut her off from her power and kept her blind to the witch realm. She—"

"That's an understatement," Lucius interrupted.

"Right." Humor seeped into his tone.

Yet again, I was the punchline. I fought back tears as intense, bitter anger rose in my chest—as if my heart was physically breaking. I had never felt so stupid. *So ashamed.*

"And as far as her access to power—it's exceptional but still not comparable to yours. I speculate it's just the Universe's reaction to the imbalance created." Daelon's voice lowered as he spoke, as if he was telling a secret.

I sensed Lucius's energy shift like Daelon had said something offensive.

"You're starting to sound too much like Amos," Lucius hissed. "The *universe* is not conscious. It is the canvas on which reality is painted. It does not feel or desire anything."

"I know," Daelon said quickly. "I've been away for too long."

"Yes you have," Lucius said, his tone changing back to a more upbeat, nonchalant air. "I even started making Nathaniel keep track of humorous moments I wanted to tell you about but couldn't. He really hates you, you know."

"I'm well aware."

Nathaniel. That was where I'd recognized him from. He was one of the men who flanked Lucius in the astrals. He stood closest to Lucius on the other side of the missing space, as if he and Daelon were Lucius's two favored men. Why hadn't I made that connection sooner? If only I had paid better attention. If only I hadn't been so trusting. Blinding nausea rose in my gut. I was going to be sick.

Lucius clicked his tongue. "When I told you to get close to her, I hadn't realized you would take it so literally. It did make the betrayal all the better, though, and her pain so much more enjoyable. Points for creativity."

I heard shuffling. I didn't know how much more I could stand to hear, but like a horror movie, I just couldn't look away. Or, rather, stop listening.

"That's very unlike you. Am I going to have to be the one who scolds *you* about honor now?"

"It was a necessity, yes," Daelon sighed. "But it was the only way to keep up the charade. It was the natural progression of things, unfortunately."

Through the heaviness of my exhaustion, even as every fiber of my being yearned to give back into the peace of slumber, red hot anger flooded my veins. This couldn't be real. There was no way that Daelon had faked any of what we had—it was too intense, too pure.

I opened my eyes to a dimly lit bedroom, vast and ornate, with white and green accents. A lavish canopy hung overhead where I lay. Daelon and Lucius stood to my left near a wardrobe, their backs turned to me.

"Tell me more a—"

"*Fuck you*," I spat. I tried to move, but my limbs were locked in place. My power was nonexistent.

Both men whipped their heads around to assess me. Lucius's demeanor barely shifted, his eyes widening ever so slightly. Daelon paled, but quickly regained his impassive composure.

"You're quite off in your estimations," Lucius muttered to Daelon. "And I take it respect for her divine ruler didn't make it into the curriculum?"

"She knows better than to speak to me like that," Daelon said, stepping forward. "Don't you, little witch?"

"Brutal," Lucius laughed, grabbing Daelon's shoulder. "Fantastic. You should be grateful I didn't go back to my original plan of killing you after that little stunt," he said, wagging his finger at me. "Really, you should be more grateful to Daelon for convincing me I'd be better off with you alive."

I glared, struggling to free my limbs from whatever spell they were under. I didn't think I'd ever been more angry or more hurt, not since my mothers had been murdered right before my eyes.

I ignored Lucius, fixing my stare at Daelon. His face was unreadable, showing only coldness in his eyes.

I didn't say anything. I couldn't begin to find the words for what I wanted to convey to this man I'd let in, despite all of my doubts, and put my trust into in such intimate, vulnerable ways. I showed him the Divine—what my mothers, and maybe even his parents, called the Goddess. I showed him my soul and everyone else's souls, too.

I kept glaring at him, my eyes boring into his, unwavering even as they grew heavy with exhaustion.

"Well," Lucius said, looking from Daelon to me then back again. "As much as I appreciate a well-orchestrated, complete emotional destruction of a person, we still have much to discuss from your intelligence mission. Let's retreat to the study."

The floorboards creaked as Lucius turned away, his expression cavalier like he'd grown bored of the entire ordeal. As my vision went awry, I watched Daelon look away, turn his back on me, and walk out.

<hr />

When I woke again, I was alone. The room was dark and quiet. It was a relief, actually, because this time I couldn't hold back a cascade of tears. It felt like I was trapped in a nightmare, and I just needed to scream and claw my way back into reality.

I sat up and assessed my surroundings, which were grand and luxurious. It was the largest bedroom I'd ever stayed in... by a lot. I rolled off the bed and onto the cold hardwood floor, pausing after a headrush left me with the spins. I was barefoot, still in the oversized sweater and leggings I'd been wearing back at the cabin.

I took a deep breath, hurrying to the tall, white double doors at the far side of the room. I wiped the tears from my cheeks. I couldn't focus on the grief that threatened to pull me under. I had to focus on the anger, or I would drown.

The doorknob was cool under my touch, and I twisted it slowly as my heart pounded. The door creaked as I pulled it open, revealing another room even vaster than the first. There was an arrangement of couches in the center, a fireplace crackling to the left, tall windows with an empty bookshelf in between, candles flickering scattered around all the furniture.

Well, I've seen prisoners with less, I supposed.

I jumped as a head shot up from behind one of the couches faced away from me. It was a girl who appeared around my age, her near-black hair cascading messily around her shoulders. She peered at me like I was the one who was intruding upon *her*, narrowing her green eyes as she yawned.

I was glad to find that my power was at least somewhat recharged, though it felt farther away from myself—more disconnected, like how it felt back on Earth. I took on a defensive stance, reaching out to assess her energy. It was guarded and apprehensive, but there was nothing inherently threatening about it. It was neutral, albeit intense and wild as it spun out all around her. It was tinged with red and deep violet, and there was a hint of something I recognized deep in my gut.

Her face merely showed annoyance. "Right," she said slowly, breaking the tense silence. "I'm Taryn. I've been tasked with... babysitting you, basically." She rolled her eyes, and I could pick up on a slight accent similar to Irish in her rich, low-pitched voice. "I don't want to be here anymore than you want me here, so we can just stay out of each other's way, all right?"

I prickled at the word *babysitter*, my nostrils flaring.

"I won't be staying," I muttered.

She laughed. "*Okay*. Good luck with that. I'm going to let the King know you're awake."

And with that, she tossed a book onto the table next to her haphazardly, got up, and walked to another set of doors on the right. I got a glimpse of a dim hallway as she slipped out, light flickering and bouncing off a golden wall.

As soon as she left, I gathered up as much power as was

available to me, thinking of the first place to come to mind—the place with the aurora borealis. I didn't know how I would be able to outrun Lucius, but I had to try. I wouldn't be waiting around to find out what his plans were for me, and surely someone in Aradia could help me. I couldn't imagine Lucius was popular with the masses.

I closed my eyes and conjured up a strong vision, and the room began to spin. With a whoosh I transported, but when I opened my eyes, I let out a frustrated gasp.

I was back in the bedroom I'd awoken in.

I tried it a few more times with the same outcome, growing more and more enraged. I couldn't stay here. Not when I'd been lied to and betrayed so deeply, not when the only person I knew here in my mothers' realm was a completely different person than I'd fallen in love with, not when all of my instincts and intuition had been wrong. Was I even as special as I'd let myself believe if none of the forces of the Universe could have warned me of Daelon's treachery?

Maybe Daelon and Lucius were right. Maybe I wasn't a threat. Maybe I was just as naïve and weak as they made me feel.

"Are you quite finished?"

I spun around to see Lucius in the doorway to my bedroom, his arms crossed.

"You can't leave, *obviously*."

I glared at him, the helplessness of my predicament finally setting in. If I wanted out, it looked like I was going to have to play a long game. There was nothing I could do right now but stay alive.

He tapped his fingers along his arm, watching me

silently. I blocked out his unnerving energy, unable to stand the reminder that I'd been kidnapped by a mass murderer.

He killed my mothers.

"Just be grateful I didn't stick you in the dungeons," he said with a small grin. "See? Despite what your little sixth sense may have led you to believe, I am a benevolent and fair ruler."

I clenched my fist at my side. "You're a fucking murderer. I can feel how unnatural your power is—like it never even belonged to you in the first place," I spat, remembering how Daelon had struck a chord earlier.

Lucius stepped forward, the look in his eyes as sharp as daggers. He stopped inches from me, his hand raised in the air like he was going to hit me. I just stared up at him, refusing to back down.

"I could strike you down right now, but I won't," he said, lowering his hand. "Because I know that you're probably having *emotions*. I've heard they can be difficult."

I drew my brows together, my breathing shallow as I held his gaze. Usually, sociopaths didn't brag about being sociopaths.

"Talk to Taryn about it," he said with faux concern in his eyes. "She's a wholly unpleasant woman, but she knows all about Daelon—so you have *that* in common." He smiled. "But the next time you disrespect your king, I will not hesitate."

He reached out a hand toward my face, and I slapped it away out of instinct. My act of insolence was met with my airway constricting, leaving me gasping for air.

He grasped my chin and narrowed his gaze. "Is that understood?"

Spots formed in my vision as I ran out of oxygen. He released me just before I succumbed to the blackness. With a flick of the wrist, he sent me stumbling backward, catching myself on my forearms as I gulped in air.

He sighed. "Lovely. I'll see you tomorrow. Don't hate Daelon too much. He was merely following orders."

He turned to leave, stopping in the doorway. "If you stop and think about it, I was the only one telling you the truth this whole time. If only you'd listened." He clucked his tongue. "Your time with the humans has made you stupid and naïve."

I vaguely heard him speak to Taryn, followed by his booming laughter before the slamming of a door. The atmosphere was quiet for a moment, and I was relieved to feel Lucius's suffocating energy leave along with him.

"You all right, love?" Taryn asked as she appeared in the doorway, her smugness softening at my no doubt pitiful appearance on the floor. "You look like shite."

I laughed in surprise, the act unleashing all manner of pent-up emotion. The laughter quickly turned into sobs as I buried my head in my hands. I tried in vain to reel myself in as I lost it in front of this stranger, but the more I fought the more hysterical I became.

Wind whistled and bore down upon the windows next to us, and I was vaguely aware of what sounded like hail beginning to pour down outside.

"Whoa."

"Can you just leave me alone, please? I want to be alone."

I lifted my head to see Taryn pulling open the blinds to stare out the window, her dark brows drawn together as she turned back to me. "So, you were the one who cursed the castle with all of that end of days business," she said, crossing her arms and throwing me an accusatory look. "I was interrogated rather intrusively over that."

I shook my head, sniffling. "I have absolutely no idea what you're talking about."

She pressed her lips together then shrugged. "Well, all right then. If you don't want my company I sure as hell am not going to beg ya. Tomorrow we can steal some of Daelon's wine and get drunk in the gardens, yeah? That always makes *me* feel better."

Still trying to stop my hysterical sobs, I looked up at her in an incredulous confusion.

"Right, sorry. Reading the room." She raised her eyebrows and backed away. "Daelon wanted me to sleep on the couch until tomorrow, but you seem to be a lot more powerful than him, so I think I'll listen to you instead. I'm in the quarters to your left. Have a good night. Or just *a night*, I guess."

I stared at her blankly. Somehow her incoherent rambling had actually seemed to calm me down.

"Oh, and don't try anything stupid. There are guards everywhere, obviously."

Not to mention I was bound from using teleportation magick. I clenched my fists, watching her leave as my power stirred.

I shoved it away. I didn't trust it anymore.

CHAPTER 24

I had no idea how long it had been since Daelon betrayed me. I couldn't be sure of anything other than that I wasn't going to be able to sleep tonight. In the dark and quiet, I could think only of him. I had never felt so alone, not even as a newly orphaned child in a strange city in a foreign country.

My mind ran through all of our time together, and I simply couldn't reconcile the Daelon that told me I belonged to him with the Daelon that dismissed me with such coldness in his eyes.

I'd managed to drag myself into the bathroom for a much-needed shower, relieved that despite the unexplainable archaicity of the castle, it still had modern amenities. I'd found some kind of nightgown in the dresser and called it a night.

I tossed and turned, the intensity of my rapidly shifting emotions spinning my magick out of control. I knew I was the reason it was raining down huge balls of ice outside right now.

I shot up with a start at the sound of a door opening and closing in the distance. Quiet footsteps sounded from the living area, and I considered if it was morning already and Taryn was sneaking back in. I wondered idly if her job as my *babysitter* was a permanent position.

At least it wasn't Daelon's job anymore.

I was seething again at the thought of him as my bedroom door eased open slowly. I pulled the sheets over myself, and my heart raced when I recognized the intruder as Daelon himself.

"Get the fuck out," I hissed.

He held a finger to his lips. "Áine, listen."

"*No*," I choked. "I never want to hear another word out of your mouth. You fulfilled your mission. You managed to gaslight me, break my heart, and gather your intel. Now leave me the hell alone."

"Please keep your voice down." He moved closer tentatively, his eyes pleading.

"As if I would ever follow another of your *commands*. You'll have to find another way to get off," I spat, fury giving a mean edge to my voice that I'd rarely heard before.

His jaw tensed, closing his eyes for a moment. "I don't have much time. I never lied to you, I swear. I'm still protecting you. I've always protected you. I'm going to help you find all the answers you need."

I shook my head. I wanted to hurt him. I knew that I could, easily.

"*Your enemies are my enemies*," he said, his voice low like it always was when he said this to me.

I opened my mouth then closed it. My power swelled, but it didn't want to hurt Daelon. Not like it wanted to hurt Lucius.

But *I* did.

I allowed him to approach me, and he stopped just next to my bed. He fell to his knees.

"Energy doesn't lie, Áine. You know that." He reached out his arm slowly, begging me with his eyes to read him.

I shook my head, tears welling up in my eyes against my will. "I wish I'd never met you."

"I know that's how you feel right now," he sighed. "But you're my home. And I'm yours. There are more of us. I know you feel it."

I looked ahead, refusing to meet his eyes.

He brushed away a tear on my cheek with his thumb, and I caught his wrist in mine, finally bringing myself to glare into his soul. He swallowed, and before I could close him out, I started to read his aura. He was... terrified. It was a desperate, erratic thing. Like the scared little boy running through the streets of a ravaged village.

I let go of his wrist quickly. I would not give him the satisfaction.

"Áine, please."

"Get out."

"I—"

"I could have killed him. I could have killed him, and I would have been free. I would've been able to finally learn about my people and my purpose out of the shadows."

"There's so much I need to tell you. That I *can* tell you, finally. That dagger wasn't going to do what you thought it would."

I raised a hand, and Daelon watched cautiously as I reached it toward his chest. Fiery energy welled up in my palm, and I didn't stop it from breaking forth through the air. I wanted him to feel exactly what I'd felt the moment I realized he'd betrayed me. I watched as he sputtered and grasped his chest, reading this shattering emotion as if it were his own.

I breathed in shallowly, preparing for the worst. If he was the man who agreed I needed to be put in my place, then here was his opportunity.

Instead, he was motionless and silent, looking at me with dark eyes that were filled more with sadness and shame than any kind of spite. He took in a deep breath, recovering from the burst of my own pain I sent into his heart.

"Get out," I repeated, slower and firmer. I had nothing more to say.

He blinked, nodding before he recoiled from me and stood. "I really do love you. More than anything in this world."

"You have a fucked-up way of showing it."

"Don't lose yourself in this place. It's easy to do. You are still our hope. *You have friends where you least expect them.*"

ALSO BY MAGGIE SUNSERI

THE LOST WITCHES OF ARADIA

The Discovered

The Coveted

The Illuminated

The Hunted

THE AWAKEN SERIES (Young Adult Series)

Awaken

Arisen

ABOUT MAGGIE SUNSERI

Maggie Sunseri graduated Cum Laude from Centre College in 2021 with a degree in Anthropology/Sociology. Thanks to the virus-that-shall-not-be-named, she was forced to halt her travels abroad and study from home her senior year of college. Thus, *The Lost Witches of Aradia* was born, the first three novels completed soon after graduating. And the series is far from over.

When she's not dreaming up new worlds, she's uncovering the esoteric secrets of the Universe, practicing witchcraft, and astral projecting to visit her pals in other dimensions. Or, you know, just drinking lots of coffee and pretending to be an extrovert. If you're dying to hear more about Maggie, you can connect with her as follows:

Maggie Sunseri
P.O. Box 1264
Versailles, KY 40383
Website: https://maggiesunseri.com
Email: maggie@maggiesunseri.com

Made in United States
Orlando, FL
02 January 2023